CHAPTER 1

*B*lood-red baroque wallpaper. It was the first thing to greet me when I managed to peel my eyes open, which was no small feat, yet nobody applauded my efforts. My mind swam as I slowly scanned the room. A wrought iron and crystal chandelier hung above me, along with a canopy suspended from the ceiling to drape around the headboard. It was the same color and pattern as the wallpaper. And not to ruin the Bloody Nightmare theme, matched the bedspread. My fingers sunk into the heavy blanket tucked around me as I picked it up. I dropped it. What an awful place. Where in the hell was I?

It all came rushing back to me. There had been vampires outside the door to the Never. Five of them. They'd been dressed like they were part of some sort of bad 1800's vampire porno. If that wasn't a big enough clue that shit was about to go down, Sven's reaction would have been. Speaking of which, where was he? I propped myself up on my elbows and looked around. There was a small hollow in the expensive coverlet by my hip. I pushed it flat to reveal tiny sticks, a long-dead flower, and a rat pelt lining the hollow. It screamed pixie. That meant Kittie had to be somewhere around here. I looked to the ornate dresser and vanity, expecting to see Sven or her pop out of somewhere, but the eerily quiet room was all I got. Well, that and a hall leading to another area. Maybe they were in there? It was a better option than the only other door in the room. Since the bed faced that direction, that probably was the entryway.

I went to get out of bed and something pulled in my arm. Hissing in pain, I looked down to see an IV stuck inside my hand. Gritting my teeth, I tore off the tape then in short order peeled the needle out in one fluid move. My breath came out in a whoosh as I let go of the pain. Ok, now to get out of this bed for real.

Mixing the stunning acrobatic maneuvers of push and pull, I made it out of bed. Still, nobody applauded. I stood, my legs buckled. Gasping, I caught the wall before I fell. What was wrong with me? Between my muscle soreness and the grogginess, it beat the snot out of any hangover I'd ever had, and I hadn't even been drinking. Not that I recalled anyway. All I remember was passing out when we'd left the Never. Everything else was foggy.

Red silk brushed against my ankles. My dress, apparently. What in the name of Dagda was I wearing? It looked like a vampire's wet dream. My lips thinned. Annoyingly, my legs still didn't want to cooperate, so I ended up leaning on the wall, the wallpaper bumpy under my hand as I made my way down the hall. Sconces hung from the walls, giving so little light I had to blink just to focus two feet in front of me. When I got closer, I saw the lights were fanged, wrought iron bats. They were suspended by chains and clutched votive candles in their claws. Now, I appreciated interior decorating as much as the next faerie princess, but I'd rather see what I was doing rather than be choked out by ambiance. The door at the end of the hall didn't help any. It was wide open, but inside was pitch black.

QUEENS & KINGS

To all of the Queens and Kings out there, thank you for taking this journey with me.

Even though it was pretty obvious Kittie or Sven weren't in there, curiosity got the better of me, and I finished my way to the room. When I flicked on the light, I winced then let out a low whistle. Black marble covered the room from ceiling to floor, including the tub that was so big it could double as an above-ground backyard pool. The sleek silver waterfall faucet combined with a sideways shower almost made me overlook the red veins running through the black marble. No doubt a nod to rivers of blood. Despite that, this was a room I could get used to.

"I see you're awake," said a woman's monotone voice.

My heart jumped in my throat. Reacting by instinct, I turned, swinging my arms up to eye level and falling into the Muay Thai fighting stance. The expression on the woman who stood there didn't change. Or should I say, the vampire standing there. Her skin was the color of paper, almost the same color as the stiff collar of her dress that bled down at the neckline into a black-satin hoop skirt. The only thing to interrupt the look was the black buttons on the starch white and a dainty black bow around her neck. She was clearly a servant. I didn't drop my stance.

"It's good that you are. The High Council had come to a unanimous vote to proceed with the trial without you. It will be much better that you are there," she said, still not blinking.

It unnerved me, but I needed clarification on what she'd said more than I needed to be comfortable, so I asked, "What trial?"

"The trial for Communing with the Fae," she said. My insides slid around. Being a faerie, that was one count I was definitely guilty of. How exactly did someone argue against facts when all of them pointed to you?

She blinked, which was the only way I knew she wasn't some sort of sick puppet. "Come. The Invitation is going to commence. You will not be late."

Goosebumps trailed down my arms. Not that I *shouldn't* be late. I *wouldn't* be late. It had a threatening tone to it. Not surprising, everything I'd seen of vampires in power had an ominous overtone. Maybe you got used to it after a while?

"Look, I don't know who you are, but I'm not going anywhere until I see Sven," I said, crossing my arms over my chest.

"My name is Dextera. Oh, he will be there," she said, a gleam entering her eyes. "It's his execution that is being planned."

CHAPTER 2

*S*culptures embedded into the walls of the hall and me clipping behind Dextera at a pace that was far too boisterous for the getup they'd crammed me into. Spilling out of my borrowed outfit wasn't something I was going to care about right now. Not when I was being bombarded with different variations of vampires ripping the throat out of wide-eyed maids every few paces. Ok, let me not exaggerate. One statue showed a vampire about to bite, yet another showed a woman dead at a vampire's feet. So technically not ripping the throat out of each lady, but whatever step they were at in the killing process, since I was a faerie and they hunted us like the drug we were for them, it all translated the same in my book. Scary as fuck.

We'd reached a set of doors at the end of the hall. So far, so good. I was alive, well, as long as having two vampire marks still counted as being alive. It did, didn't it? The thought didn't sit easily as I breathed through the steady clop of my heart.

Dextera threw the doors open, and the horrific images behind me were washed away by the mammoth room in front of me. Its ceilings, vaulted high like a cathedral, had bone-white ribs laced over black of night scenes depicting blood, sex, and death. As if that weren't enough, far below the gruesome scenes were *actual* vampires. Not just the kind froze in nightmares. Even though the milling crowd was doing nothing more menacing than pointing with lace-dripping cuffs and swishing velvet skirts, I found myself rooted in place. It wasn't just the scenes above and behind me. It was the deathly stillness. It wasn't natural in a room full of beings. When I'd first gotten with Sven, I had thought it was because I was calm around him. Vampires were just scary stories before that. I'd never met one. So how was I supposed to know he'd been a vampire?

Thinking of him calmed my rioting stomach. Vampires weren't all bad. There were more instances of good ones than him too. There had been that one woman from The Gathering I'd been at...what was her name? And her husband too. They'd been good people. And I couldn't imagine Sven, being the wonderful person he was, would be the Master of a Coven that wasn't at least filled with halfway decent vampires. Right? Feeling eyes on me, I swung around. The tight bodice of my borrowed costume made it slower than it should have been. Court fashion was the worst.

A vampire with a burgundy velvet waistcoat and lace that dripped over the head of his glossy cane stared intently at me. Tor Mór, two seconds in this place, and I already had unwanted attention. Sweat dripped down my spine. His chin dropped, and his eyes flared. Then, lifting his cane jauntily, he strode over. His gaze held mine. By the time he reached me, my heart was pounding like a bird trying to get out of its cage.

He licked his lips, his fang poking from underneath his thin lips.

"Unless you want to get fucked, bitten, or both, I'd suggest you rid yourself of that fear immediately. I can smell it from across the room," the vamp said, leaning on the cane he obviously didn't need as he looked me over like I was prime rib.

My mouth worked, but no words came out. What did you say to someone who just met you and told you they wanted to fuck you while they were ripping out your throat?

"That's enough, Alwick," Sven said, coming up behind him.

Outfitted in a black suit with a matching black vest and red shirt underneath, he had my blood pumping for very different reasons as he strolled up next to the vampire. Or was it vampyr? How did one even tell the difference between the two when they weren't decked out like old Hollywood socialites?

The man slinked backward like his favorite toy had been taken away. "I'm just warning your pet, Sven. You'd do well to watch out for your Black Swan before someone else takes her away from you. She smells...intoxicating. Even I find myself tempted. And that hasn't happened for a millennia."

"She is Claimed," Sven said, taking a hand and pulling me behind him.

His hand was hard on my arm.

The vampire's hair tickled the back of his ruffled collar as he threw his head back and laughed.

"You and I both know that can be changed if another is more powerful than the Maker. And might I remind you that nobody is less powerful than a vampire, Master or no," Alwick said this with a snide look.

Ok, he was definitely a vampyr. Vampyrs considered vampires less than because they were bitten rather than born. His smile dropped as his gaze came to rest on me again. Closing his eyes, he inhaled deeply. Then he opened his eyes and shook his head with a rueful grin before walking away.

Sven turned to me. His rich brown hair seemed to be deeper than usual. I didn't know if it was because he was wearing black instead of his signature dark blue or what. All I knew was that I was about to combust simply from looking at him. Seeing him in the flesh again after almost having died in the Never felt so good. Butterflies fluttered in my stomach. Everything in me wanted to pull him in for a kiss, but this wasn't exactly the right time for that. Not that I cared about what was politically correct, I was more concerned about keeping him alive. We were at his trial, after all.

"I can't promise that isn't going to happen again," said Sven with a nod at Alwick.

I blinked at his complete lack of notice of me. After not seeing him for so long, I would have thought he'd have other things to say first. Like how much he missed me. Or how much he loved me. I mean, there wasn't even a smile or jokes about how the vampyrs weren't going to leave me alone because of how sexy I was. In fact, he had barely even glanced down at my borrowed outfit, which was smoking hot, if I do say so myself. It had a hood, boots, and a long jacket, but to say it was modest would have been a joke. The bulk of the outfit could laughingly have been referred to as a leather trench with a hood. However, it was missing half of the front, exposing a set of matching bikini underwear. Not to mention it was only held together by strings that laced up the entire length of the back. Suffice it to say, it was doing a terrible job at being a coat. With their mesh that questionably held leather straps together, the stiletto platform boots didn't do anything to keep me warm either. But I could have been wearing a burlap sack with POTATOES emblazoned on the front for all of the attention he paid me. Suddenly, it became hard to breathe, and I don't think it had anything to do with the leather.

It took me a couple times to clear my throat before I decided to avoid what was really bothering me. It was something I excelled at. "Why did he call me Black Swan?"

"Black Swans are non-vampires who are lovers," he said, shifting his gaze to roam over the crowd that had started to gather.

My face flamed. He didn't exactly look overjoyed by the thought. I was saved from saying anything by a hush that fell over the gathering. Everyone turned to a dais I hadn't seen through the throng. It was butted up against an elaborate painting of the Garden of Eden. Except in this vamp version, Adam had Eve bent over a stone bench. Blood was pouring down her creamy throat. Lilith stood in the background, her lips curled in pleasure over her fangs as she watched the scene. I shivered.

I was still processing the scene and all of the gruesome additions they'd made when the first vampyr strode out. He wore a frilly black button-down tucked into leather pants. Pants that took backstage to knee-high boots as his floor-length jacket billowed behind him while he strode to one of five black leather thrones on the stage.

"The High Council," Sven said, leaning down to whisper in my ear.

His breath sent shivers down my arm. A woman from the stage drew everyone's gaze. As she glided across the stage, I could feel the air being sucked out of the room as everyone held their breath. Whether it was out of reverence or fear, I'm not sure there was much of a difference in this crowd. She was a gothic vision. Her regal burgundy dress didn't dare move as she glided across the stage. The lace cuffs on her bell sleeves mixed with lace spilling down the front of her dress and frothing around her feet. Her face, framed by a black leather, ruff collar, was whiter than death. Of course, her color was no doubt exaggerated by the black, horned headdress she wore. A dark lace veil, spilling off the back of the bridle, was pulled to the side by vampire girls as she lowered herself into the center chair.

The woman's black lips looked disapprovingly over the crowd, yet she said nothing.

Watching the stage, I leaned over to ask Sven who that was when her eyes snapped to me. I slowly straightened back up. I could ask later.

A vampire stepped military-fashion from behind the curtain. Compared to the others, with a white cravat under a buttoned vest and long coat, he was dressed conservatively. He looked at the matron. When she nodded, he bought up a summons in front of him, his top hat never moving from his head.

"We extend this Invitation to Sven Sivertsen, Master of the Sun Down, New York Coven, for the charge of Communing with the Fae. If found guilty, this sentence carries the penalty of death."

I swallowed hard. That sounded a little too final for my blood. The crier rolled the parchment back down with white gloves and then turned on his heel and walked into the wings.

I shot a look at Sven under my lashes. He stared straight ahead, as cool as if he'd just been told the weather. What was his deal? Could it have something to do with his heart? Well, lack thereof, considering he'd given it to me? Was he regretting that decision?

Another man stepped out from the wing. His curled powdered wig rolled past his shoulder blades swaying as he prowled the length of the stage. Pausing at periodic intervals, he leveled intimidating glares into the crowd.

Finally, he stopped and held up a finger. "The Fae. They are vile, wicked creatures."

I blinked away the red that was trying to creep up my

throat. That seemed like a bit of a stretch. Ok, sure, we had been kidnapping children for Changelings since the beginning of man. But, that had stopped when we moved into our mounds, the faerie realms. Yes, the Changelings were pissed about that, but we had to. We'd moved into the realms to make the vampires think we were extinct. And nobody would think we were extinct if we still kept taking kids. No matter how careful we were in planting baby Changelings in their places, a clever mama or papa would discover one. That kind of word traveled quickly. But we put the babies back when the Changelings turned 18, so we weren't all bad, were we?

The powdery wig vamp wasn't done. Ticking off his fingers, he said, "These wretched creatures would trick, maim, and murder our kind. Many of us have lost brothers, sons, even mothers to their deceit. Still, others walk to this day with scars from their run-ins with these earthbound devils."

His arm swung dramatically over the crowd that was becoming more and more agitated. Feet shifted, and hooded eyes kept glancing my way. I looked them in the eyes. I couldn't let them know that I was shitting my pants.

This could go bad. Quick. A group that was so close we almost were rubbing elbows nodded, shifted to look at one man sympathetically. Peering through the gothic forest of men surrounding him, I could barely make out his face. Then, when one particularly ruffly tree moved, suddenly, he was entirely visible. Half of his face was melted off to reveal a gaping hole where his eyeball stared back at me. I stumbled back. Could what they were saying be true? I thought vampires had been the ones who'd hunted us?

"But we showed our power." Cheers met his gripped fist. "Our movement to hunt and exterminate the fae nuisance was a total success. Or was it?" The fervor around him died as solemn expression stole over him. "I am here to tell you, my friends, it was not. The fae exist still. They are back to finish what they started. In fact, I tell you we have one here in our very midst!" he thrust a finger at me.

This time my face did blaze red, and my eyes went wide. Ok, this was officially a fuckery bomb. Gasps came from all around as vampyrs alternated from leaning forward with eagerness to back in shock. One woman near me fainted dead away. All I could do was blink at her. Vampyrs fainted?

I settled on stepping away from her silk skirts that spread on the floor like pooling blood. When I did, I backed into a woman. I turned lightning quick, whether it was to apologize or to defend myself from the fight that was undoubtedly coming, I didn't have time to reflect on because I'd just laid eyes on the most angelic vampire I'd ever seen. She had sandy-blonde hair spun up in a strong coif with floating tendrils that deliberately tickled her neck and temples. With a closed look, she looked me up and down. Then the moment was over.

"If this atrocity was not egregious enough, one of these beasts was brought into our midst by one of our very own." He leveled a stare at Sven that would have made a Catholic mama proud. "Sven Sivertsen has committed one of the most treasonous acts a vampire is capable of, Communing with the Fae, and the Council is calling for his death."

Thunderous applause and calls for his head mixed together to create chaos that echoed into the belly of the cathedral. It was a headhunt. My stomach rolled. As my gaze moved from one overzealous, deathly pale face to the next, something gray caught my eye. It was the size of a three-year-old mistake and flashed behind a pair of velvet breeches before disappearing under a hooped skirt the size of Rhode Island. No, it couldn't be.

The woman on the state in the center throne leaned over

to the man in the leather pants. He listened intently as she spoke in tones too low for anyone else to hear. Another movement caught my eye, and I looked back to where I'd seen the gray earlier. I groaned. A tiny little goblin head peeked out, the giant skirt resting on his wrinkled brow. His knobby elbows shined the parquet floor as he waved to me. Mabye. Or Maybe, as I liked to call him, looked far happier to see me than I was to see him. Couldn't I deal with one demented species at a time? I gave him big eyes that said, "what the hell are you thinking?" as the chatter around me died effectively as if it had been stepped on by a giant.

The vampyr the woman in charge had been talking to had his hand raised. "On behalf of the High Priestess, I, Raven Cel Tradat, recognize your Invitation for Sven Sivertsen. If this transgression has indeed occurred, we agree the punishment is fitting for the crime. In two midnight's time, we will proceed to the Masked Ball. Three more midnights will signal the start of the Unveiling."

A ball? Why were they having a ball? Why did nothing in this undead jizz-fest make sense? The excitement was as thick as blood as everyone started talking at once. I stilled. It wasn't that I didn't share in their joy. I didn't. It was more that I felt something inside me. It felt...ugly. Like something was sniffing at my soul. And it wasn't looking to play nice. Looking for the source, I saw the High Priestess staring into the crowd. Directly at me. With death in her eyes.

CHAPTER 3

"So, are you looking to get you or me killed?" I asked, my hands on my hips as the little goblin slid his feet along the carpet.

"Why did they give you such gross carpet?" Mabye asked, stifling a shudder.

I opened my mouth to tell him to stay focused but shook my head when his words registered, "What are you talking about? This is the nicest carpet I've ever seen, and I'm faerie royalty, remember? To say I've seen some nice carpet is an understatement."

"But it's so...squishy," he said, screwing up his face as he wriggled his gnarled toes in the thick carpet.

"They call that plush. Now, stay focused. What are you doing here?" I asked. He was harder to keep on track than an evil spirit.

"Oh, everything's going to hell in a head basket," Mabye said, padding his dirty feet over to the bed.

I cocked my head. "Ummm...do you mean hell in a hand basket?"

He grabbed onto the pillow top and climbed up it, smearing dirt across the red bed skirt. "That's what I said."

I shook my head. "Ok, it wasn't, but why is everything going to hell in a hand basket?"

"Head basket." He corrected with a cat-like growl as he finished pulling himself up. He shoved the temporary pixie home onto the floor. My lips flattened. I was going to kill him. Nobody would miss a goblin, right? He waved his spindly fingers. "It not matters. You can't stay here. It is unfit," he said, pushing at the fluffy bed with a look of disbelief widening his mouth enough to where his razor-sharp teeth just poked through.

"Not that I am arguing that I should stay, but what's wrong with the bed?" Of all of the things in this wretched place, the luxurious surroundings was the one thing ticking all of my faerie boxes.

His red eyes squinted. "What do you mean, 'what's wrong with it?' You're our God. You can't live in such a place."

Tor Mór, that's right. The goblins thought their god, Baboloki, was still inside me. My heart squeezed as I thought of what the brave, fabulous goblin had given up for me. His life. In turn, I'd promised to take care of his people. Something told me if his cranky pint-sized soldiers knew I was responsible for his death that not only would the goblins not let me look out for them, but they'd be back to where they were a month ago. Trying to kill me.

With a shrill laugh, I waved a hand to the side. "Well, I mean besides the fact that it is quite clearly too soft. No, I don't sleep on that atrocity. I sleep," thinking quickly, I turned and pointed to the floor. "There."

His mouth thinned. Dagda be damned, he didn't buy it.

"Not much better," he said with a grunt as he swung off the bed to land with an *oomph* two feet away.

"Maybe, why are you here?" I said, sitting on my hands before I throttled him with them.

Blinking as if he remembered he was here for a reason,

his features darkened. "Our people are being eaten faster than rotten sauerkraut at a smoking ceremony."

"As in still being killed? That's rough," I said, pushing the distracting blonde curtain of my hair out of my eyes. "Who is the unwelcome buffet goer?"

He suddenly became very interested in the chandelier. "We sorta need you to figure that out too."

I rolled my eyes. Of course, I had to figure that out. Goblins were inherently evil little shits, leaving a sycamore tree-long suspect list, especially when considering the rest of the worlds, realms, and veils.

"Ok, while that sucks, why are you here?" I asked. Ok, yes, I had an idea, but I was still hoping there was a way out of it. There was too much on my plate right now, as is.

"You must avenge us," Maybe said, throwing his fist in the air like someone who knew nothing about death.

"Avenge you?" I blinked. Being a goblin vigilante was more than I'd bargained for. "Just how do you want me to do that?"

"Rip out their spine? Tear off their heads and make them dance? It's really up to you," he said with a yawn.

Yeah, ok. Literally, none of those were on the table. I wouldn't be tearing the head off of anyone.

Shaking my head, I held out a hand, "Ok, ok. Let's back up."

A no-nonsense knock on the door cut me off. It didn't take a seer to know shit would hit the fan if the little goblin was found in my room. Can we say fae red flag? Thanking Danu I'd locked the door, I glanced wildly around. The laundry chute would have to do. Without thinking, I scooped Maybe up.

With quick steps, I whispered to the cradled little goblin. "You can't be found here. The vampires can't know I'm a faerie."

His eyes, barely visible over his round, gray belly, rolled. "Just tell them you're a goblin god."

He clearly wasn't getting the point. Another knock came, this one more staccato. Whoever it was clearly wasn't happy at being kept waiting.

I picked him up. He felt...comforting, like a hairless cat. "Look, Mabye. I don't know how to help you. I don't know where this Blood Spire we're in is, but I can't travel to your caves and back in three days. And I have to be here for Sven's trial proceedings."

That was as much as he was going to get for clarification. I was seven hundred and ninety percent positive as a goblin he wouldn't understand the intricacies of the vampire legal system. Not that I was in the mood anyway. I didn't want to do anything other than nap. For a couple decades.

"Oh, it's no worries. We have come to be near our God. We are right down the road," he said, his eyes crinkling in happiness.

"That's great," I said with total insincerity as I hefted him to the chute. With a sigh, I reminded myself I had told Bab I'd help the goblins in his stead. "Fine, I'll meet you there when I am done here. Wait, where are we going again?"

"Hell's Gate," Mabye said, swinging his feet.

Of course, that's where they were staying. At a thermal theme park. Why not stay in the middle of a tourist destination? I wanted to slam my head against the wall.

"Ok, fine. I'll be there, but for now, you've got to go," I said.

"You got it, Pretty Princess," he said, right before I tossed him down the shoot.

I barely waited for the clang of goblin on metal shoot before I sprinted back to the now-shaking door. "Coming!"

Without breaking stride, I threw the deadbolt and whipped open the door. Sven stood there in all of his glory.

Was it my imagination, or did the light from the hall put the tiniest halo around him? I sighed in relief.

"Thank...God, it's you," I said, catching myself before I called my own god. No sense giving fodder to prying ears. Because if there's one thing you could be certain of in a vampire house, it was that you could never let your guard down. "Get in here."

"I thought you might have some questions," Sven said. His unruffled body language belied the fact that I'd just finished manhandling him by pulling him inside and subsequently slamming the door after him.

I threw myself at him, my lips cutting off anything else he had to say. Little zings traveled up and down my body as he took a second to register that I was kissing him and return the kiss. It had been so long since I'd kissed him in person. Since we'd decided to give it another chance, our kisses had been just through our metaphysical connection. But there was nothing like the real thing. Nothing like the moistness of his lips on mine. It was like a drug, and I wanted more. Deepening the kiss, my legs failed me. He caught me with those rippling muscles. I gave the taught cords a slight squeeze as he broke the kiss to right me. Dazed by lust, I blinked to clear my head. Crooking a silly grin at him, I resisted the urge to hip-bump him. For all of the unreal chaos going on around me, at least he was by my side again. It had been so long.

He didn't return the smile. I frowned.

"How are you feeling?" he asked, walking into the room.

I followed him.

"Besides, the fact that I'm stuck in a whacked-out vampire church and you're about to die because of me, just fine, thanks," I said, not bothering to keep the sarcasm out of my voice.

"Though the High Council is headed by the High

Priestess, you are not in a church. You are in the Blood Spire," he said, bowing in reverence.

My frown deepened. Maybe it was just me, but I couldn't get on board with honoring a system that was about to slice and dice me like a butcher at the county fair.

"However, I did not mean emotionally. I meant physically. Are you feeling well?" Sven said, turning to face me again. He didn't meet my eyes, though. Instead, he looked me up and down. The act would have excited me if he had an ounce of I-want-to-rip-off-your-clothes in his eyes. But there wasn't.

Really taking the time to measure how I felt, I answered honestly. "Oddly weak. But beyond that, I'm ok. What makes you ask?"

"You've been sleeping for two months," he said, putting a hand on my shoulder. The comfort of his hand softened some of the blow, but my insides rioted at the news anyway. Then he felt down my arm, and I realized he wasn't trying to comfort me. "Your muscles have atrophied."

The news was almost as shocking as his cold regard. I mean, sure, Oganess had mentioned I could fall into a coma when I stepped into our world from the Never. But I guess I'd thought with Sven giving me his heart and the spell stuff, I assumed that no longer applied. It looks like I was wrong. As far as his coldness, a wriggling feeling wormed inside of me. Was it because I had his heart? Guilt ate at me with the thought.

I shrugged his hand off me, not liking how he was touching me. If it had been a caress, I would have reveled in it, but as is, it was just cold. But I couldn't face that with him. His rejection, especially if it had to do with his sacrifice for me. Because if he lost his feelings for me, just what else had he lost? Panic bubbled in my chest, and I pushed it down. "Whatever. I'll do push-ups and some squats. What's going on with this trial and what do they mean faeries have been attacking?"

"To answer your first question, it would seem that despite the safeguards we've put in place, word has spread that you are a faerie." My blood ran cold. Clearing his throat, he continued. "Since Communing with Fae is considered one of the highest offenses, I am being put on trial to see if I have broken the law. As far as your second question is concerned, the past is very unclear as it pertains to faeries. It is common knowledge that faeries have attacked our covens for some time. Only the past few hundred years have we began proactively lashing out against them."

I leaned away from him. "What do you mean 'we' have been lashing out over the past few hundred years ago. Didn't you say that you are only like 228?"

"You are correct. What I mean by that is vampire society, as a whole," he said, as if that explained everything.

It didn't.

I put my hands on my hips. "So what you are telling me is you really have no idea what faeries have done or not done?"

"I suppose that is fair to say. However, that doesn't change the facts. The matter at hand is the fae are viewed as highly dangerous, so they are kill or be killed," he said with a shrug.

Unless they could be tamed and used as a drug supply. Nobody seemed to care when it came to getting their fix, but that wasn't being addressed was it? No, it was this ridiculous idea that we were terrorizing an entire race. Despite the complete ignorance, that wasn't what stuck in my brain. No, it was the fact that for once I'd gotten what I'd wanted: for faeries to be recognized as the powerhouses we were. And frankly? It sucked big time. Because of it my life and the man I loved was on the line. And how did you prove that you were something you weren't? That was a trick I'd tried a lifetime to pull off, and I'd failed every time.

CHAPTER 4

"*S*he ain't Ba," said the goblin on the throne, sticking his finger in his ear and swirling it around. I could hear the *shlick, shlick* of ear wax from where I stood on the boardwalk.

Who would have thought creatures of myth and legend would choose a theme park for their temporary home? Then again, nobody would consider goblins intelligent. But maybe they were smarter than I gave them credit for because they hadn't been spotted by tourists yet. Sure, their gray bodies blended in with the gray mud and rock of the geothermal reserve, but you'd still think *someone* would have spotted them. My eyes went to the tiki posts at the entrance of the Hell's Gate attraction where the goblins had decided to put their throne. Maybe they had been spotted, but tourists just thought they were part of the attractions. That would be more logical. Speaking of logic, who in the hell was that on the throne? The uglier-than-usual goblin was definitely not the goblin queen I'd stolen Bab's bone from.

"If there's anyone here making themselves out to be something they're not, it's you. Where's Moreanna?" I asked, leaning against the demonic font that read ATE in the HELL'S GATE wooden sign.

"We don't know," said Mabye, skimming his feet over the sulfur pool.

The imposter king jumped up onto the pile of slate serving as his throne. "Lies! She's dead, I tell you! Eaten by The Beast!"

One of the goblins bathing in the rotten egg-smelling water didn't bother to stop slathering the murky liquid into his armpit. "You ain't King yet, Dik."

I shot Mabye a look. "Dick?" I mouthed. "Dikeledi," he mouthed back. Oh, well, at least, I wasn't about to step into the middle of a fight. Name-calling was always the first step. That, ladies and gentlemen, was what you called experience.

"P's and Q's. Soon, Mogapi, you will see," said the knobby-kneed goblin on the throne, a grin cocking his mouth. Then, he frowned as if remembering my presence and turned back to me. "Who are you to question my authority? You have no rule over us."

"She's Ba," said Mabye, slapping my calf in support.

My leg stung as his too-long fingernails scratched me through my jeans. In my room, I'd found my tank top, leather jacket, and jeans. Those, not to mention some Burger King on the way over, had me feeling a tad normal, at least. Which was great because it kept me calm enough not to punt the "helpful" little goblin at my feet. The throned goblin didn't look convinced by my unofficial spokesman. What worse was that other goblins were also starting to tilt their football-shaped heads at me in question.

Tapping my foot, I wracked my brain. Talk about a serious What Would Bab Do? moment. No matter what I said, they'd question it. And it wasn't like I could call Bab from the dead. The thought stopped me. Or could I?

"Don't take my word for it. Take his. Do you want to talk

to him?" I asked, pretending like the mere suggestion didn't send a storm of butterflies rioting in my gut.

"You bet I do," said the goblin flopping down with a snide smile curling his lips.

I gave a disgusted sigh. "Fine, let me get him."

Closing my eyes, I fluttered my lids as I rolled my eyes into the back of my head. After a second, I jerked my body, sending it convulsing, and then flailed my arms. I carried on for a few more seconds. Wait, that was probably too long. Stopping with a long exhale, I flopped my arms to my side and lolled my head back.

Snapping my body up rigid and straight, I stomped the rickety walk once for effect. Cat-like hisses and gasps echoed from around me. One goblin even splashed and ran out of the water, his wide feet making slapping noises as he ran into the woods.

Making sure my eyes were rolled in the back of my head, I snapped my eyes open.

I fluttered the lids as I deepened my voice and spoke in drawn-out tones, "What evil befalls you, my children?"

A hush descended over the waiting goblins. Nobody dared move.

Finally, a goblin spoke as the thick beads of her necklace picked up hefty chunks of mud as she bent low. "Nothing, Protector of Goblins and all that is Bad."

"Nothing?" I said, doing my best roar. "You have the nerve to pull me from my rest and place pain upon my chosen host for Nothing?!"

"Not, not nothing, Your Badness." Dik was quick to add. "We did not think the faerie held your person. In fact," he said, standing a little taller, "I still don't believe it. I require proof."

I resisted the urge to roll my eyes for real this time. Thankfully, I knew precisely how Bab would respond to this.

Bringing my head up like a serpent about to strike, I said, "Proof? The only proof you will get from me is when I play She-Loves-Me-Not with your head. I am your *God.* Now, bother me no more. You will speak directly with my host. I have spoken."

Ok, maybe the last was a tad much. I couldn't take it back now, though. Finishing my performance, I flopped my arms down and slumped my head back again.

I waited. A geyser burst in the distance, but beyond that, all I heard was the buzzing of mosquitoes. No splashing, no squish of mud between toes, no suck of stabbing daggers into 'unimportant' flesh. All was quiet. I don't know how I managed to keep the smile off my face as I brought my head back up and resumed a normal stance.

Blinking as if coming out of a daze, I looked down at Mabye. "Did he come?"

He merely nodded at me with large eyes, the red-bodied, blue-legged frog he'd been eating squirming, half-eaten in his mouth.

I looked to the goblin on the throne. His face was almost white; it was so pale.

"I still don't believe you." He lied. If the color of his face wasn't indication enough, the mud spraying from his dangling foot as it shook would have been. "But no mind. It no hurt to accept help."

"If you would like to talk to him more about it. I'd be happy to bring him back," I said, blinking coyly at the scared-shitless goblin.

He shook his head fast, his earring slapping his hollowed cheeks. "No, no, need. We are happy to do whatever you want, give whatever you need. Poisonous frogs. Spears. Control of our people while you are here. It's all yours to command. You are our freeloader, after all."

Freeloader? My eyes went dark. I'd had about enough of the little goblin.

Mabye must have seen my anger because he pulled at my pant leg. I leaned down.

"It's our highest honor for a guest," he said.

Ok...satisfied, if a tad confused, I stood up and nodded.

"I accept your gracious hospitality." With a loud clap that made the goblin closest to me dive headfirst into a rock outcropping, I said, "The first thing I'm going to need is for you to move to the Sodom and Gomorrah pools. The sprays will shield you from visitors. There's no need for you to get noticed and hexed out of this place by a Tohunga." I said.

The local witch doctors would do it too. They didn't play around.

"But we like it here at Hell's Gate. It's cozy." Complained one of the goblins in the pool. Mogapi shot him a look, and he scurried out of the pool. "That's ok. I'm getting all pruney anyway. Gonna dry off on the rocks over at Gomorrah before I go in for another dip. I heard it's comfy there too."

I raised my eyebrow. If water that exceeded the boiling point was considered comfortable, I'd been doing it wrong all this time.

The spell broke, and everyone started moving at once. Their naked little gray bodies were disappearing faster than pixies could fly. That wouldn't have been a problem if I didn't need one of them to tell me more about what was going on. And I'd be damned if that "one" was going to be Mabye. He was equal parts so-ugly-he-was-cute and brainless.

I pointed at Mogapi. "Can I speak to you?"

The goblin nodded and walked out of the pool. Unlike the others, he wasn't completely naked. Tied to his feet were once-white bandages. From the agile way he climbed the rocks to get to a pile of clothes on the bank, I doubted the strips were for anything other than protection.

"Hey, where's Kut?" I asked Mabye. With her no-nonsense, military mind, she would have been the perfect goblin to ask for help, but she was nowhere around.

"She dove in after the monster killing us this morning," Mabye said between loud crunches of frog bone.

My lips curled in a begrudgingly tender smile. Of course, the fierce warrior had. She would never sit here bathing while her people were dying.

That she only went this morning gave me pause, though. "Wasn't she around for the other attacks?"

"Yes, but she was never close enough to follow. The beast only comes up to grab one of us, and then they're gone again, quicker than a maggot can blink," Maybe said.

Ok, that was a visual I didn't need. "If you know this, I assume that means others saw the attack as well. So what are we looking for?"

"Nobody saw a thing. We just heard the sploshing of whatever it was jumping into the gate to hell," said Mogapi, buckling his belt over his layered chimera pelt tunic.

I raised my eyebrows. He must have been quite a fighter to have procured something like that.

"Don't get too excited. I'm just a Ranger. A demi-god traded it in exchange for me keeping his secrets," he said, seeming to know what I was thinking.

No doubt, he got that reaction all of the time. You didn't see Chimeras every day, and to have their pelt was even rarer. But a goblin and a demi-god? How exactly did that happen?

Though it had nothing to do with the investigation, I was intrigued. I couldn't help asking, "What demi-god gave you a chimera pelt?"

He gave me a come-now look before he slipped on his cloak and hood.

It was worth a shot. "So if you're a Ranger, that means you're good at tracking. What have you seen?"

"Well, there were prints, but they were wiped half-clean by the time I'd gotten to them," he said, pointing to the basin.

"Do you mind if we have a look?" I said, already hopping down from the boardwalk before he could say anything.

"Knock yourself out," he said, pointing towards the back of the pool where the gray mud slipped into the murky depths.

When I reached the sloped bank, I spotted the prints. Or partial prints. I rubbed the bridge of my nose. Wiped away. Is that what we called the goblin butt cheeks rubbing out everything but the four toe prints? Of course, all beasts had roughly the same shape when it came to fingers, hence the name. I grimaced. There was no avoiding it. Wedging my heel into the sloshing mud to anchor myself so I didn't slip, I knelt to look at the print.

"Well, it wasn't a cat," I said, leaning closer to run a finger over the faint marks above the nails.

"How can you tell?" said Mabye, wedging his face between mine and the paw mark.

"There are claw marks. Cats don't leave those. Move, would you?" I said to the back of Mabye's head. He kept moving closer and farther away from the print like he was zooming in on it.

"So demanding," he said but complied with a frown.

When he moved, I got a better look again. "From the squashed tips and how spaced out they are, I'd say it probably was a dog. And...was that singed earth?" Then, suddenly, what Mogapi said earlier clicked into place. "Wait, is this like the real Hell's Gate? As in the *actual* gate to hell?"

"Now, you're getting it," said Mogapi, his pointy teeth

gleaming in the sun as one side of his mouth curled up in a grin.

"Ok, that narrows down our suspect list quite significantly. Do you know of any dog in hell that would come up with no other purpose than to grab a goblin snack and then go back down?" Even as I asked the question, a horrible thought tickled the edge of my thoughts. The hairs on the back of my neck stood up. I prayed to Danu that it was anything but what I was thinking.

"Oh, I don't know. Do you maybe mean a dog who can't resist goblins and pops them like cockroaches in a hooker hotel?" asked Mogapi, reaching under his hood to rub his bald head.

I nodded, my twisting gut not wanting to be the first one to say it.

Mabye smeared frog blood across his forehead as he stared at me, a dawning horror in his eyes. "Cerberus-"

"The guardian to the gates of hell. *The* Hound of hell," I finished.

One word summed up the goblin's fate. Screwed.

CHAPTER 5

"*N*ot that I wouldn't love to see a stake or two through his heart. Tell me again why you're going to a ball to celebrate Sven being offed?" As she sat in the vanity's ornate curve, Kittie surveyed the last touches I put to my makeup.

"Who knows," I said, as I furiously blended the edges of my eyeshadow out into a softened wing. "Who knows why they do anything in this crazy ass place?"

The cry of bending metal made my eyes bounce to the laundry chute and back to the mirror in front of me to check that everything was in place. My hair was in an elaborate updo that consisted of a pulled-apart side braid with trailing pieces, black feathers and red crystals that looked like drops of blood that slipped from the spray. Why now? The shoot had become Mabye's favorite entrance into my room since he'd discovered the vampires only did laundry at night. As if to emphasize his arrival, the porthole door clanged, followed by a small thud.

I fished the ruby earrings out of the porcelain cup they sat in.

"Come, immediately. This is bad. So bad." said Mabye, his leather skirts swishing together as he ran to me.

Why did he always have to be a drama king? I looked over, giving a start when I realized he had already reached me and was picking at my sheer skirt.

Pulling it out of his hands, I said, "This isn't a good time, Maybe. I'm required downstairs, like now."

His face screwed up at me. "You are leaving this room like that? But you are ugly. Uglier than normal."

He was no doubt referring to the black confection of a dress I'd been instructed to wear. It was entirely made of sheer lace, from the fitted bodice to the full skirts. A sheer skirted overlay was the only difference between the top and the bottom. At least the harness bra and high-waisted underwear they'd given me kept it from being entirely indecent. Not that the slit, clear up to my girly bits, gave that hope any wings to speak of.

I slipped the earrings into my lobes. "Well, it's a good thing I'm not looking for your approval, isn't it?"

"You can't leave. You must come. Right away. Things have went to hell in a head basket," he said.

"Again?" I asked, rolling my eyes, pinning the fasteners on the back.

"Does this have to do with the hell dog eating you guys?" asked Kittie, suppressing a yawn as she reclined on the curved, black wood.

"Yes, yes. That is exactly it," he said.

"Look, I told your sorry-substitute-for-a-king that I was coming up with a plan. It's only been two days. These things take time," I said.

Truth be told, I didn't know what to do. I'd spent the entire time holed away in here, talking to Kittie about it. Right now, the best solution we had was to do what legend said Sybyl had done, put sleeping herbs in Cerberus' food.

But considering he was eating goblins, it seemed far-fetched to have all of them carry bottles of sleeping pills until one of them was eaten. And then there was tracking and all of that hassle until the hound finally fell asleep. Talk about a giant PITA. The next best option I could think of was trying to trap him. Still, even though I had my powers again, the idea of trapping *the* big kahuna Hell Hound was a scary fucking prospect. That's why I hadn't said anything yet. There had to be another solution. I just had to find it.

Out of the corner of my eye, I saw something pulled down from my vanity. "No time, I tell you. It's went to hell in a-"

"Head basket, I know," I said, reaching down to pull my lace, black metal masquerade mask out of his hands. "Why the sudden tizzy?"

"Well, we moved to the Sodom and Gomorrah pools, just like you said," he paused, waiting for my approval, like an eager puppy. I smiled and nodded to keep the story going. "Well, Cerberus came to find us. We ran, but he grabbed Bontle. But the beast didn't go back to the gate. He went into the woods."

My mind blanked out in panic. Ok, this was the one time I agreed with the little goblin. This was bad.

"What if Cerberus found the gate and went back?" I asked, the black pearls clanking on the thick, wooden top as I set the mask back on the vanity. I mean, that was possible, right?

Maybe shook his head. His ears flopped with the violent motion, "No, Kut had followed him back out and has been watching the gate. Cerberus is on the plane."

On the plane as in roaming the human world. I let out a long breath.

"So wait...I'm not super up on my underworld creatures, but doesn't that mean nobody is preventing the dead, demons, hellspawn, and all of that fun stuff from leaving hell?"

Maybe nodded gravely with his big eyes, looking up at me.

"Faerie farts," said Kittie, who'd sat up.

I sighed and slumped back in my chair. "That can't be good."

Not quite how I would have put it. Especially considering me and a bunch of goblins were the only thing keeping Earth, and all of its ungrateful inhabitants, safe.

I must have looked quite fucked, and not in a good way, because Mabye put a hand on my forearm. "One nice thing is one of the ugly monkeys watching the shooting pools ran away to leave her tiny monkey. It's been serenading us with the most melodious song."

It took me a second to realize what he was talking about, but I finally got it and closed my eyes. From the peaceful smile that had been on his face, I could tell he was trying to make me feel better. It wasn't working. Quite the opposite. I wasn't a violent person, but I was 10 seconds away from cuffing the evil little goblin upside the head.

When the urge to either slap him or my forehead subsided, I clarified. "Are you telling me you took a human child?"

"Yes, they are quite delightful the way they sing all day and night," Mabye said, bouncing on his toes. "You can borrow it, if you like. It will help you feel better."

I swallowed. I wouldn't lose it. I would be fine. "Ok, Mabye, take that baby and put it in front of the gates. The workers who arrive in the morning can find it and return it to the mother." When he opened his mouth to protest, I held up a hand. "I don't care if you've named it, adopted it, initiated it into your clan. I. Don't. Care. Return it."

He nodded.

"Great, go and make that your number one priority," I said, waving my arms at him to get him moving.

The Diet Coke of Evil presence still didn't budge. It took some serious packing to stuff down the urge to scream.

"What are you still doing here, Maybe?" I asked as I slipped my foot into my dancing shoe.

"I'm waiting for you," said Mabye, with head-splitting obtuseness as he watched me thread the ankle strap through the dainty gemstone buckle.

I stopped long enough to look up and will him to combust on the spot. When he didn't, I finally said, "So are creatures coming up from hell?" He opened his mouth to speak. I held up a hand. "Yes, or no."

His foot shook as he opened his mouth and shut it a few times and then landed on. "No."

"Then go home, Mabye. Come get me if they start wandering through." Trial or not, I couldn't let all of hell overrun Earth because I was trying to play nice with the vampires.

"Your will is my duty, Protector of all that is Bad," he said, bowing low.

The room felt noticeably hotter. I wish he'd stop calling me that. However, I couldn't exactly tell him why it bothered me without giving myself away, so I gritted my teeth and kept my mouth shut. With any luck, there wasn't a special circle of hell for people who lied to an entire species. Looking at the wall clock with the breakaway bats, I stood up.

Swishing out my skirts, I said, "You've got to go. Sven is going to be here any minute." Then to Kittie I said, "It's pretty obvious we aren't getting the solution to this Cerberus thing ourselves. Can you get with Iris to see if there is anything she can think of to tie him back to Hell?"

"You got it," Kittie said with a mock salute as a knock sounded at the door.

Turning to Mabye, I said, "Yeah, you've got to go."

He pulled the cow skull hanging over his crotch up, his belly peeking out from under his stitched leather square of a shirt with the movement. "I'm going. You just focus on saying something rotten to that man, so he doesn't puke on you the second he sees you."

All I could do was shake my head as he grooved paths into the carpet as he dragged my puffed vanity stool over to the laundry chute. He flashed his bony goblin butt cheeks at me as he climbed onto the vanity and, of course, once again as he hefted himself into the shoot.

Turning around to give me a thumbs up, which I returned with a tight smile, he lost his grip and went tumbling down. As the shoot rattled, all I could do was be grateful he was gone. Inadvertent peep show and all.

My mind turned to the vampire that was undoubtedly at my door. Things were bound to be awkward. The last time I'd seen him, I essentially told him I would make him love me. At the time, it seemed like a perfectly reasonable plan. After all, he wanted to love me, and I wanted to love him. He just had no heart, was all. Surely, love could be found in other ways. I mean, scientifically speaking, emotions were a mental thing anyway. Maybe, if I got his brain firing for me, other parts would too...if you get what I mean.

The rap came again. I gave a start. Oh, nice. I'd just been staring at the door. Well, might as well make the most out of this outfit and put my theory to the test. Adjusting the slit on my leg so it was as scandalous as possible and putting a confident you-want-this smile on my face, I threw the deadbolt and opened the door. It was Sven alright. My heart slammed in my chest the second I laid eyes on him. In a fitted tuxedo that followed the curvature of all the right places, he was everything any red-blooded woman would want. With a strong jawline that peeked out of the bottom of his black, full-face mask, he screamed of virility that would bend you over the bed and kiss you senseless before you had a chance to remember your own name. Blue eyes so clear you could drown in them pierced through the simple leather with scrolled metal edging as they roved over me. His tumbled, dark hair and height were just the cherries on top of his eye candy sundae.

Too bad he was looking at me like you'd look at your sister.

"Hi, there," I said, in a sultry voice.

His eyes flickered. He knew I was acting flirty.

Instead of responding to it, his eyes weren't unkind as he offered me the crook of his arm. "Ready to go?"

Well, I'd been hoping for more, but I'd take kind over indifference any day. At least it was something to work with. Said every person in the Friend Zone ever.

Linking my arm in his, we made our way to the staircase in silence. The silence stretched on as we glided down the double-wide staircase. That was fine by me. Sure, one of my goals tonight was to woo the shit out of this man, but I needed to know what I was walking into first. We were heading into a room full of vampires, after all.

The stairs opened right into the ballroom. Glossy wood stretched over the entire length of the floor like a satisfied lover. The same polished face climbed the walls too, but here it was interrupted by black panels and framed by silver edges that spun into flirty curls. For all of the beauty below, the real spectacle was above. The same silver swirled edging was here, but instead of black in the center, the silver continued to wave and dip to form a spider's web. A giant spider chandelier in the web's center crawled along the entire ceiling, glittered menacingly.

Underneath the watchful red crystal eye of the spider, dancers swirled and dipped. Leather and lace masks sat upon the pale faces of the undead, making it hard to determine who was who. Not that it mattered much, they were all a threat, when it came to me.

We'd reached the bottom of the stairs, Sven stepping down first to hold a hand out for me. It was an outdated gesture, and it took everything in me to keep my eye roll in my head. Even if he didn't take into consideration that I was a Muay Thai master, had I not walked down the entire length of the stairs without breaking my neck? It was these kinds of insinuations that drove me crazy, and every other day of the week, I'd say something. Today, though, surrounded by a room full of old-fashioned vampires, I kept my irritation to myself. No need to ruffle feathers, especially dead ones.

I put my hand in his with a demure nod. My years at Court were the only reason I even knew the meaning of the word. When we stepped into the crowd, they parted like faeries at a witch convention. Was this a standard part of the custom? Or was there that much fear because of the fact that I was a faerie? It was a thought that had me doing a lot of blinking.

Unruffled by the separation, Sven moved us towards the center of the floor, which was empty also since the look-but-don't-touch bubble seemed to flow with us. Maybe, it was part of the pomp and circumstance after all. As we reached the center of the floor, he extended his arm out. I knew the move all too well and went with the motion to circle wide like a good dance partner. When we'd reached the center, I'd come full-circle back into his arms. It was then that I noticed there was no music. I would have liked to think it had to do with the fact that I was wildly attracted to the vampire, not even a foot from me, but I had the feeling it had more to do with the fact that the rite was officially underway. And we were the star attraction.

We stood, staring into each other's eyes, and as much as I willed my body not to, I sank into his spell. I loved this man. We would keep each other safe. Sure, he didn't love me, but that was temporary, right?

Being that we were on a dance floor, the first downbeat of the waltz shouldn't have flipped my stomach, but it did. When Sven pulled me close with a quick grab, I came alive, my heart slamming in my chest a million miles a minute. With the first step, my mind forgot we were on display for dozens of vampires. It even forgot I was solely responsible for Sven's trial and impending execution. All I could think about was this man in my arms and a love that swelled with every sweep of our arms and synchronized step of our feet to the haunting notes that coaxed us on. He twirled me around to a cast of violins that pleaded with us to stop. Still, he only conceded when the lighthearted notes of a piano came to play on top of it. He honored it and me by dipping me with a smile on his face. My heart fluttered, and I returned his smile with one of my own. Then the lovely notes dropped away to leave only a clever cello that had snuck in to flirt with my dark side. With a gentle tug, he pulled me up. Holding my hand high, gave my hand a light turn, and I knew that he wanted me to twirl. So I did once, twice, and almost three times before he stopped me by wrapping an arm around my waist to pull me flush against his body. The sudden pressure sent frissons of heat dancing through me, and I breathed for a few seconds to slow the zings racing down my spine. The music played on, so I stepped away, but he snapped me back against him with a harsh grip on my elbows. Feeling the hard length of him behind me had me melting, and when he brought a hand up to cup my throat. Even the harsh reality of a snare drum wasn't enough to pull me out of the magic of his touch. He finished the move by winding his hand lower, down my front. And I had a wild thought. Would he caress me in front of all of these people? When he grabbed my waist to hold me close. With his other hand, he bared my neck and laid a long lick that sent cold goosebumps blossoming over my skin. It took me a second, but I realized the last notes of an imploring xylophone had already faded into nothing under the watchful eye of the ballroom.

I flinched as something hit my shoulder. Then another touch came on my hair. I brought my hand up to catch one of the blood-red petals as they rained down around us. It only took seconds for me to realize the attendees were casting them at us. Bathed in blood by vampyrs.

"May blood wash them clean," Sven said as the blood fell between us.

My adrenaline spiked at the meaning. What other blood would be spilled tonight in this twisted ritual? Mine? Sven's? The questions hung over us as dancers whirled in, one by one, to join us. Before long, vampyrs moved in dizzying circles, close enough to reach out and touch. They flowed around us as we stood still, the last of the petals fluttering down, echoing the riot in my gut.

Sven placed a hand on my elbow. Lowering his voice, he asked. "Are you ok?"

Was I ok? What a ridiculous question. I was about to get the love of my life killed. Not to mention that man in question didn't even love me anymore. Unable to speak past the lump in my throat, I shook my head.

"We are required to dance no longer. Let's get you some room to breathe." Sven said, putting a hand on the small of my back.

Holding a hand out, he guided me to the wings. When we had made it to the back wall, I began to breathe a bit easier.

"Thanks," I said, releasing a deep breath as I rested against the cool paneling.

He nodded and leaned against the wall too. We sat there for a moment, processing our own separate thoughts and emotions. I was so grateful that a man as wonderful as Sven had come into my life. Even if we were going through hard times right now, he was still a friend. That much was clear. When he looked over and raised an eyebrow, I realized a smile was on my face. Warmth seeped into me. Maybe, it was time I sucked a little less at this making-him-fall-in-love-with-me-again thing.

Scooching closer to him on the wall, I stood there for a second, just feeling his presence as we watched people mill about, chat, and laugh together. If it weren't for the periodic stares and flared nostrils of interest my way, one could almost forget they were blood-thirsty pricks.

Not wanting to let the shared intimacy between Sven and I go to waste, I thought of what to say. Should I tell him he looked good, but he'd look even better between my legs? Or should I say he looked as edible as a hot-out-of-the-fryer chalupa? Both options flew from my mind, though, when Alwick appeared. Between a velvet cage that shrouded him almost entirely from view and a pewter mask shaped into a wolf's head, it should have been hard to identify the wretch. But I knew it was him by the cane in his hand and the way he stood. It was a posture that begged me to punch him in the face.

"You're looking well. Positively mouth-watering, really, Miss Vanguard," he said, with a low bow that held more than a trace of mockery.

Resisting to pull the slit of my skirt together, I pushed off the wall with my heel to stand straight instead. "You're not welcome to look."

His laugh tinkled like crystal, grating on my nerves.

Ignoring Sven, he moved closer to me. I shifted, unable to move any farther back because of the wall behind me.

"That was quite a performance on the dance floor, mon chéri. I must admit, I felt your call. And I have decided to answer it." he said, deliberately showing fang under the silver muzzle of his wolf's mask as he bit his lip. The blood in my veins froze at his declaration. He continued on, "When Sven is dead, I shall Claim you for my own."

My hands trembled at the image his words created. Sven's dead body at my feet. This monster sinking his fangs into me, making me do Dagda knows what. There was no telling what part of the vampire lifestyle Sven had spared me from. I'd experienced all of the benefits of being claimed by a vampire and very few of the drawbacks. I wasn't ignorant enough to think there weren't more. They were a tragic species. Cursed even, and some were undoubtedly wicked. Yeah, that wasn't happening.

"Over my dead body," I said, uncurling my fists when the stinging sensation alerted me to my freshly manicured nails digging into my palms.

Alwick groaned and closed his eyes in pleasure. After a moment, they fluttered back open, and he swayed closer. "If you keep talking like that, I might not be able to stop myself, and I'll have to take you before he's dead."

Faster than I could blink, Sven shoved himself between the vampyr and me. Alwick laughed as he fell back a few steps, never losing his balance.

The blank mask matched Sven's dead tone, and even I shivered when Sven said, "Disrespect me, do you? Take more care, Alwick. Before you find yourself dead."

The sudden movement drew the attention of another vampyr. At hearing Sven's threat, she stumbled over to drop an elbow drunkenly against the tuxedoed shoulder of another. Her hair, a shiny black curtain, fell off his broad shoulder as she tittered.

Blood in her wineglass sloshed over the sides, coating the stem and beading onto the velvet coat under her elbow as she said, "Says the vampire. What are *you* going to do against a vampyr?" Then her eyes honed in on me, raking me up and down.

"What are *you* looking at?" I asked, mimicking her mannerisms. Sure, she scared me a little bit, but you couldn't let bad people see your weakness. They'd exploit the hell out of it all day long.

"Just looking for stolen jewelry. Dozens of baubles have went missing since you got here. Why just yesterday I had a beautiful amulet go missing. It had a gorgeous red diamond that set my outfit off just so," she said with a sniff.

"Well, I don't feel like much of a miracle, so I think we can rule out coma-stealing," I said with a raised eyebrow.

Sven must have sensed me losing control because he spoke up, "Vampyr may he be, but I'm still a Master. Aren't I?"

She snorted, using the back as leverage as she tossed the remaining contents of the glass back. It dribbled down her chin as she sneered.

"Of the smallest coven in the bloodline. And aren't they being attacked even as we speak? How do you know you're really still a Master?" Dropping the glass, it splintered onto the floor. Her silver-spiked stilettos crunched over it as she staggered over to him. Coming an inch from his smooth, leather face, she leaned in, "Even I could be Master of your coven if I wanted to. Care to play, vamp boy?"

Sven "If you're looking for a fight-"

He cut himself off as the vibrational equivalent of a midnight thunderstorm soaked me to my bones. My body was alive with electricity, but it felt weighed down like all I could do was open my arms and let it consume me. What in the name of Dagda was that? I shook my head to clear the fog, but it had a hold of me. Blinking, I looked around to find the source.

There standing where the drunken vampyr had come in was the right hand of the High Priestess. Raven. For the occasion, like Sven, he'd donned a leather mask. His was in the shape of a raven's head. Strips of leather had been fashioned into stiff feathers around the slanted eyes of the mask while the remaining mask broke down into a wicked beak. The sharp end shone in the soft glow of the chandelier. Raven wore the same floor-length jacket and knee-high boots over black leather pants combo as he had the other day. However, he'd switched out the sensible black button-down for a sheer number that offered tantalizing glimpses of his sinewy chest. I exhaled, probably too loudly. Smooth, Cy. Pulling a face, I looked around. Thankfully, nobody had noticed. No, every eye in our unlikely foursome was on Raven. As it should have been. He strode towards us with the same force as if he'd come out of the mist straight from a pirate ship. The electricity dancing across my skin was definitely coming from him. It reminded me so much of my own lightning, but this power was different. It pushed at me, willing me into submission the closer he came. When he was right next to us, it beat at me with an intensity that I had to fight standing to keep from falling to my knees.

The blue of his eyes pierced us, one at a time, reading our soul. When the dark flecks of his eyes searched mine, the need to confess all of my sins overwhelmed me. I swallowed. Hard. After a few heartbeats of perusal, he moved on, finally settling on Alwick and the drunk vampyr.

"I believe you have somewhere to be, Ambrosia," he said, his voice menacing. Predatory.

The woman swished her glass our way, spilling the rest of its contents onto the floor. Blood splash, warm on my foot.

"Waste of my time, anyway. Come find me when you're done with the trash, won't you, love?" she said, her eyes raking over Raven as she slid away.

He didn't so much as blink in her direction. His eyes never left Alwick. When he made no move to leave, a slow smile stretched over Raven's lips. The eager look was enough to make Alwick's eyes narrow to slits in his wolf mask. Then he gave a nod before turning to leave. His cloak brushed against my bared leg. From the way he lingered a heartbeat, I knew the touch hadn't been accidental. It was a silent message that said we weren't finished.

Even though Raven didn't turn to watch him leave, the lines of his shoulders said he was very aware of the vampyr's movements. His posture relaxed when Alwick disappeared into the crowd. And then, like a light switch had been flicked, the submissive pull vanished. My eyes fluttered closed in relief at its absence. Tor Mór, what was I doing? I popped them back open. Forgetting where I was had dangerous written all over it. Letting your guard down around predators was a great way to get you dead. Even ones that looked like they had stepped out of a dream. Dreams could become nightmares in the blink of an eye.

Then he turned his attention to me. If I thought he'd given me his entire focus before, I'd been sorely mistaken. This time I felt the pull of his stare like a drowning pool, pulling me under. I shook my head to break the contact. Vampyrs could get in your head. Plant ideas there that weren't yours. I'd been on the receiving end of that before and didn't want to play that game again. Still, it felt like Raven wasn't doing it on purpose. Like he was just that powerful.

I was still wrestling with waves slamming into me one

after another when he spoke. "My dear. You shine brighter than any diamond in the room. How is it that our Sven has found such a treasure before I have shown you true pleasure? Thank the Mother, we have nothing but time. All you have to do is ask, I am but your willing servant."

My eyes had turned into saucers. Flying saucers. The kind that swallows you up whole and takes you to another planet. It wasn't that I wanted him. I mean, I did. What red-blooded woman wouldn't crave that slice of walking sex pie? Of course, I wouldn't accept his tantalizing offer. What I wanted from Sven was something this man could never give me. And I was going to find a way to get that from him. One way or another. But holy tamales, Raven was *hot*.

My tongue sat thick and useless in my mouth, but he must have been able to sense my answer. He clicked his own and shook his head. "More's the pity. By the by, I must steal Sven from you. Do forgive me."

Wait. Raven was taking Sven? That went a long way to clearing my mental fog. Sven met my where-in-the-fuck-do-you-think-you're-going look with a regretful one of his own. He had known this was coming. Well, for Dagda's sake, he could have told me. I didn't have a problem being alone. In fact, I quite liked it sometimes, but that didn't include when I was in a room full of vampires.

My heart hammered in my chest as men and women pass by. Some stopped to stare me dead in the eyes before moving on. I was under no illusion that this dress had somehow made me a hundred times sexier. Alwick, Raven, bells- all of them, they were attracted to the one thing they couldn't understand. The one thing they'd sensed but couldn't see. My blood. It was like a drug to vampires and vampyrs alike. So standing in a forest of them made my legs weak and me more than a little dizzy. I didn't even have my powers to rely on.

All it would take is one bolt of lightning from my fingertips to not only put the nail in Sven's coffin but seal my own fate.

Squaring my shoulders, I took a few stabilizing breaths to ease my light-headedness and walked into the crowd. The way the first couple I pushed between stared at me was quite funny. However, by the time I'd reached the edge of the dance floor, I was no longer laughing. The air was thick with anticipation. And all eyes were on me. I could hope they were waiting for me to jump onto the floor and do a tap-dance version of Peter Pan, but I doubted it.

A vampyr across the floor caught my eye. He was wearing all white. And even though his hair was lighter and how he held himself was all wrong, my mind jumped to the vampyr who'd kidnapped me to be his on-call girlfriend slash personal food source. Thomas. It wasn't him. Everything in me told me it wasn't. Sven had killed him. He was dead. My pulse jumped nonetheless when the vampyr started to weave through the crowd. He wasn't coming this way. Was he?

My mind zipped with thoughts as a hand slid into mine. It was small and soft. Neither was it insistent or demanding. Instead, comfort radiated from the gentle tips. My lips pressed together. Rather than jerk my palm out of the delicate one that held mine. I looked at it. The hand was whiter than a ray of sunshine, and its golden nails looked out of place in this land of black and red. I followed the hand up to its owner, somehow already knowing who it would be. It was the angelic vampire from The Invitation. She wore a gold blind mask. Wings sprouted out from the side, joined in the center by an ornate cross. The theme continued at the bottom of the filigree mask where small gold crosses dangled, laying against her cheek as she smiled at me. I thanked Danu her eyes were hidden behind her mask because I'd already felt her pull. These vampires radiated a power the likes of which I'd never seen. What made them different from the others I'd seen?

"Come. Dance with me," she said, her accent making her voice soft and wide.

I shouldn't. Going willingly into the arms of a vampyr was a terrible idea with a capital what-the-hell-are-you-doing, even if we were just dancing. But I found myself nodding anyway and going with her as she led me onto the dance floor. For some reason, I couldn't explain, she felt safe. She brought my hand up. When I didn't move into position, she reached for my other one, seating it snugly in hers. I had half a second to wonder who would lead before she started spinning me around the dance floor. We moved in wide, graceful arcs. I marveled at the way she led me in a way that was all woman, more coaxing than a man's dominating hand. If possible, it was more potent because it implored me to be a part of the dance rather than demanding submission. It begged and pleaded, meanwhile giving me everything I'd want and more.

I marveled at the way she moved. How the rigid line of her gold, strapless dress was at odds with the delicate way she whirled around the floor.

"All of these vampyrs watch you and wonder what you taste like. You are a heady prize, indeed," the woman said, her hold solid but gentle as she swung me around to the music.

"Do you?" I kicked myself, knowing I shouldn't ask, but couldn't help myself.

She laughed. The sound delightful, like a bird's song. "Of course, I do." As she spun me closer and turned me in time to the music, her voice dropped to a whisper as she said, "A faerie is a rare catch indeed."

Despite her sweet demeanor and calming presence, her words made me cold all over. She hadn't said fae. She'd said faerie. But there was no way she could have known what I was. Could she? Whatever she thought she knew, I had to stop that line of thinking. Immediately. Sven's very life depended on it.

I laughed, the sound high and tight even to my own ears. "What a ridiculous-"

"Your secret will stay with me. And don't you worry. I only bite the willing. If that be you, I'd love to oblige. Otherwise, you are safe with me. You have nothing to fear."

Her words racketed around inside my head. Safe. With a vampyr who, of her own admission, wanted to drink my blood, who knew who I was. The thought didn't sit well, but all of my instincts had hit the snooze button like the midnight hour it almost was. I was at a loss. Usually, I trusted my gut. In my line of work, you had to. But none of it made sense. How did she know what I was? Why wasn't she telling anyone?

"Why?" I asked, executing the swing together and coming apart move the dance dictated.

"Why what? Why only bite the willing?" she asked, bringing me close, her skirts swishing against mine as we moved in time with the music.

"No, why... the kindness? Even if unneeded." I added, unwilling to come out and admit I was a faerie as I moved away again.

Her movements came to a quiet end as the dance did. "I suppose because I see some of the old me in you. Someone who means no harm. Who only wants to help those less fortunate. That is to be cherished, not turned."

While her words had me patting myself on the back for my sparkling intuition, what she was saying hit me as we stopped moving since the music had ended. "You are a vampire. Not a vampyr."

She gave a slight nod, her curls springing with the movement. "I am."

I wanted to ask more. Ask if she had been a faerie too, but I didn't dare. Not here.

"But I thought all in the Blood Spire were vampyrs besides Sven and me," I said.

"Unlike your Master, the rest of us like to stay under the radar. It is a safer place to be," she said, with a twist to her lips and a shrug of her bare shoulders.

The way she said Master sat like week-old pizza in my gut. I didn't like to be reminded that someone had control over me. Even if the person in question was wonderful and let me be me. I shrugged off the feeling. I couldn't change the facts. For now, it was enough to know we weren't the only ones here not vampyr. For some reason, I didn't understand, it made me feel...safer. A silly thought considering both could rip out my throat and enslave me just as efficiently. But I held onto it.

"What's your name?" I asked.

"Catherine of Sienna." She gave a slight bow and then inclined her head in acknowledgment to the other side of the room and said, "Speaking of which, he is here."

Thank, Danu. I whirled around so fast I had to check if I gave myself whiplash. But Sven wasn't here to keep me company. He was on the other side of the room on a stage with steps leading up to the small platform he stood on. It held all of the charm of burning a witch at the stake. Sven stood in the center of it, naked from the waist up except for his leather face mask. His muscled triceps made his arms look huge as he spread his arms. Wide, open.

What in the name of Dagda was happening? My stomach clenched. I was sick of not knowing what was going on in this forsaken place. I wanted to go to him, to prove to myself that he was ok. But I couldn't. I stepped on my foot to keep myself rooted in place. This was all part of the ritual. Part of the process. My going up there would do nothing but embarrass Sven, if not break some kind of stupid vampire law. There seemed to be a million of them. And I thought faerie law was extreme.

Four women dancers, clad in black teddies with strings of red sequins dropping down to form a half-hearted skirt, danced onto the stage. They wore blind masks of red lace with horns made of bone jutting out from each side. Their bodies popped, flashing the red sparkles like spurts of blood as they moved towards the stage.

"Their motions tell the tale of the crime," Catherine whispered close to my ear, her heavy Dominican accent sending shivers up my spine.

When the dancers were within a foot of the stairs, they dropped to the ground. Slithering a few steps up the stairs only to drop back down to the hard, black planks. They writhed and gyrated like snakes in a frenzy around Sven's feet, coming up to caress around his bare feet and slide up inside his dress pant leg. My jaw tightened. Then they fell back onto their knees, away from him. The move didn't calm my nerves, though. Undulating their bodies, they reached towards him. Then without warning, they spun on their kneecaps and turned towards the audience, stopping in a flourish of sequins. Making the same motions to us, they danced and interwove their arms into each other's. Finally, they broke free to reach their arms in a wordless plea to the audience. It was then that one of the dancers fell with a flourish. Crawling up the stairs, her body popped in time with the jarring music that had slowly seeped into my consciousness. When she reached him, she threw her arms out, unfurling giant black bat wings from her back as she rose to her feet. She swept her arms in wide arcs. My stomach jumped as the fabric concealed Sven, only offering glimpses of his stoic masked self. All of the dancers flew back, dropping to the floor, motionless. Seconds later, the woman creating all of the chaos went limp and fell at his feet.

There stood the High Priestess. Her mask was an infinity symbol on top of a two-barred cross. It jutted high to hold a thick, black veil that framed her eyes, so pale that they looked white, and her pencil-thin brows. She stood behind Sven. My chest tightened. I wanted to scream to Sven to run. The woman at his feet rose again, climbing his body with flat hands. She was asking for it. When she stood once again, she caressed his head, her red nails flashing in and out of his dark hair. Then she removed his mask, extending it in with a quick sweep.

"The Unveiling is about revealing the truth," Catherine's voice brushed my ear as my heart pounded in my chest.

The Priestess lowered her head to Sven's neck. My hand flew to my neck.

"They aren't going to-" I sucked in a breath when Sven's face contorted as the Priestess sank her teeth into him.

Black blood ran down his neck and chest in a thick curtain. Though he never screamed, the pain was plain on his face. Time seemed suspended as he was soaked in his own blood. I don't know if it was a test or what, but I was done with it. I went to move forward, but I was stopped with a hand around my wrist. This time I knew who it was and threw daggers at Catherine. She gave a quiet shake of her head. I gritted my teeth. Everything in me screamed to get him, save him, but her imploring eyes said that would only make it worse for him. Sinking all of my faith in the fact that he was to be held for trial still, my chest rose and fell, heavy and fast. It went against all of my instincts, but I made myself stay. Painful seconds stretched on before the High Priestess finally raised her bloody mouth. And looked straight at me. The warning clear in her eyes.

a teenager with more swagger than he deserved walked past our wooden topped long table at Hell Pizza. I wanted to trip him. Dear Danu, did I ever. Maybe it would wipe that smug look off his greasy face.

Sighing, I looked back across the table. If I was being honest with myself, that was probably the real source of my frustration. Sven. He'd agreed to come out on a date, but I don't think building a connection with me was why he was really here. Not that it felt like it was starting to matter. When I first suggested we go out for pizza, I never imagined we'd end up at a place called Hell Pizza. Between the goblins issue with *actual* hell and this hell-on-earth trial we were a part of, I'd had my fill with everything hell-related at this point. But of course, this was the closest pizza place. And our date night dinner had to be pizza. We'd had it on our first stakeout together. I thought it would bring back memories of when we'd really started to fall in love after our lust-filled, rocky start. I know overlooking something as mammoth as getting bitten painted me a sucker. However, Sven really had done everything he could to prove how much he had messed up the first time around, even going so far as to give me his heart to bring me back to life. Wasn't that a love worth fighting for?

I said yes. So here we were. Whoever said true love was effortless never sat across from someone, trying to rekindle a love that had somehow grown to feel impossible, over fast-growing cold pizza. I hated cold pizza.

"Don't you like deluxe?" I asked, knowing full well he did as I nodded to the untouched pizza on his plate.

"It's fine," he said with a shrug.

I smiled; it was empty. A clatter of pans in the kitchen crashed in the silence that yawned between us. This was not going like I'd thought it would. Maybe, he needed a nudge in the right direction.

"Do you remember when we had pizza last?" I asked, wrapping my tongue around the cheese dangling off the end of the pizza. Or I tried to. The cheese was hard and didn't come when I pulled it, so I ended up biting it off like an angry chihuahua.

"Of course, I do," he said, a spark flaring in his eyes.

Hope flared in my chest. What piqued his interest, I didn't know. Sure, it could have been me and our love. But more than likely, it was the bloodthirstiness of staking out a killer. Whatever it was, was fine by me. I'd take anything that resembled emotion at this point.

"Me too," I said, leaning on the table to get closer to him, never close enough. The smell of earth and cinnamon tickled my nose. "It was incredible how you helped me put that killer behind bars. His sister would have died if it wasn't for you."

Sven shrugged and pushed the still whole piece of pizza to the center of the table. "I respect what you do for a living. Being a bounty hunter can't be easy. Tracking down people and bringing them back alive? Are you kidding? It would be so much easier just to kill them."

I sat back in my bench seat. So much for warm and fuzzies.

"That seems to be your species' answer for everything. You know there *are* other solutions," I said, my mind going to his impending trial.

"But none so effective," he said, with a sardonic tilt of his lips.

"Maybe, you'll think differently when you're dead," I said, fear making the words a freight train I couldn't stop from passing my lips.

All he did was shrug. I wanted to scream. Why couldn't he care about his future just a little bit more? Oh, yeah. That's right, because I had his heart. I dropped my head in my hands. Talk about cyclical issues.

My frustration wouldn't help him. Instead, with a herculean effort, I took a deep breath and focused on him. "So, what's the plan for your trial?"

"Our trials are not so different from the human trials you are used to. The days of guilty until proven innocent are over. Now, we are given the opportunity to prove our innocence."

"Oh, yeah. That was quite the 'opportunity' you were a part of last night," I said as I motioned to his now-healed neck.

Regeneration. Don't we all wish we had it? He merely shrugged at my angry words.

Tor Mór, I had the hardest time keeping my feelings in check when I was worried. I looked away. "So, what's the plan for keeping your butt from frying anyway?"

"We just have to prove that you aren't fae," he said with a smile.

I gave him a droll look. Leaning over the table, I whispered, "Kind of hard to do when I *am* one."

A smug look accompanied the raise of his eyebrow.

"But they don't know that, do they?" he whispered so close to my lips that my heart tripped over itself.

I moved over to his side of the table. Talk about a subject we didn't want to broadcast across the restaurant. At least that's what I told myself. Easy to say, harder to believe when my thigh brushed his as I straddled the bench. I tried to focus on what he was saying. You would have thought it would have been easy, considering it was life or death we were talking about. Let's hear it for a starved sex drive.

Snorting, I pulled my Coke over. After taking a noisy sip, I continued in a hushed tone. "Kind of hard to keep a secret when all they have to do is dip a fang in. Seems to be everyone's favorite pastime in your little *community*."

He knew I wasn't happy. I could tell as much by the set of his shoulders. So why was he smiling? Frowning? Something?

"But that's the thing," he said, crossing his arms over his chest. The movement brushing his leg against mine. Did he do that on purpose? I shot a look at him. There was a glint in his eyes, but the sparkle held no hint of wanting to jump my bones. Bummer.

Oblivious to my inner turmoil, he continued on.

"One of the perks of being Claimed is being bitten without permission from your Master is forbidden. So your blood is mine." His grin grew as he held his hands up cockily.

Part of me wanted to roll my eyes even while my veins sang at his claim. But outwardly, I reacted to neither. I had more pressing questions. "So, what are the exceptions to that little rule?"

As part of Law Enforcement's "good-guy" side, I knew a thing or two about how the Law didn't always apply to those executing it. And from the way everyone had been sharing their "sides" like it was some sort of family reunion potluck, it smelled of that kind of law.

"The only exception that exists is if they can prove probable cause. And no wings, no cause." Sven sat back as if that were check and mate. When I didn't look convinced, he leaned forward. "If you don't have wings, the prosecution won't have a leg to stand on. Everything else is purely conjecture. They won't kill me based on speculation."

I winced at his words. Reaching into my pocket, I rubbed the coin I always kept there. As part of the spell to seal one of the doors in the Never, I'd given up my wings. Yes, that was just as traumatic as it sounded. Not only had it been painful as the eternal torment of a lich's binding spell, but the haunting words of Oganess kept floating back to me. "Flight, wings, and ancestors, yours no more." It was inconvenient as hell while I was trying to sleep. What had the words meant? Just what had I done by giving up my wings? Now that closing the doors was off our plate, I really wished I could ask her. Yes, she said we'd always be connected, that I'd never be alone again. And while I did feel their presence, feelings only went so far. What I wouldn't give for an actual conversation with the headstrong, teen sorceress I'd come to think of as family. Gods be, any of the Kamikazes, for that matter. They were the only real family I'd ever known.

Weeding through the thoughts made me feel like I was picking through a bramble bush, but I finally remembered what Sven and I were talking about. And it was still a sore subject. "For your information, it's not a smooth canvas back there. It's pretty obvious shit went down," I said, gesturing to my back.

He looked at me for a long time. Then he reached for me before his brow crinkled, and he ran his hand through his hair instead. From his actions, his struggle couldn't be more apparent. He wanted to be there for me but didn't know what to do. The thought lightened some of the fear in my chest. At least he was reaching out to me. Maybe, he remembered some of what we had.

"Do you want to see?" I asked, my mouth suddenly dry. Revealing your scars to someone was a very intimate act. Maybe that's why it was so important to me that he saw them. To remind me that our love was real and worth fighting for.

Searching my eyes, he finally said, "If it's something you're ok with."

"I wouldn't have offered if I wasn't," I said, wrinkling my nose up at him to lighten the mood.

He laughed at my antics as I turned around and shrugged off my jacket. Moving my hair over my shoulder, his laughter stopped. With delicate fingers, I felt him traced the bumped pattern. The slashes barely resembled the glorious wings that had been there. And that included the tattooed version before they had sprung out of me like some magical jack-in-the-box.

"They did this to you?" Sven asked, his voice tight. Hard.

Was he angry? The hope of any emotion from him was burned away by a blush that burned my cheeks. Technically? Yes, but it's not like I'd been forced. It had been Stupid Move 75,001.

"It was sort of my choice," I said, not wanting to get into details. It had been Stupid Move 75,002 and 75,003 that had led to not only the doors being opened in the first place but the sacrifice of my wings to close them.

He let out a sigh, the sound sudden in the almost empty pizza joint. With a pitying look that made everything in me want to take it all back, he quirked his lips and said, "We'll just say you were in a house fire."

The idea didn't make me feel any better. My lip curled as I looked out the window. "I suppose-"

I cut myself off as a movement outside the window

caught my eye. A teal streak darted into the darkened alley that was tucked against the side of the restaurant. Well, that's a fuckery bomb.

"Give me a second, will you?" I asked, already standing up even as I said it.

Never taking my eyes off where the flash had disappeared, I made my way out the door into the quickly cooling night air. The sound of metal crashing against metal rang out as I made my way to the alley. When I rounded the corner, the back of a teal creature greeted me. His wings beat fast as he crashed two trash can lids together in glee, which didn't pose a problem for him because his wings were miniature compared to his body, so they were useless. I let out a tired sigh. An imp. I mean, why not? My night might as well add to it Hell's pain-in-the-ass.

Continuing to crash his new toys together, his heart-shaped tail barb dragged on the pavement behind him as he turned to offer me a profile. Navy striped horns that bled from teal to gold jutted out from a face that could disgustingly be described as nothing else but cute. He suddenly went still, his body going rigid as something caught his eye. My gaze trailed his to a man, passed out against the graffitied brick wall not four feet from him. A cigar in the imp's mouth glowed red in the dark. Then smiling, he held the lids aloft and took a step towards the peacefully sleeping form. I suppose that meant I had to help. I rolled my eyes at myself. As if I would have walked away anyway.

"How about you put those down instead?" I called in a clear voice that I reserved for skips and stupid people as I made my way unhurriedly down the alley.

The cigar drooped as his grin fell. A laughingly perplexed look came across his face as he turned towards me, his big, gold eyes glowing with a mischievous glint. When he saw me, though, even that dropped from his face.

He rolled his eyes and let out a disgusted sound, turning up his palms. The trash can lids dropped with a clang and a wong that echoed down the short alley.

"Oh, look. It's Cy Vanguard," he said, raising his hands and moving his shoulders in a prissy movement.

How in the name of Dagda did he know who I was? Yes, I was a faerie princess, but we didn't exactly consort with denizens of Hell. Not even the Unseelie did. Even though I was all kinds of confused, I didn't show it. Imps were like kids. If they thought they had a leg up on you, they'd be all over it like ants on cakes. I just kept walking towards him. Slowly. Deliberately. He shrank in on himself as I drew closer.

"Taking down Kroni wasn't that impressive, you know. He was over a millennia old. That's practically having one foot in the grave and one on a banana peel. Anyone could have pushed him into the grave. Satan's balls, even I could have," he said, spitting.

Chewed up bits of his cigar landed in a ball on the ground. He was nervous. Good. Stopping a foot from him, I crossed my arms over my chest. His belly jiggled as his body vibrated with fear.

It hadn't been my choice to fight the Devil's number one muscle, but when the prince of hell tells you to fight someone to save your friend, you don't have many choices.

Ignoring my apparent, newfound celebrity status, I looked down my nose at him, focusing on what important, like why a creature from Hell was on Earth. "Why are you here, imp?"

"Imp? Imp, she says. That's just plain rude, you know. I've got a name." He thrust his belly out, disgruntled. I merely raised an eyebrow. He averted his eyes. He was still watching me as he let out a belabored sigh and said, "Brazzi."

This little guy was past my nerves and making no sense.

Wondering if there was any law against throttling a citizen of Hell without just cause, I asked, "What?"

"My name is Brazzi," he said, straightening in pride.

"Fabulous," I said, my tone making it clear this line of conversation was anything but. "Now that we're nice and acquainted, why don't you tell me why you're here?"

"I felt like it," he said with a shrug that said he did everything he felt like. Not surprising since imps, as a general rule, did everything that popped into their heads.

"Did you get here through the Gate?" I asked, afraid I knew the answer already.

"Maybe I did and maybe I didn't. Maybe it's up to you to find out, and maybe you won't," Brazzi said, dropping a giant ash from his cigar with a flick against his foot that looked like it belonged to a six-toed kitten.

Screw it. Getting a solid answer from an imp was about as likely as getting blood from a stone. "Why don't you fuck back off to Hell? You aren't welcome here."

"But I just got here," the little imp said with a flabbergasted hand on his thick hip.

My jaw ached from grinding my teeth. Even though I didn't know if I could attack him, I knew one thing I could do. Scare him. Tapping the closest ley line, magic flowed into me warm, lapping at my consciousness. With a flick of my hand, I pretended to inspect my nails and released a tiny spark. And just like that, my hand lit up. Lightning flashed and crackled, licking up my forearm and over my fist. Then I looked back down at the imp. Way down, he barely came to my thigh. The color had drained from his face. He schooled his features into a flat set again.

"Whatever, I don't want to be on this boring plane anyway. There's a human trampoline I have to get back to. Until we meet again, Ms. Vanguard," he said as he padded away.

"I'll kill you if I find you topside again," I called after the little imp, not convinced he was actually leaving.

He turned to stop and look at me, hitting me with the full force of those adorable eyes. "I get it. I get it, Faerie Queen. I'm leaving," he said, dragging on his cigar once more before he threw it to the ground and sauntered around the corner with a brave set of his shoulders. The golden barb of his tail trailed after him like a security blanket.

With another belabored sigh that was starting to sound like my mating call, I walked over to the lit embers smoldering on the dirty pavement.

"Since when are you Queen?" Sven asked, leaning a shoulder against the window of Pizza Hell as I walked around the corner.

"Since never," I said, grinding the thick cheroot under my glossy red heels.

What a waste of a good heel. The night, not the cigar. I hadn't had any hopes for the bad habit. The same couldn't have been said about my date, though. I'd had plenty of wishing on a star notions about that.

"You know he's not likely to go back," Sven said, pushing off the wall as I finished my Good Samaritan moment.

Maybe it was the heels. Perhaps it was the growing unease that had started to nibble at me ever since I'd spied Brazzi sneaking into the alley. Or maybe it was the yawning night that had my inhibitions disappearing like a faerie light in the morning. Whatever the reason, I didn't know if my motives were pure or wicked when I asked him, "How do you feel about another stakeout?"

CHAPTER 7

"*W*hy are we outside the thermal park?" Sven asked as we sat in our Ford Fiesta rental, facing the employee entrance.

Being careful to avoid the steering wheel, I shifted my right leg against the door for the 100th time. I didn't want to bump the horn and attract unwanted attention from the night security, but I just couldn't get comfortable. This was my go-to position on a stakeout, but my leg wasn't cooperating. It didn't understand why it had to be propped up instead of the usual left leg. Why couldn't the world all drive on the same side of the road again?

"Mabye said Hell's peeps hadn't been coming through, but we just saw an imp. And since Mabye is...well, a goblin, let's just say I have my doubts about if we can trust him. So we're at Hell's Gate to make sure he is right and there aren't more of that imp's friends here."

"Like the actual gate to Hell?" Sven asked as a woman carrying bags that looked about as big as the ones under her eyes wandered out of a door labeled Employee's Only. After assessing the dumpster like she'd rather throw herself in, she tossed the two bags in and went back through the door with a slam.

"The one and only," I said, shifting my leg back down.

"So what's the plan if we happen upon one of these dastardly creatures of the Underworld?" asked Sven, a teasing note creeping into his voice.

Considering vampires were descended from Satan like we were descended from God, it made sense that he found this situation ironic. It was. I was in a car with a descendant of Satan looking for all things Hellish. Oh, irony. How she hated me.

"Well, I suppose it depends which creature we happen upon, doesn't it?" I asked, flipping my hair.

And it really did. You wouldn't send an imp back the way you would send an ifrit back. The thought made me stop. Danu help us if a hellspawn came. I was fresh out of sorceresses that could send them back.

We watched the back of the building. Nothing moved behind the stacked barrels, over the pallets thrown into a nonsensical pile, or even as much as a wayward wrapper dancing across the parking lot. As far as stakeouts were concerned, it was pretty typical. A lot of nothing. So far the annoying little goblin was right. Thank Danu for that.

I really should lean over. Make a flirty comment. Maybe even drop the neckline of my shirt to expose some skin. But suddenly I didn't want to fuck him as much as I wanted to be there for him. Giving him my time was the best way to thank him for what he had done for me. For the favor I'd never be able to return in measure, no matter how long we both lived. But I could show him I cared. That, at least, I could do.

"So how did a little coven in the Catskill area become a big player in New York City?" I asked, diligently watching the lot of nothing going on in front of us.

"We are the only local supplier of Heaven's Tears," Sven said.

Faerie's blood. My people's blood. His tone didn't make any apologies, though. I wanted to be angry at him for that, but I had to stuff it down. It seemed counterproductive to what I'd set out to do anyway. Besides, he hadn't known his Uncle had been keeping faeries as glorified cows until I was kidnapped. And then we burnt the place to the ground. Not intentionally, but it still made me feel good to think about it that way.

Remembering we were having a conversation that didn't center around me, I asked, "Since your supply has stopped, doesn't that make you less attractive to wannabe master vamps?"

Since we'd freed the faeries and destroyed their supply in the process, it seemed like a fair assumption to make.

"No, because the faeries giving us blood was only reserved for higher members of the coven, everyone thought we had a supply. And they don't believe a supply of that magnitude could be contained in one small house," he said. I inwardly rolled my eyes at that. One person's house was another person's 23,680 square foot mansion, I suppose. He continued on. "Now, they think we are hoarding the supply, so it's actually made attacks on the coven more frequent. Honestly, I don't know how much longer we can keep them at bay." His eyebrows pinched together as he looked out the window.

I let my air out in a loud whoosh. What a shitty position. First, he'd accepted the role of Master, even though he didn't want it. And now, on top of that, death was knocking at his door because of that same responsibility. What did you say to that? Sorry about your luck? Bummer? Both responses were sure to earn me an eye roll. And rightly so. Even though I didn't know what to say, I knew one thing. It made me love him even more. Only the strongest, rarest of creatures didn't give up when saddled with an enormous burden. And death was undoubtedly the greatest burden of all.

My heart warmed. I wanted to kiss him. Tell him it was going to be alright. All of those lies you wanted to hear during a time like this. What would he say if I did? Would he accept my kiss? My love? Knowing that he couldn't return it? Or maybe it would trigger something in him. Make him remember what we had? What we could have again. It was worth a try. Holding my breath, I slid closer to him.

"I believe one of your dastardly fiends is over there," Sven said with a nod over my shoulder, breaking the spell.

My brow wrinkled. So much for having some fun. Trying to ignore the voice inside me complaining as loudly as a two-year-old, I looked to where he pointed.

My eyebrows rose to my hairline. "Does that even count?"

Sven chuckled. Ok, yes. Technically speaking, he was right. There *was* a being from Hell here. The lowest of all of the beings that is. A familiar.

The black cat's hindquarters waggled as it readied itself. Then it sprung onto the barrel without a sound. It made its way effortlessly from one barrel to the next, with one uncertain paw in front of the other.

Clenching my jaw, I opened the door. "I'll be right back."

At the click of the door, the familiar looked over, its eyes flashing blue in the dark night.

"Do you need backup?" Sven asked, keeping his face blank.

"Oh, haha," I said, closing the door on his laughter with a smile of my own.

Any other day, I wouldn't think twice about seeing a familiar on Earth, especially blue-eyed ones. They were bound to witches, after all. However, there was no witch to be seen. That paired with the imp I'd seen earlier made this worth a conversation, at the very least.

The cat swung her graceful head, eyeing me like a queen oversaw her subjects. Trust me. I had enough experience on the topic to pen a novel. This queen, however, I didn't have any second thoughts about walking up to.

"Where's your master?" I asked when I was in range for only her to hear.

"Meow," it said, settling its tail against the outside of the barrel and lifting its head as if turning up its nose at me.

What this little pain in the butt didn't know was that I'd had my fill of obstinate devilish folk today. Setting my hand on the metal ring of the barrel, I opened up to the nearest ley line. With a thought, I felt a faint buzz as I released a jolt of current through my fingertips. The cat screeched and lifted its tail high in the air.

"Of all of the rude, insufferable things," she said with a haughty puff of her chest.

I merely raised an eyebrow.

She sniffed and looked away. Looking back, her whiskers drooped as she frowned. "If you must know, my *witch* hasn't come into her powers yet."

"Then shouldn't you be in Hell?" I asked. Since I didn't know everything about other magics, I wanted to make sure she was where she needed to be before I jumped to conclusions.

"Should is a word used by inferior creatures," she said, wiggling her bottom as she settled back down onto the top of the barrel.

"Let me rephrase that. Aren't you supposed to be in Hell?" I asked, my jaw beginning to ache with the effort of holding back the scream starting to build in the pit of my chest.

Yawning, she lifted a paw. "Technicalities. The real question is would you want to be there? They're insufferable.

Constantly whining about torture and eternal damnation, it's positively exhausting."

A lousy answer was still an answer.

"Ok, so you're supposed to be in Hell. How did you get here exactly?" I asked, sweeping a hand around us.

"Here? Oh, there was a pile of diapers with what undoubtedly was feces in them. I most certainly wasn't going past that. And then when I got to the pools, I smelled rotten eggs, also, out of the question. So I came over here, and when I saw the rats on the ground, I decided to wait them out on these barrels. Not exactly a settee, but it will do in a pinch. Rats are dirty little things. Did you know they carried the plague-"

I held up a hand to cut her off. She drew back like I'd insulted her mother.

Whatever, I didn't have time for pretentious familiars. "I mean, how did you end up on Earth?"

Her shoulders relaxed again. "Oh, well. When I strolled by during my half-moon ritual walk, I noticed Cerberus, that noisy canine, was neglecting his duties- doing Satan knows what. The gate was wide open, and him nowhere to be seen. Really a lazy beast."

I shook my head. Yep, just what I thought. Hell's citizens were just breezing through without a care in the wind. And if a familiar could get through, there was no telling what else had gotten through already.

With a sigh, I said, "What's your name?"

"Radi," she said, tossing her mane like she was a lion on the safari. "It's short for Radiance."

Of course, it was. Let's completely ignore the fact that she was as dark as a black hole. "You really should go back to Hell."

She lifted an eyebrow and said, "You sound boring enough to be there. Why don't you go in my place?"

I narrowed my eyes at her. She squinted back at me. I laughed. Of all the cheeky little beings.

Shaking my head, I said, "Good night, Radi."

A huff was the most response I was getting out of her, which was fine. I had more things to worry about than a rogue familiar. She wasn't going to do anything more than shame a few kids who, frankly, probably needed it. I had bigger things on my plate, like figuring out a way to send Hell's higher-up-the-food-chain denizens back. Because Danu knew where a familiar dwelt, a hellspawn was sure to follow. And I had no clue how to send one of those back.

CHAPTER 8

I looked at the glow stick necklaces in my hand. They looked right at home against the backdrop of the dirty club bathroom's floor. It still weirded me out that the vampyrs were so cocky in their command of the entire world that they let me come and go as I pleased. I mean sure I wasn't on trial, but weren't they afraid I'd tell someone about them? I mean there had to be *someone* vampires were afraid of. Wasn't there?

"How exactly do these work again?" I asked, my face scrunching up as I tried to stuff what Kittie had told me in there.

"You crack it like you busted some bones, and then you shake it like a baby, and then you lasso it around their neck like you're hog tying your least favorite Aunt, and then you clip it in place like...like a glow stick necklace." A poster stuck to the bathroom door proclaiming, "Fozzy Coming Friday," bobbed in and out of view as she explained it for the second time.

No doubt she'd added the similarities this time because she thought I didn't understand the first time. Oh, I had. Perfectly.

I ignored everything wrong with her examples. One issue at a time. "Like a glow stick necklace. On whichever Hell's many residents have wandered onto Earth."

"Exactly," she said, crossing her arms and nodding approvingly.

"Right, I got that the first time." I swallowed and tried again, unable to believe I had to actually say it. "My problem comes in with the fact that you all are asking me to clip a *glow stick* on a *being* from *Hell.*"

"You sure you aren't Queen yet? You're so drama," she said, rolling her eyes.

Careful not to touch the side of the stall of the club's bathroom, I shook the magical glow stick necklaces at her. "These suck." At least it was something. It was a lot better than the nothing I had right now. Sighing, I stuffed them into my purse. "Did Iris tell you how we're supposed to tie Cerberus back to Hell's Gate?"

"She said the Cerberus problem is as tricky as a two-toed troll. Right now, she only knows how to send Hell's peeps to the inner circle of Hell. Not actually tie them there," Kittie said, flying up to land on the coat hook.

Stuffing down a growl of frustration, I said, "Well, thanks for the necklaces. They'll buy us time if nothing else. Now, can you go back and see if Iris found a way to bind Cerberus to the gate yet? Because without him guarding the entrance, everyone I send down is just going to pop back up. And I might have more to do than being Earth's toll booth operator."

"Sure, it's not exhausting at all flying the globe over and over." She stood up and stretched her wings. She really was doing a lot to help me. Maybe someday I would show her how much I appreciated it. Then she said, "It's a good thing you're not a pain in the ass at all."

That did a lot to help ease my guilt. I was still trying to

figure out if she'd done it on purpose or if she was just a little jerk when she zipped out of the stall.

"Be careful!" I called after her.

Throwing the latch on the stall door, I made my way out too. This was a cluster of mammoth proportions. Barely registering the heavily-graffitied door to the bathroom as I pushed through it, I told myself everything was going to be fine. I was probably worrying for nothing. I readjusted my purse with the magical glow sticks in them. I'd just hoped and prayed these worked.

As I ducked and dodged through the dancers, they parted to reveal Sven lounging against the club's dingy wall, just where I'd left him. Then the gap closed again, and he was gone. I'd excused myself to go to the bathroom when Kitty had dusted me to get my attention. Even though I didn't love that we'd been in public when she'd done it, it was the best possible option. Glitter was as a staple in a club as trees were in a forest. I was glad she'd come and found me. I felt a whole lot more comfortable with a weapon, any weapon, that would send the creatures back to Hell. Sure, the necklaces weren't ideal because the banished could find their way back, but since these bad boys sent them back to the inner circle of Hell, that would give me time. Speaking of which, now that I had a way to send him back, even temporarily, I should probably get down to Hell's Gate and wrangle one of these around Cerberus. Maybe that would give us enough time to tie him to the gate. Permanently this time.

Any other day that ended in Y, I'd be itching to take care of Cerberus this second, but I couldn't go. Not now. Not on the eve of Sven's trial. I was an emotional wreck, by what I still couldn't shake was his looming death. That was actually why we had come out, to take our minds off of what lay ahead. Admittedly, it had been my suggestion. Partly because I didn't want to be alone and partly because of my seemingly doomed quest to get Sven to feel something for me again. The latter was probably why we'd spent most of the night holding up the wall with our backsides rather than the dancing I'd suggested in the first place.

The sea parted again to find Sven in the same place, in the same position, I'd left him. He looked sexy and completely unapproachable in a black tee, black jeans, and a closed-off expression. He was still here, at least. That was a plus.

I gave him a smile as I settled in next to him. To his credit, he returned my smile and then turned back to watch the dancers. Their feet were so close to us, it was a wonder they didn't step on our toes. At first, I watched them too, shocked to find most people moved barely at all. With their arms close and their bodies swaying from side to side, they moved with all of the liveliness of passengers on a subway. However, there was one particularly amorous couple in the back who caught my attention. They moved differently. Pressed close together, they dipped and swayed, the language of love clear on their faces. My heart squeezed. They rocked side to side, moving in time. Reminding me of how not so long ago that had been Sven and I. The man bent his love over, swirling low with her and then coming back up. Their hips moved in unison as she smiled up into his downturned face. Attune to her every emotion, he answered her grin with one of his own. My pulse thrummed through my veins. What I wouldn't give to have that again with the man that I loved. The man that was right next to me but could have been a million miles away for all of the emotional connection we had at the moment. Screw that. I could do something at least rather than sit here and be miserable.

Deciding to keep the conversation on neutral ground, I asked, "What do you know about Catherine of Sienna?"

"She used to be higher in the Council, but she fell out of

favor," Sven asked, his shoulders easing at the light conversation.

At least I'd picked a good topic. Besides, I had to admit the golden vampire intrigued me.

"What did she do?" I asked, shifting on my feet, my butt already going numb.

He gave a sardonic tilt of his lips. "Sometimes, you don't have to *do* anything to fall out of favor. People just do. But in the case of Catherine of Sienna, nobody knows. It was like a switch. For centuries, she was the High Priestess' right hand. And just one day, she wasn't."

"She had to have done something. I wonder what she did that was so awful?" My mind raced at all of the possibilities, not all of them bad. Because let's be honest, being in favor with the High Priestess probably entailed some shady ass shit. The whole council felt dirty, corrupt. Except Raven. But that might have just been that hot vibe he seemed to wear like a second suit.

"Are you nervous about the trial tomorrow?" I pretended like I was watching the dancers still, but my focus was tuned to the man next to me.

"Not at all." His muscles rippled as he shrugged, his own eyes never leaving the dance floor.

Something told me he wasn't watching me the same way I was watching him. Silence stretched on, cold and unwelcoming. He might as well have a blinking neon sign above his head that said Not Interested.

Still, I pressed on. "I am. I hate the thought that something could happen to you. I can't shake the feeling that people just *know* that I'm a faerie."

"Nobody in The Blood Spire knows what you are. Hearsay is not fact," he said, thrusting his chin out with the declaration.

As if strong body language meant anything. I wish it did.

It would save me a lot of talking in my day job as Bounty Hunter and Private Eye.

Ignoring his posturing, I asked, "How can you be so sure? I mean, what if word got out from your coven?"

"All that knew what you are have died. And if anyone does suspect, they wouldn't speak out. They are loyal to the death." His face was hard as he looked around the dance floor.

"Ok, yeah. I get all that, but aren't there laws against going against the High Council? Don't they like rule all of you? So wouldn't it follow that they'd be shit salad if they broke those rules?" I asked, running a hand down my borrowed red silk dress to straighten it. Borrowing from a vampire's closet gave you lots of reds and blacks. Big surprise there.

"To the death," he said, this time turning to meet my gaze.

I met his blue eyes, taken aback by the intensity there. Everything in me wanted to revel in his gaze, soak him in. But it was too soon for something like that. I didn't want to push him away.

Rolling my eyes, I turned back to pretend-monitor the dancers. "You seem pretty confident for a guy who has people trying to take him out at every turn."

"Of course, I am. Why wouldn't I be? We are a small group. Brought together through these last hundred years by Jerrick. We're family." This time a small smile accompanied the statement.

My brow furrowed. The brief glimpses of emotion Sven showed confused me. Was he picking feeling up from his memories? He only seemed to show any kind of feeling when what he was talking about surrounded past emotions. The problem was when the moment passed, so did the emotion.

While my wandering mind was worrying paths trying to figure that out, something about what he'd said clicked like a puzzle piece. "Jerrick was your maker, wasn't he?"

After a brief silence, he nodded. I dropped my head against the wall. This time the far-away look wasn't feigned as the full enormity of what he'd done for me hit me. He'd killed his maker. For me. The only reason Jerrick hadn't mind-controlled him was he'd never believed one of his own would kill him.

Love surged in my chest, an overwhelming feeling that threatened to pull me away. He'd done so much for me. Kept the secret of my race. Killed his Maker. Tor Mór, he'd even given me his heart. I'd be damned if when he needed me now, I wasn't going to be there for him anyway I could.

Pressing my lips together, I grabbed his strong hand in mine.

Confusion knit his brow as I pulled him onto the dance floor. "That's the oddest lead-in to a dance I think I've ever seen."

I took the statement as a compliment and laughed. The old Sven liked my quirky habits. Since he used to adore them, this new and not-so-improved Sven could at least get used to them. Placing his hands on my hips like he'd done so long ago, I linked my hands around his neck.

As I moved my body in a teasing game of touch-and-go against his, he looked at me, his body angling away from me. "What is your aim exactly?"

"Making you love me," I said, pulling him close again as if it was the most normal thing in the world.

His brows furrowed at me as the crystal blue of his eyes stared into my soul as if he were trying to figure me out. He was trying. Maybe it wasn't trying to feel, but he was making an effort towards me. That's all I could ask for. For now.

My throat felt thick. Since tears and arousal didn't go together, I spun around in Sven's arms. I wanted him to want me. To *feel* something. Pushing back, I ground and rolled against him. After a few moments, I felt the most surprising thing. He was enjoying it. Like *really* enjoying it. I giggled. Lit up, the bittersweet feelings vanished. The world faded away as I brought my arms up to wrap around his neck. He pulled me up, and I melted onto him. He pressed against me with firm hands as he slid down my body and back up. The movement was hesitant. I stiffened but then made myself relax. He wanted more, but there was an unsureness to his moves like he didn't know how to marry the instinct inside him without emotion paired to it. With a groan, his head cradled my neck. His mouth kissed along my neck. Unthinking, I tilted my head. When I realized what I was doing, I stopped myself. Was I really offering myself up to him? He'd already had my blood. How could I trust he wouldn't cross the line and give me the third and final mark?

I blinked my eyes. Torn, the world came back into focus.

That's when I saw her.

A demon. Her golden skin glowed in the pulsing lights. Her equally gold mane looking like stop animation as she flipped and played with it. Numerous men surrounded her, all vying for a chance to dance with her. Clad in the standard Slave Demon uniform of a Princess Leia-style bikini, it wasn't a surprising development.

Why? Why did this have to happen now when I was just getting a reaction out of Sven? He wanted me. Well, he wanted something. I didn't know where the feeling was coming from, but it was definitely something I could work with, not to mention a far cry closer than I'd gotten until this point. So why, dear Danu, why did a demon have to show up now, of all times?

It took an Odysseus-style effort to unclench my jaw and turn to Sven. Still, in the throes, his eyes were hooded, and his expression dark. Standing on tiptoe, I pulled him towards me. He hesitated but let me.

"There's a demon over there. I have to go take care of it

before it does something crazy- like complete an errand for the Devil," I said, hating the words even as they came out. This good person crap was for the birds.

Sven nodded. His expression was empty as he pulled away. Everything in me screamed. All of that progress killed, just like that. I wanted to wrap him in a hug, to cling to him. Instead, with no sense in my head, I made myself turn towards the wayward demon.

The way she clung to one eager male, in particular, made me pick up my pace. Jamming my hand in my purse, I grabbed the first glow stick I could find. With a kick to each of her prey's legs, she opened his stance up. Then she bent at the waist, dropping low. I cracked the magical glass inside the plastic. With deliberate movements, she ran her hands from his feet to thighs. Danu, please don't let this potion leak on me. The last thing I needed was to end up in the inner circle of Hell. Flinching, I shook the wand, releasing the magic into the chamber. A soft purple glow radiated from the tube. By her raised eyebrow and smile, the creature was pleased with her findings. She thrust both of her hands through her hair and tossed it back, the golden locks cascading like a waterfall through the air as she stood back up. It was quite a show, and I wasn't the only one watching, for very different reasons though, I'm sure.

She had just flung her target's arms out to the side and made a show of turning them from side to side when I came up behind him. Confident he'd be happy with me if he knew what she had planned, I grabbed a fist full of his hair and pulled him back. Gravity did the rest as he dropped to the floor. Displeasure contorted the monster's face as she narrowed her black eyes on me.

My jaw tight, I pulled a ley line. "Yeah, the party's over."

I didn't know if she heard me over the music, but it didn't

matter. The end result would be the same. As long as this damn necklace worked, that is.

She hissed at me even as she stepped her cloven hooves around the drunken man at her feet. He reached out to pet the soft fur that started at her knees but was pushed out of the way as she clipped past.

"I don't know who you think you are, but you are about to find out who I am the hard way," she said, her smile hard.

"I'm Cy Vanguard, Princess of Knockaine, and I couldn't give a fig what your name is. Slave demons are all the same to me. Useless." Releasing the Kundalini Energy from my heart chakra, I twisted the energy I'd pulled.

Immediately, a wall of glamour appeared around her. Since she wasn't going to stay still, no matter how nicely I asked, I had to keep the radius small. That way, I could still fight and maintain the trickle of energy needed for the enchantment. The man on the floor made the sign of the cross over his chest and backpedaled out of view. All I had done for the minor illusion was repeat the space around her. Simple but effective. Though, to the naked eye, it looked like she'd disappeared. I got why he'd been freaked out by it. Nobody else seemed to be phased. Let's hear it for drugs and alcohol. They messed with the mind better than any faerie magic ever could.

"That's right. You're the demon killer." Her black fingernails flashed as she wagged a finger at me. "But you got lucky with Kroni. He was old."

That was the second being from Hell that had said as much. I frowned. Maybe, I wasn't as impressive as I thought. Or, more likely, that was just the propaganda they were waving around down in good ol' Satan's paradise.

"Well, if the second in command was so weak, that doesn't say much for your little home turf, now does it? But whichever way you slice it, *you* at least are going down," I said, bringing my fists up.

She had barely gotten out a laugh when she lunged at me, no doubt wanting to catch me unaware. Too bad for her, she wasn't the first shitty person I'd had the utter displeasure to know. As if we were dancing, I moved just as quickly. Her brows knitted together. Apparently, she had believed the lies spread in the underworld. Too bad for her.

Clearly, a quick learner, she phased when she came at me this time. Her body morphed into a gold blur. I moved out of the way, but she must have anticipated where I'd go because she was on me. She grabbed my wrist. Slinging herself forward, she tried to use her momentum to slam me to the ground. I put my leg out to catch myself. It worked. Thank Danu for my heightened abilities, or she might have actually succeeded. It only took one good ring to knock you out.

She tried to use her body weight to rock me forward, but I braced again. Then I twisted the hand she held and grabbed onto her wrist. She blinked owl eyes at me. Obviously, she didn't know that all faeries trained in Muay Thai. At the same time that I rotated my hips to break the hold, I punched out with my free hand. Her face felt like concrete as I connected with it. With a shriek, she stumbled back. Quick to follow, I wrapped one hand around the neck. My other hand gripped the necklace. I posted that fist onto the back of her neck, too, in a cradle. Using leverage, I swung her to my left shoulder, clutching her close.

Clearly not a Muay Thai fighter, her arms flailed as she tried to break free. I smiled grimly. Nobody told her that if I rested on her crown, she'd have to come inside my arms for control. Now, there was just the little matter of this damn necklace.

Muay Thai fighter or not, the chick was damn strong, it was either that or the fact that I'd been laid up in a bed for two months. Whatever it was, it took every ounce of my control to keep her locked down. Since she was still invisible, I'm sure I looked insane to anyone watching. My breath came in ragged gasps as I fought to connect that damn plastic connector while keeping her in the hold. Time and time again, I thought the piece was going to click together, but every time I thought I had it, the post slipped free.

"Fuck!" I screamed against the bucking demon as sweat trickled down my neck.

Then the unthinkable happened. My hands slipped. And the hold broke.

This wasn't happening. Clutching wildly, I gave a Hail Mary and blindly jammed the two pieces at each other right as she bucked me off. My teeth clicked together. Pain radiated up my ass as I skidded across the rubber floor. Jarred, but out of time, I lifted my fists to combat the coming attack.

None came. I separated my arms just enough to see what was happening. A brilliant light radiated from the demon as she clawed at the glow stick. A whoosh blew my hair back as a fiery circle flamed alive around her. Wincing, I watched as the fire licked and lashed out, stretching into deadly ropes. One by one, the cords wrapped around her until, faster than the blink of a newt's eye, she was cocooned in it. The light grew hotter and whiter. Then the light flared purple and blinding. And she vanished. The echo of her screams was the last thing to be heard as I stared at the scarred, empty space where her body used to be.

CHAPTER 9

Clipping across the massive Oriental rug, I saw my prey. Full of grace and poise, the room-sized fireplace cast an angelic halo around her. In this case, "room-sized" meant freaking mammoth. Shocker there. Everything in the Blood Spire was larger than life. Even the chandeliers above me in the "common" room I stalked through right now were grander than most luxury hotels. Without a doubt, vampires had taken one chapter from modern culture. Supersize everything.

"Miss Vanguard, to what do I owe the pleasure?" Catherine of Sienna asked, not taking her eyes off the dancing flames as I came upon her.

"I wondered if I could...borrow you a moment?" I asked, trying to keep the ticking-time bomb strain out of my voice. We needed to make this faster than a pack of pixies at a candy convention. The trial was going to start any minute.

Her gaze flicked to mine. I darted a meaningful glance at the pair of vampires chatting under a portrait of some vampire who must have been important. I could tell by the way his cloak flapped majestically over the backdrop of a bloody battle scene.

"Of course," she said with a smile and nod to the hall I'd come from.

We moved away from the comforting heat. This place was freezing. I know vampyrs were technically born and not dead, but you could have fooled me with the temperatures they kept here. It smacked of a morgue's cooler.

I took in the black marble pillars and green velvet-curtained alcoves. If nothing but consistent, the nooks had murals painted in them of- you guessed it, vampires and their victims, along with a general theme of world domination. Ego much?

After we'd walked for a few minutes, she said, "You have my undivided attention."

"I'm nervous about the upcoming trial." I started off.

"As you should be," she said, her expression grave.

My heart rate jumped at her words. Well, that wasn't helpful. "Is there anything we can do to...help Sven's case?"

She paused. Choosing her words carefully, she asked, "Since you aren't a faerie, why would anything extra be required of you?"

My mouth worked like a fish out of water. "I mean no offense, but we are talking about vampires. Would you honestly have me believe they won't pull any funny business?"

"Now, that I didn't say." Catherine shrugged, drawing out the moment, then stopped to hold my gaze. I was quick to follow her somber lead. Her brown eyes bored into mine with a quiet intensity before she said, "You should be prepared for anything."

Then, as if she hadn't just freaked me out, she picked up her skirts and started walking again.

I blinked through the bramble of thoughts and the emotions that treated my stomach like a bouncy house. This was going to be a shit salad. I knew it. There had to be more she wasn't telling me. Maybe she didn't feel comfortable telling me. I mean, she barely knew me. Then again, we had so many secrets already. I got the feeling that she wanted to say more but didn't know what to say. And for some reason I couldn't explain, I think it had to do with the High Priestess.

Scrambling to catch up with her, I caught her arm. "Why did you lose favor with the High Priestess?"

Her steps faltered, if only for a second. It was enough. Jackpot. Quick to resume her footing, her lips thinned. But I knew I had her. She blindly walked on for only a few seconds before changing her course to walk along the right side of the hall.

Never missing a beat, she flicked her hand out, pulling the velvet curtains loose from their bindings. What was she about?

"Dark secrets are locked behind doors which should not be opened." The drapes swooshed down with heavy thuds, punctuating her words.

After at least a dozen alcoves had been hidden, she did an about-turn. Sensing she was wrestling with something, I stayed quiet as I followed. A few heartbeats later, she looked down the hall both ways and dipped into a random, now-secluded, recess. I ducked in after her.

Her words were urgent and low. "But it would appear you are the key to unlock this secret. So listen and listen well, for this is for you and your ears only. Yes, many years ago, I was the right hand to the High Priestess. However, she turned me out because she fell in love with a man, but he did not return her love."

Not ready for this turn of events, let alone such a vague explanation, I scrunched my eyebrows and cocked my head to the side. "That doesn't make sense. Why would she blame you for him not loving her?"

"You misunderstand me. Mercy didn't blame me for Fer

Fi's ambivalence towards her. She cast me out because I wouldn't give credence to or spread her rhetoric of lies. And I was ostracized from my own coven because of it." She said in a harsh whisper. Her hand had curled into a fist.

But I'd only heard bits and pieces of what she'd said after she said Fer Fi. My Uncle. Granted, since he was my mother's brother, I hadn't seen him since my father died, but it was hard to forget the shapeshifting dwarf who struck fear in legends and townsfolk alike. I could understand why the High Priestess fell in love with him. Talk about right up her alley. It also made perfect sense why she'd been heartbroken. He only loved himself.

"What lies?" I asked, wincing.

Being that my family was a part of this, I so didn't want to know, but I was never one to bury my head in the sand if something involved me. No matter how painful. And I'd say me being in a trial one of my family's psycho ex's presided over definitely counted as "being involved."

"That faeries had been abducting, maiming, and slaughtering vampires," she said, folding her arms over her chest.

"So why are faeries being killed off outside of the Blood Spire if vampires are so afraid of them?" I asked, biting the inside of my lip.

"Originally? That's simple. Retaliation. We are a prideful people. Just the idea that a species thought they were above us was enough to call for their blood. Add in the slights against us and the ensuing headhunt was inevitable. Now? I suspect it has less to do with an age-old grudge and more to do with what was discovered during the hunt. That the high you can get from faerie blood has no equal," she said the last with a sympathetic twist to her mouth.

I stepped back as the pieces came together; my legs hit the couch behind me. I sat down. I needed it at this point.

"So you're saying you all haven't been attacked by faeries?" I asked, slow to make sure I wasn't misunderstanding. She laughed a thick, wet laugh. Well, that was mildly insulting, but I moved past the prick to my pride. "But what about the victims?"

She dismissed the thought with a wave of her hand. "All paid, sworn to secrecy on a fate worse than death. Nothing was left to chance. Everything was elaborate and deliberate. Listen to what I tell you, for it is the truth."

"So she deceived her entire race because she was rejected?" I asked, wanting to make sure I understood.

She gave a bitter smile and nod. "So do you see now why you and Sven are in such trouble? Heed my words. No one can bite you. Or it is the end of both you and your Sven."

Her words dropped like a cement block into my stomach, effectively killing off all thoughts of my screwed-up family. I stared at the shadowy ceiling above me. Yep. Total shit salad.

Shaking her head, she looked at me and choked out a whispered, "I'm so sorry," before throwing open the curtain and walking away as fast as her legs would take her.

I didn't have to ask what she was running from. She was trying to outrun the monster that had become her life. The nightmare that my very presence made her face. Well, wasn't I just a beacon of joy and light?

But more than her words sat with me. It was even more than the knowledge that my Uncle had messed up more people's lives than in my own species. It was the fact that without Sven's presence in the Blood Spire, I would be dead.

With a haggard sigh, I stood up. I'd only taken two steps when Sven all but dashed around the corner.

"The trial is starting now. We must go," Sven said, barely raising his voice for it to bounce down the hall to me.

My stomach twisted. Dagda, where had the time gone? I'd

known time was running short, but I had no idea I was out of it. Holding my wrap dress together, it flapped against my legs as I jogged to him. He picked up his pace to match mine. Soon, we were racing down the halls, the opulent surroundings barely hitting my radar as Catherine's bombshell ricocheted around in my head. My uncle and the High Priestess. Did she know I was his niece? The thought crawled up and sat in my throat until I pushed it back down. No, if she suspected, I'd have "disappeared" already. No, right now, I was just a representation of everything she hated. They said hate wasn't the opposite of love. It was snuggled up close next to it. In situations like this, it was all too easy to see how true that was.

We dashed around the second corner. Thankfully, my hair stayed put in its convenient but dressy pulled-apart side braid. The carpet gave way to marble, and my breath came faster.

"Stick to what we went over," Sven said, dodging a Roomba as we continued to jog down the hall.

Sven's defending attorney had met with him and me this morning. At least that's what I assumed he was. Nobody had expressly told me as much, big surprise there since nobody told me anything here, but considering we'd rehearsed for the thousandth time what we were going to say, it seemed like a safe assumption. The problem is this wasn't what we'd rehearsed. I just doubted the prosecution was going to stick to the script. And though I'd been on the witness stand before, it hadn't been a matter of life or death for the man I loved. I swallowed hard as I acknowledged that my survival, too, was on the line.

"Be calm. Stay cool. Don't pay them any heed, no matter what they may say. You don't want to give them cause to suspect anything. If your reactions are called in to question, they may accept that as probable cause." He continued on, and I don't know if the string of hushed reminders was for him or me.

I snorted out a laugh. "Are you kidding? Vampires freak me out, no offense. The way I feel right now, one could just whisper in my general direction, and I might faint."

"You're not going to faint," he assured me as we rounded yet another corner. Two imposing double doors greeted us. A chill came over me as he continued on. "Just remember, nobody can bite you without my consent."

All the while he was speaking, Catherine's words rang in my ears. Prepare for anything.

"It's a good thing we're going into a room full of meek, mild-mannered vampyrs that don't think they're better than both of us combined," I said, sarcasm dripping from each word as we reached the entrance.

Finally, we came to a dead stop. Sven looked at me. Gulping to slow my breathing, I looked at him. He looked cool and calm. Not at all like we'd just raced what amounted to two city blocks to get here. At least that was one of us. Taking a cue from him, I let all of my breath out in a whoosh. This was it. I was as ready as I'd ever be. I'd just taken a deep breath to steady my nerves when Sven threw open the doors.

I could have been spared some of the production of the move, but taking in the room in front of us, I realized that was the least dramatic thing I'd be seeing for the next few hours.

The doors opened to a two-story-high room with pillars formed into the corners. A domed ceiling topped it all off. The entire place was made out of stone, except for a marble staircase. The bottom portion started off as rounded, gradual steps that grew to form a semi-circle landing. Three vampires stood on the stage. One was the vampire who'd been making all of the fuss at The Invitation. A frown tugged at my lips. He was the Prosecution and a Grade A asshole.

Next to him, looking decidedly more relieved at seeing us, was our attorney. The third vampire off to the side didn't move. On second thought, maybe he was a wax statue. What a terrible decoration.

But none of that was the focal point. That was at the top of the staircase. Glossy and black, an imposing dais stood out stark against the white stone, demanding respect. A quick count of the empty seats showed seven. For the High Council, no doubt.

That's where any half-hearted attempt at normalcy ended. Behind the rounded edges of the first steps, two colossal gargoyle statues loomed, dark and ominous, over the courtroom floor. They rose high to flank the main staircase, the tips of their heads stretching up to reach the currently empty judges' seats. The carved monstrosities each held out a hand that came up level with the semi-circle platform.

In front of the spectacle were vampires. Hundreds of them were sectioned off into two groups. Packed tighter than a baker's corset, the only breathing room between them was a blood-red carpet that ran through the center of the crowd. This same carpet crept up the staircase, only stopping to blanket the first landing. Scary or not. I could do this.

Holding my head high, we started down the plush carpet. Hatred beat on either side of us like crashing waves, threatening to pull us under. A petite vampire dressed in frills met my gaze full on. Ice dripped from her whole being. With a silent hiss, she bared her fangs.

"Nothing like the coziness of walking to your own execution," I whispered, barely moving my lips as I broke eye contact at the clear threat.

Sven reached out to give my hand a quick squeeze. My chest lightened at the touch. To know that he supported me even during his darkest hour meant so much. Sooner than seemed possible, we were climbing the shallow stairs to the awaiting attorneys. With sure steps, Sven went to stand with his counsel. I went with him but was stopped by the lawyer indicating the gargoyle with a proffered hand. I looked from the statue back to him, confusion knitting my brow. That couldn't be the star witness box he'd mentioned. No way he wanted me to stand on that. For Dagda's sake, I had heels on. That would be hell to stand on.

When I didn't move, his previously kind smile widened like I might be daft and nodded to the gargoyle's hand for good measure.

Stuffing my grumbling deep down, I pasted on my good-girl smile and went where I was told. The lawyer should have appreciated my compliance more than was currently showing on his face. I did what I wanted. The compliant sweetheart act hurt a bit. Promising myself I'd do something only for me later to make up for it, my steps slowed as I got to the sculpture.

The floor crested and dipped. You know, like a *hand*. I grabbed the behemoth's giant thumb for support and stepped onto its palm. Just as awkward as it promised, I weebled and wobbled around until I finally found a place I could wedge my heel in and brace my bottom against to keep upright. Good enough.

Just as I got settled, everyone's eyes went to the dais above. Craning my head to get a better look, I caught the last of the members of the High Council as they filed in, adorned in matching robes of black with bone collars stained red. A shiver skittered down my spine.

Forcing myself to notice something- anything, else, I saw Mercy, the High Priestess, sat in a slightly raised seat. However, it was Raven that sat in front of the gavel. I ignored the little relieved bubble in my chest. Hello, brain. It wasn't as if Mercy had less power just because she wasn't holding the clacker. Wasting no time on ceremony, he cracked it against its wooden plate. "Do you wish to make an opening statement?"

"Yes," said the prosecution with a grave nod.

"We do," said our attorney with an equally solemn bob.

My stomach turned.

"You may proceed," said Raven with a wave.

The prosecution stepped to the center of the floor. I had the urge to run out and push him off the platform. Anything to keep this from happening.

"Your honors, today you will hear the tale of a vampire who has committed the highest sin: Communing with the Fae. Today, we'll bring forward witnesses that show, with no thought but to his own self-serving base desires, he's thrown his relationship with the fae in the face of his entire race. It will show he lacks respect for the victims or the atrocity of the acts committed against us as a whole. You will see why we are calling for the end of the undead life of Sven Sivertsen."

As he went back to the front of the platform, chills skittered up my spine. I don't care how good of a poker face I had. It didn't get any more real than the open threat to Sven's life in front of everyone. And fuck everyone if they judged me for not wanting him to die. I'd think that would fall under being a decent being, not only fae.

Sven's attorney was quick to replace him. "Your honors, today you will see the story, not of a man who has committed the highest of all crimes. No, today you will hear the story of a good man who has stepped up and taken on a burden he didn't want for the good of his coven. And instead of being lauded for this admirable act, his tale is being twisted and corrupted. And for what? All for the purpose of his seat. That it may be opened and occupied by those whose quest isn't for justice but for power. However, this day, we know that justness will prevail."

Eerie quiet greeted his upturned hands. He left them there for a few seconds before moving back to be with Sven again.

Raven didn't so much as crease an eyebrow as he said, "Thank you, counsel. Will the prosecution call their first witness?"

"Yes, we'd like to call Richard Bram to the stand." The lawyer's voice rang out as bats cried out above.

I looked up in time to see a man drop from the ceiling at lightning speeds. Tor Mór, a jumper. My heart pounded in my chest as I stepped forward to catch him, but his descent slowed at the last minute. Confused, I rocked back, sitting back against the cement gargoyle as the man alighted with a gentle foot onto the red carpet. That's when I noticed the wire attached to him, hidden by his cape. This whole place had gone round the bend. Two small boys dressed in black came up and unhooked him as he walked with purpose to the other gargoyle's hand. A woman sashayed out in a catsuit, cop uniform. Were these people for real? On the verge of laughter, I looked around. Except no one else was laughing. I immediately sobered.

When he was in the witness box, he turned towards me. He didn't look even vaguely familiar.

"Please raise your right hand. Do you promise to tell the truth, the whole truth, and nothing but the truth so help you lest you be struck down by Satan himself?" she asked, her voice saying she clearly meant business as it rang out.

"I do," he said, giving her his widest, open-eye stare.

She nodded and walked back down the steps, the bible in her hands swinging had an infinity symbol on top of a two-barred cross emblazoned on the front. On the one hand, it made sense. Vampires weren't born from God. Satan was their father. On the other hand, it was just another slap-in-the-face reminder of how far down the rabbit hole we were.

The prosecution ambled over to the man. "Mr. Bram. Would you say that you know Sven Sivertsen rather well?"

Sven's jaw tightened. That's what I thought. Likely he didn't know this guy from Adam either.

"I do," the vampire said, not even having the decency to flinch.

"And can you please kindly point out for the court Mr. Sivertsen?"

His mouth flattened dramatically as he said, "There's the bastard."

Jeers erupted from the audience. The gavel cracked. "Order."

No other shouts came.

Lawyer Asshat didn't even try to hide his smile as he said, "Would you care to explain to the court your relationship with Mr. Sivertsen?"

"Happy to. He'd always come down to Madame V's toting his wares," he said with a disgusted frown, looking Sven up and down.

I'd never seen someone begging so hard for a throat punch.

The attorney held up a hand. "By wares, you mean Heaven's Tears."

"Yeah, that's the stuff. We tried to tell him we didn't want it, but he claimed he was getting it good from the source, if you know what I mean," Richard said, with a leer at me.

My hand tightened into a fist behind me as I gritted my teeth. This was it. This was when I needed to control my temper. Danu, but what I wouldn't give to go over there and smash that liar in the face.

The lawyer proceeded to ask more questions, but I stopped paying attention. If I was supposed to not react to what this clown was saying, that was the best way. Do this. Don't do that. Sweet Danu, talk about exhausting. Between helping other people and fixing my own screw-ups, I'd been strung out for longer than I cared to think about. What I wouldn't give to just have a day of relaxation. Maybe, next time I was out at Hell's Gate, I could get into one of those mud baths. I could feel it now, all warm and relaxing. Letting the crazy flake off with the dried mud. The counsel stepped away, bringing my focus back to the present.

"Would the defense like to cross-examine the witness?" Raven asked, his face as impassioned as if he were discussing the weather.

"Yes, your honors," said Sven's attorney, adjusting his suit as he stepped forward. "Mr. Bram. Isn't it true that you are kitchen staff at Madame V?"

Richard crossed his arms over his chest, "That's right. You got to get your foot in before they'll pony up the better jobs."

The attorney looked down at his notes as if searching for some information. "And isn't it true that as kitchen staff, you have never actually interacted with Mr. Sivertsen?"

His hands worked his biceps as he struggled to come up with an answer. Finally, he said, "Well, no. I didn't talk to him exactly, but I saw him plenty. I knew what was going on. We all did. It was no secret what he was about."

"But being that you never spoke to him, you can't say for sure what he said or what he was even doing at Madame V's." The lawyer challenged, widening his stance and looking Richard dead in the eyes.

"I didn't have to. Everyone was talking about it. It was common knowledge." Richard's voice climbed octaves as if it were literally climbing his tall tale.

"But you didn't talk to him directly," the lawyer pressed.

The vampire's jaw worked, anger blazing out of his eyes. Finally, he bit out. "No."

"Then all of what you have said is speculation. No further questions, your honors." The attorney turned and made his way calmly back to Sven amid shouts and cries from the audience.

"Order. Order." Raven smashed down his mallet. Then barely pausing, he said, "Prosecution, you may call your next witness."

"We'd like to call Victoria Standish to the stand," said the asshat attorney.

As if on command, the stairs next to me sprung up like a jack-in-the-box. My heart hammered in my chest. Tor Mór, I knew they were trying to keep me off balance, but were they trying to kill me? A woman in a skintight black bodice and matching silk hot pants walked down the ramp, her thigh-high boots striking the metal ramp. As she hit the lights, the shine from the blood-red crystals falling in lines from her decolletage down to her waist blinded me. I winced. Only when she moved over to the other gargoyle hand did I get eyes on her again. My mouth went dry as if I'd swallowed cotton. This woman I recognized. She was the hostess at Madame Violet's. The one I'd seen when I went there to find Sven after I'd decided to give him a chance.

The woman with the police cap and the leather jumpsuit stalked back to the box again. In a refrain that should have made her tired by now, she said, "Please raise your right hand. Do you promise to tell the truth, the whole truth, and nothing but the truth so help you lest you be struck down by Satan himself?"

Victoria popped her gum. "Yeah."

The prosecution was on his first question before he'd even reached her. His words, however, didn't match the heat of his actions. "Ms. Standish, you're the hostess at Madame Violet's, correct?"

"That's me," she said, stretching her gum and wrapping it around her finger over and over again.

"Do you know Mr. Siversten?"

Obviously, having watched the first testimony, she pointed to Sven. "Yeah, that's him right there."

"So would you say you saw Mr. Siversten on every visit?" the lawyer asked, looking back and forth between the two as if trying to judge the validity of her statement.

"Yeah, for sure," she said, stuffing the gum back in her mouth and beginning to pop it again.

"And what would you say the primary purpose of Mr. Siversten's visits were?" the attorney asked, pacing in front of the gargoyle's hand.

"That's easy. Drugs," Victoria said with an unimpressed shrug. "He's a pusher."

"A pusher. That's a pretty bold claim. A pusher of what?" Pressed the attorney. His fingertips forming a steeple in front of him, as if trying to figure out the world's problems instead of it being the leading statement we all knew it to be.

"Heaven's Tears, faerie blood," she said, lifting her palm up as if to say, 'who cares?'.

"Faerie blood!" he shouted, turning so his voice boomed over the crowd. Never letting his piercing gaze leave the rapt attendees, he asked, "Would you say he sold Madame Violet's a good amount of faerie blood?"

"Oh, sure. He was in every week with a new batch. It was way more than anyone else had. There was no way he was selling with that kind of frequency without being able to get a fresh batch," she said, licking her lips.

The slight movement made my stomach sour. Was Victoria Standish a user? Is that why she made it her business to know when they came in?

"And where do you think he got this 'fresh batch' from?" His stance made it seem like he was asking the audience to draw the conclusion instead of Victoria.

"Oh, I don't think. I know." She pointed at me. "Her."

Her gaze collided with mine as my eyes flew wide. I

couldn't help it. I did not expect to be called out like that. The weight of everyone's censure pressed down on me. Gods be. Quick to recover, I rolled my eyes and crossed my arms. I didn't know if it was too over the top. Still, considering the theatre level quality of everything else, I went with it. I was so out of my depths here, but it was either swim or sink. And even when not given a choice, I'd choose to swim all day long, even if it was the wrong stroke.

"Thank you, Ms. Standish. No further questions," said the asshat with a cocky smile and a nod that made my fist itch.

"Would the defense like to cross-examine the witness?" asked Raven.

"Yes, your honor," said Sven's attorney, moving away from Sven to come to stand in front of the witness stand. "Ms. Standish, what is your primary function as hostess?"

"To help people who come in," she said, shifting on the gargoyle's hand. She was clearly getting uncomfortable in those heels too. I stuffed any type of commiseration down. She was trying to kill Sven and, by proxy me. I'd be damned if I felt bad for her.

"Madame Violet's is quite a busy place. I'd imagine you have all kinds coming in that have all kinds of different needs," he said with a sympathetic eyebrow.

"It can get crazy, yeah," she said with a shrug.

"I can only imagine. It would seem safe to say that there are times you are away from your coffin stand, correct?" he asked, squinting his eyes as if just walking into a thought.

"Yeah," she said with a shrug.

"And since you aren't always at the door, isn't it safe to say that you might not see everyone come in?" I asked, pointing at her to make a point.

She saw it coming too. Her mini caplet popped up on her shoulders as she crossed her arms. "I mean, I see most everyone."

"Most, but not all. Is that correct?" the lawyer pressed.

"Most likely not, I guess," she said with a frown that said she didn't like where this was going.

I on, the other hand, loved it. Make her squirm. Let the High Council see that she didn't know what she was talking about.

"And since you're not always up front to see everyone come in, isn't it possible that you don't *actually* see Mr. Sivertsen every time he comes in?" Sven's attorney asked, raising his eyebrow.

She held up a hand. "Well, I mean...it's not as if..." Then she shook her finger at him as if to prove a point only to drop it and answer with a dejected, "Yeah."

I wanted to dance. Yes, that's right, swiss cheese her testimony.

Not basking in his small win, he continued on. "You said that Miss Vanguard was who he got his supply from. How did you come to this conclusion?"

Uncrossing her arms, she laughed. "I mean, come on. Look at her. All she had to do was walk in, and you can tell she was scared out of her gourd. Before we killed them faeries off...or *thought* we did, they were all running scared of us. They knew what they did to us. Knew we'd make them pay. And we did. So yeah, there's no doubt in my mind she's the supplier with how he has her wrapped around his finger."

"But you have no proof." Pointed out the attorney with open hands.

"Besides her coming in shaking like skeleton bones asking for Sven and him having fresh faerie blood, you mean?" she asked, her lip kicked up snidely.

"No, I mean actual proof. Like something you could present to this court," he said, with a flourish of his hand to the High Council.

She snorted. "That kind of proof? No. Who's got that kind

of proof? That lying cheat right there's the only one who's bitten her. Why don't you go over and take a sip of the twit right now? That'll change your mind real quick."

I froze. My greatest fear had been put out there. The one piece of evidence we had no counter to. My heart was slamming against my chest, but outwardly, I feigned a yawn. I didn't need to look to see people were watching.

"No further questions, your honors," he said, walking back to his floor space with Sven.

When Victoria passed by, she threw me a glare that would have made a frost giant proud and walked down the steps to disappear into the throng.

Raven had already moved on. "Prosecution, you may call your next witness."

And so the trial went with one shitty witness after another. After the first few, it was easy to ignore the parlor tricks of their entrances. Panels falling away. An 'accidental' grab of my ankle as one came from behind the gargoyle statue. A bird swooping down to narrowly miss my head before it dropped a scroll in the asshat attorney's hand. Even the wax vampire coming to life. Everything had been designed to set me on edge. But it didn't take me long to become numb to it. Also, with it came a slowly blossoming hope in my chest as I realized two things. One, all of their testimonies were weak. Two, none of Sven's coven members were present. He'd been right. They were family, and they wouldn't sell him out.

Based on speculation and hearsay, the case was as leaky as a porcupine's umbrella. To pass the time, I stared through the skylights. The stars were hypnotic in the black night sky. Twinkling, they whispered to me. Called to me to get lost in their secrets. In the infinite possibilities.

The testimony of the current witness floated into my consciousness, and I looked back to the witness stand. It was the man who had stumbled into the room Sven and I had been in at the Gathering.

"You heard me. I said she was in the closet with him while my pet and I were playing," said the man, referencing the closet we'd ducked into when trying to get away from Thomas as he threw a cocksure elbow around the gargoyle. His frame was wide, thick. How had I ever mistaken him for the wiry vampyr who'd been obsessed with me?

"So they were engaging in voyeuristic behaviors." The prosecuting attorney clarified.

"Yeah, too bad too. All she would have had to do was ask, and I'd have gladly shown her what a real vamp tastes like," said the black-haired vampyr with a cocky grin.

When he saw he had my attention, he threw a wink at me. I gnashed my teeth at the overt gesture. As if it wasn't bad enough, the entire courtroom thought I was a hussy.

"No further questions, your honors," said the prosecuting lawyer as he stepped away.

Proving that the gods were real, Sven's lawyer declined to cross-examine. I did have to suffer through more winks, nods, and kissy faces, but it was worth it because the brazen vampyr actually left. The next thing out of the prosecuting attorney's mouth erased all thoughts of his creepy come-ons.

"For our last witness, we'd like to call to the stand Sasha Simone," said the prosecuting attorney.

Sasha? Sven's friend? It couldn't be. I darted a look at Sven. If his posture was anything to go by, it most definitely could be, and without a doubt, it was a surprise. This time there was no fancy entrance. Instead, the massive doors quietly clicked open, and in walked the diminutive blonde. Her flapperesque style dress screamed Old Hollywood, just like all of all the vampyrs I'd met before coming to the Blood Spire. Was the dress a regional thing? From how big her eyes were and how her hands clutched each other like she was holding an evening clutch, it became easy to see she was scared shitless. Not looking Sven's way, she sailed past him. As she was sworn in, my mind worked over what this might mean. Her testimony could change everything. How much did she know about what had happened in Jerrick's house? Had she talked to Thomas? Did she know I was a faerie? And more importantly, did she have proof?

"Ms. Simone, please explain your relationship to Mr. Sivertsen." The prosecution strutted over, his head held high.

He knew he had something in Sasha. Fuckity, fuck, fuck fuck.

"We're...friends," she said, peering through the glamorous fall of waves across her left eye.

Sven's hands tightened into fists. I wanted to go over and give him a hug. This was just not ok. Friends didn't do this to friends. Before, I couldn't have said this, but now that I was starting to grow quite a group of them, I felt something like this was just understood.

"As his friend, would it be safe to assume that you know of all of his romantic interests?" he asked, pacing in front of where she stood on the giant gargoyle's hand.

"Not all of them, but most of them. That is correct," Sasha said, her hands fluttering at her sides.

"And can you explain to the court his relationship with Miss Vanguard compared to the other romantic interests that you saw him with?" he asked.

Her hands fluttered around her neck. "Ummmm...more intense. Possessive even. Which makes sense since she's the only person he's ever claimed. He'd do anything for her."

I'd been the only person he'd ever marked? For some messed up reason, I didn't want to begin to analyze, the knowledge made me warm, glowy.

The attorney stopped to look at her. "And why do you think that his attraction for her was so intense?"

"Why...why, I couldn't begin to guess, I'm sure," she said. A high-pitched laugh bubbled out, and she pressed a hand to her chest.

"In your guesstimation, would you say that someone being a fae would spur such a strong reaction?" He asked, his eyes piercing.

She squirmed under the ferocity of it. "Well, I suppose."

"You suppose," he said, with an approving nod, and started to walk again. "You've met Miss Vanguard, have you not, Ms. Simone?"

Sasha's voice came out, stronger this time, as she said, "I have."

"Where did you meet?" he asked.

"At a Gathering at Jerrick's house. He always invited Heinrich and I, even though we had our own coven. Friends of the family, you could say."

"And were you attracted to Miss Vanguard when you met her?" he said, not stopping his pacing.

She blinked, but to her credit, she didn't flinch as she said, "I was."

"Would you say it was an...intense attraction?" he asked, stopping to level her a look.

"I...well, I suppose you could say that," she said, crossing her arms and uncrossing them again.

"Was there anything else you saw at the Gathering that seemed odd?" he asked.

"Yes, Thomas, rest his soul. He sent for Sven. I heard him tell one of the messengers to tell Sven that Jerrick needed him out in the stables. Then Sven left, and I saw Thomas go into the ballroom."

"And why did he go into the ballroom?" the prosecution asked.

"To get Cy alone. I think he wanted to convince her to leave with him. Honestly, since he was a vampyr, I don't understand why she didn't. She would have been much more comfortable than being with a vampire. Well, of course, that was before Sven became Master of the coven," she said, with a nod of approval to Sven.

Holding her gaze, he remained stone-faced. At the rebuff, Sasha's eyes darted back to the attorney. I didn't blame Sven. I'd be pissed, too, if my friend was in a trial against me on the prosecuting side.

"Tell me, do you know if Thomas was a user of Heaven's Tears? Faerie blood?" the lawyer asked.

"Oh, yes. Most of the coven was, they were suppliers of it, after all," she said, with a laugh as if that should have been obvious.

At the understanding tone, my stomach flipped. I could hardly get used to the idea that vampires drank blood to stay alive, let alone that they had different types of blood on hand, like fine brandy. My people's blood being one of those.

"Back to Thomas and Sven. What would you say their relationship was up until that point?" the lawyer asked, stroking his chin.

Sasha waved a hand in the air loftily. "They were like brothers. Jerrick raised all of his coven members like that. Those two were no different."

"Brothers. But yet, you say Thomas went in deliberately that night to take away Sven's girl. A girl, to your very admission, he was fiercely possessive of." He paused and shook his head. "What do you think it would have taken for Thomas to throw a brotherly relationship that spanned hundreds of years?"

Swallowing, Sasha admitted, "Quite a lot."

"Quite a lot, indeed, One might even say Thomas couldn't help himself because he knew what Cy was. A faerie. And as a user, he needed her like he needed the very air that he breathed. Rest his soul." The asshat rested his elbow on the gargoyle's thumb as he tilted his head, regarding the diminutive blonde and her soft waves. "And you know that, don't you, Ms. Simone? You know what Cy is. The only thing a drug-addicted vampyr would turn on his brother for."

"I…" she cleared her throat and tried again. "That is. It could be…." Stopping, she shook her head. "What I mean to say…."

The lawyer stood up a little straighter, his eyes growing dark. "She's a faerie, isn't she, Ms. Simone?"

"Well, that's one of those… it's hard to…" she trailed off, covering her hand with her mouth.

"It's a very straightforward question, Ms. Simone. Is or is not Cy Vanguard a faerie? Yes, or no." he said, leaning over her.

Her hands wrung each other like she was trying to squeeze the last drop of water out of a hair towel.

Had she seen anything? Had she heard anything? The hair on the back of my neck lifted. Was this going to be the end of Sven? Of me?

Finally, she threw her hands in the air. Squeezing her eyes shut, she screamed, "I don't know!"

The lawyer's face blazed red like he'd eaten a ghost pepper. Clearly, this wasn't what they'd rehearsed. From Sasha's obvious distress, I wondered what they were doing to force her to be on this stand. Was it her husband, Heinrich? Was he in trouble? The thought sat hard in my gut. Sure, they might be vampyrs, but the Simone's were still good people.

"Well, you might not know. But the rest of us know the answer to that. No further questions, your honors," the prosecution said, his mouth compressing in a line as he flung himself away from the gargoyle thumb and walked back to his post.

"Would the defense like to cross-examine the witness?" Raven asked, the scene having caught his full attention.

"No, your honors," Sven's attorney said, his face showing no emotion.

Oh, this guy was good. I was fuming right now, and I didn't even have to represent Sven's case.

"Defense, do you have any witnesses to call?" asked Raven as Sasha all but fled from the stage.

Part of me felt terrible for her, but I was more pissed that she'd agreed to stand against Sven in the first place. It's not like she could claim ignorance. She knew what was at stake. Death.

With the coolness of an autumn breeze, Sven's attorney said, "Yes, your honors. We'd like to call Joseph Blackwood to the stand."

A man with sandy blond hair and a gait that made me like him immediately parted from the front of the crowd with decidedly less flair than the other witnesses.

After he was sworn in, Sven's attorney asked the first question with a hand on Sven's shoulder. "Mr. Blackwood, what is your relationship to Mr. Sivertsen?"

"We were raised in Jerrick's coven together for the last two hundred years. He's like a brother," he said with a nod to Sven.

Sven returned his nod with a smile. I didn't know if memory had recalled the bond or a show for the court, but it made my chest warm. With our whirlwind romance and unconventional courtship, I hadn't gotten to see many intimate parts of Sven's life. I wanted to know everything right that second. If only time could standstill, and I could learn all there was that made him uniquely Sven.

Patting Sven on the shoulder, the lawyer walked towards the witness stand. "Can you tell me about Sven?"

"He's a stand-up guy. Us vampires are usually a little rough around the collar because that's the way we like it. You know, giving as good as we get and all. But Sven was always cut from a different cloth. Always a by-the-book kind of guy. He'd stop things before they get out of hand if you know what I mean. Would always look out for the rest of us. He even looked out for us when others in command at the time didn't."

"So would you say that you are happy he's coven master?" the attorney asked.

This time there was no holding his smile back as he said, "For sure, we all are. Well deserved, for sure."

"You said he's a 'by-the-book kind of guy.' That doesn't match the other testimonies we've heard today. Why do you think that is?" the attorney asked.

He scoffed and put his hands in his jeans pockets. "Because those other witnesses don't know nothing. They don't know Sven at all, let alone how we do in the coven."

"So, with all of your knowledge of Mr. Sivertsen, what are your opinion of the charges held against him today?" the attorney asked, careful not to look at me.

"Absolutely, stupid. Sven is the most law-abiding vampire I've ever met. Hell, half the time, I wonder if he is a vampire. He's so straight and narrow. Ain't no way he's guilty of these trumped-up charges."

"Thank you, Mr. Blackwood. No further questions," said Sven's attorney walking away.

"Would the prosecution like to cross-examine the witness?" asked Raven, stifling a yawn.

"Yes, your honors." said the prosecution, stepping out. He didn't bother to stop his stride when he asked Joseph. "Since you were a part of Jerrick's coven, that makes Sven your master now, is that correct?"

"He is, and he's doing a damn fine job of it," he said, with another nod of approval to Sven.

"How is it exactly that Mr. Siversten came to be master again?" asked the asshat.

"Like everyone else becomes master, they kill the current master," said Joseph with a laugh, looking around as if asking if this guy was for real.

"But you testified earlier that you all were like family. Why would Sven kill someone who was family?" he asked, scrunching up his forehead in exaggerated confusion.

This time Joseph had a little less puff in his chest. "Because he had to. He didn't have a choice."

"Why did he have to, Mr. Blackwell? What happened that made Mr. Siversten feel like he had to kill the man who was like a father to him?" the lawyer asked, with a smile crooking the corner of his mouth. Joseph's mouth thinned. The attorney's smile faltered. "Let me remind you that you are under oath. Lest Satan's hounds come drag you away. Answer the question."

He gritted his teeth, and the words seemed torn from him as he answered. "Because Jerrick was going to kill his girl."

"Can you be more specific? Who was his girl?" the lawyer prodded.

"Her," Joseph said, dropping his head as he pointed to me.

The crowd burst into jeers and shouts while the lawyer smiled. "No further questions, your honors."

My shoulders ached with the need not to go over there and throttle that attorney. He was painting Sven to be nothing more than a mindless killer. If he had been there that horrific night, he would have seen there was really no choice at all. Jerrick was killing me. What was Sven supposed to do? Just let me die?

It took longer for Raven to smash his gavel again. "Does the defense have any further witnesses?"

"Yes, your honors. We'd like to call our last witness to the stand, Cy Vanguard," said the attorney, and all of the gazes in the crowd swung to me.

Any other day, I wasn't shy to get in front of a crowd, but

my steps were hesitant as I climbed off the gargoyle's hand. I made a show of being careful and let them think it was because I wanted to be safe, but in reality, it was because I was petrified to be the one thing standing between Sven's life and his death.

When I got to the witness box, I was sworn in by the same lady. She had a mole on her cheek. Sven's lawyer walked over, and even though we'd rehearsed it a thousand times, my heartbeat increased.

"Miss Vanguard, are you now, or have you ever been, a fae?" He asked.

My heart rate sped up. Before giving up my wings, yes, I was a faerie. But was I now? I thought of Oganess' words 'Ancestors, no more.' Was I a fae? Did I even have a people anymore? I worked to keep my face neutral. For some reason, it was much more challenging than I'd thought it was going to be. It was too long. I was waiting too long.

My stomach clenched hard as I blurted out, "No, I am not."

Please, Danu, let that not be true.

The prosecuting attorney's eyebrows furrowed once and then went smooth again.

"But many other witnesses have said otherwise tonight." He countered with a frown.

"None of them know me," I said, my voice tight. The cold wash of anger that came over me wasn't feigned. It was real. I was sick of people judging me and not knowing me. I tried to stay calm whenever anger came over me, but this time I let it come. Let it clear my head.

"All faeries have wings. It has been said today that you have these same wings. If you are truly not faerie, bare for us your back so that we may see your humanity for ourselves," he said, with a sweep of his hand.

This time I was all for the dramatics as I stepped

forward and began to undo the belt of my wrap dress. If I was about to get undressed in front of a crowd of strangers, I'd at least like it to have some fanfare. Turning around, I dropped the dress dramatically, letting it catch on the crook of my arms. If I didn't have to expose my ass, why do it? A backless dress would have been so much easier, but the attorney wanted to make the revealing of my scars a dramatic moment. It was a good thing I didn't have self-esteem issues, or that would have hurt. There was nothing like being told a part of your body was shocking to make you want to run out and buy a half-dozen turtle necks.

I concentrated on the fact that I was wearing a strappy halter bra and a matching high-waisted bikini as the lawyer proclaimed dramatically, "What happened here?"

Even if we hadn't planned for this moment, I'd have known what he was referring to. The patchwork quilt of scars that ran the length of my back. Unlike the murder victim who'd been kidnapped by Thomas, they weren't neat marks where my wings had been ripped off. No, these scars spanned from the top of my neck down to my lower back. It was as if the magic had ripped them from my soul, starting where my wings came out and then scorching everywhere they had touched.

Choking back the traumatic memory of how they'd been ripped from my back, I'd said, "I was in a house fire."

I knew my voice was thick, but it was too hard to hide the hurt. Besides, I figured house fires would be traumatic for people too.

"You poor thing. You may put your dress back on. I have no further questions," he said and walked away.

As I threaded my dress back together and the prosecution confirmed that he would like to cross-examine, I couldn't help but wonder if Sven's lawyer did part-time work on

Broadway. He was good. I started to go back to the witness box when a cold touch on my shoulder made me freeze.

"You may stay as you are," said the prosecuting lawyer.

This was fine. It wasn't as if Sven's lawyer hadn't asked the same thing. Letting out a deep breath, I turned to the audience.

"Miss Vanguard, tell me about your relationship with Mr. Siversten?" he asked.

"Well, things went a little fast at first. We got caught up in the heat of our *mutual* attraction," I said, making sure to highlight the fact that it hadn't been some blinding faerie lust that drove Sven to me. "But then, we settled back and really took time to grow a deeper relationship."

There. Simple. Just two people navigating through this messed up "modern society" to build something meaningful with each other. There was no talk about things that didn't apply to the case, like his betrayal and my stupidity of letting lust override logic.

"Would you say you're in love?" he asked, the word sticking on his tongue like tar.

The words didn't want to come out because they were too real, too raw. But since I knew they would help Sven's case, I said them. "I would, but I don't know that he would say the same."

The lawyer laughed, a genuine, hearty thing that bounced along the cement walls. "Oh, I don't know about that. I think you could make anyone you wanted to fall in love with you."

I ignored the blatant taunt. He wanted a reaction out of me. That was the only way to get probable cause for someone to bite me. And this was his last chance to get it. I'd be damned if he succeeded.

Unperturbed, he continued on. "In fact, I can prove it. Your honors, we'd like to call Alwick Creighton to the stand."

As if by magic, Alwick appeared. He stormed up the

stairs, his cane barely touching the stairs as his cloak billowed behind him like an old-time horror movie. Distrust wormed in my gut as he neared me. What was he doing here? And the lawyer couldn't do this, could he? I must not have been the only one to think that because Raven started to speak. Grateful for the interruption to this sham of a trial, I looked over my shoulder.

"But you already have a witness on the stand, and you've had your chance for additional-" Raven began but stopped when Mercy leaned over and whispered in his ear. He went very still but then nodded and said, "This is highly unusual, but we will allow it."

What? They were going to allow it? How? I was the witness being questioned. How did one even question two witnesses at once? But logic or not, Alwick was here. Stopping next to me, he gave me a smoldering look that made my skin crawl before turning to the prosecuting attorney.

"Mr. Creighton, when did you first meet Miss Vanguard?" he asked.

"Last week," Alwick said.

"And what was your impression of her?" asked the asshat, as if Alwick's attraction were as serious as an oil spill in the Atlantic.

I fought not to roll my eyes.

"Immediate awe. She stole my heart," Alwick said with a hand over his own heart.

Dagda, this was torture.

"You say she stole your heart. Can you elaborate?" asked the lawyer.

I shifted on my heels. I'd rather he not.

But since I didn't have a say here, with a bow, Alwick said, "I'd be happy to do so. There's something about her that draws the eye. It's subtle, delectable. But the closer you get to her, the more you want to reach out and grab hold of her." I swallowed hard. "You want to pull her to you. Claim her. Make her yours." Then he turned to the audience. "You feel it, don't you? The pull? The need?" Shouts from the crowd came back to him. He turned to me again, his eyes plundering my depths as if the key might be there. "It's real. And why? Why this pull?" Right when I was about to close my eyes, so he couldn't bespell me, he broke our eye contact. He looked back to the storm brewing in the assembly and grew steadily more animated. "It's not like she's some great beauty." I blinked. Ouch. Sure, I wasn't Beyonce, but I was a solid Michelle Williams. I opened my mouth to tell him he wasn't precisely Zak Efron but closed it again. My only job was to not have a reaction. By Dagda, I could do this. People's nods to each other didn't help much as Alwick started to pace around me in circles, eyeing me as if he wanted to devour me. Someone had to stop this. There's no way they'd let this continue. But he pressed on. "I get how Sven would have done anything for her. I, too, even after such a short time knowing her, would do anything for this sweet little bud." No? We weren't stopping this? We were just going to let this go on? Suddenly, he grabbed me around the waist and pulled me to him. I lowered my eyes, not meeting his gaze, not because I was scared but because he'd see the hatred there, the fury. "I can feel her blood calling to me. Singing to me. Taste me. Take me. Make me yours." His mouth moved to my neck. This couldn't be happening. They said he wouldn't bite me. Couldn't. No response, Cy. They couldn't get a reaction from me. Sven's life depended on it. I wanted to look to Sven, to his attorney- to anyone, and plead for them to make this stop. Before it was too late. My heart pounded in my ears as his teeth scraped along my skin. A scream built inside my chest.

"Are we about done with this? Or are we going to listen to

another hour of this pathetic vampyr going on about how much he wants to fornicate with the first available woman that presents herself?" The defense attorney said in a bored voice.

Snickers from the attendees turned Alwick into a statue. He growled, the sound vibrating the delicate skin of my neck. My jaw clenched. If I had picked a time to provoke a vampyr of questionable sanity, it wouldn't have been when he was within chomping distance of my neck.

Raven's voice was bored as he said, "Enough, Alwick. You've proven your point."

"No further questions for Mr. Creighton, your honors," said the prosecuting attorney.

He'd made his point. I thought bitterly. My thoughts were brought away from him as Alwick's hands worked on my sides.

After several heartbeats, he moved his head to my ear and whispered, "You two think you're so clever. You just wait. We'll see who has the last laugh."

Without another word, he loosened his grip. Slanting me an egotistical sneer, I itched to slap off his face, he stepped away from me. As relieved as I was to have him away from me, a part of me wondered what he meant by that as he walked off the stage. Something told me that wasn't the last I'd be seeing of Alwick Creighton.

"Isn't it true, Miss Vanguard, that you are a fae?" asked the asshat, apparently, not catching a clue.

"No, it is not true," I said, lifting my chin as my ribs pressed in. Belying my calm, jitters worked through my chest.

He gave me a chiding look and then looked back to the audience with a roll of his eyes. "You're telling me truthfully that fae blood doesn't run through your veins."

"That is what I am telling you," I said through gritted

teeth. Did I need a box of crayons and construction paper? What was it going to take for this guy to get it?

He leaned in close, his starched suit grazing my bare arm. Too close.

Inhaling a deep whiff of air, he said, "You smell utterly delicious, Miss Vanguard. You do realize faerie blood is...unique...spicey...intoxicating."

Oh, he definitely needed crayons. Or a two-by-four upside the head. It took everything I had in me to meet his eyes. I just wanted this to be over.

With a shrug, I said, "Since I am not a fae, I did not realize that."

The smile crinkling his eyes said I hadn't pulled that off as convincingly as I'd hoped.

"Oh, I think you do. In fact, I call for a motion for your blood." He finished the declaration with a sweeping raise of his fist.

Noises crashed in the back of the courtroom, and the crowd cheered with abandon. Then the chanting started. "Blood. Blood. Blood." My stomach curdled. One particularly rowdy group of vampires stalked up the steps. My insides turned as I looked back to the dais for help. They were the ruling body. Were they going to let this go on? Was my slip enough to end Sven? End me? The High Priestess watched it all with a growing smile as feet pounded the stage. A crash came, and I turned back to see a shard of glass had appeared in one of my would-be attackers' hands. Six of them. I think I could take that many. But if I fought, would I be just giving more weight to their case? Probably, but I'd be damned if I just sat there and let them beat me to a pulp.

The pounding of the gavel came, and I nearly fell to the floor in relief. The group of vampires exchanged looks. Would they still attack? After a few silent back and forths punctuated by more rapping of the mallet and shouts for order, the impromptu dagger dropped soundlessly to the plush carpet. When they turned and left, I let my eyes close in relief. That had been too real for my liking.

"What does the defense say to this motion for the court to test Miss Vanguard's blood?" Raven asked, with barely a lift of his lips.

"We respectfully decline the request," said Sven's attorney, with a slight bow.

Raven cocked his head and squinted at the attorney. Clearly, this was an unusual refusal. "On what grounds?"

This time Sven spoke up, his voice ringing through the rafters, silencing all. "On the grounds that her blood is mine and mine alone. I have not shared Cy and never will. She is mine." My heart soared. It was what I'd wanted to hear ever since I'd woken up. Sweet words. His love. It took everything in me not to run over and wrap myself in his arms.

Sven's lawyer cleared his throat as if the mere act of a wish could take away Sven's words. "As has been pointed out here today, your honors. My client is territorial of his claim on Miss Vanguard. And to speak frankly, with all of the...interest in her, who can blame him?"

Raven sat back, looking between the two of us with an unreadable look on his face. After a moment, he let out an exhale and, with a half-smile, asked the prosecution, "Do we have probable cause to overturn this declination?"

The attorney sputtered. "You mean besides that she's a bloody faerie?"

Raven looked down on him, much like a lion looking down on its next meal. "Facts, counselor. Do we have facts that show probable cause that Miss Vanguard very likely is the faerie you claim her to be?"

"Her wings, your honors. One of the witnesses testified that she had wings," the attorney said in a puff of indignation.

"Right, and if she did, in fact, have said wings, I would

agree with you, counselor. However, all I see is a woman who has been badly burned and a trial that has gone on too long for what is reasonable, customary, and far past what could have been deemed as my good graces hours ago. So, unless you have anything to add, I suggest you let us adjourn before you are witness to what my bad graces look like."

"We have nothing to add, your honors," Sven's attorney said, barely able to keep the smile from his face.

The prosecuting attorney turned redder than any vampire I'd ever seen and finally spit out, "We also have nothing further, your honors."

Raven gave an approving nod. Then, without consulting any of the others, you could feel the room deflate as he said, "Motion for blood declined. It looks like these love birds, as odd as it is, aren't into sharing. We will take a brief recess while we adjourn. Upon our return, we will announce the verdict."

With a crack of the mallet, the High Council rose and shuffled out of the court. I could feel Mercy's displeasure like a fist. That couldn't bode well. Pushing her displeasure out of my head, I focused on the grueling trial we'd just been through. We had done the best we could. Now, all we could do was wait.

Sven's attorney put a comforting hand on my elbow. I looked to him to say thanks, but he was just telling me to go join the crowd. Sure, he'd worded it like a suggestion, but the look in his eyes said Get Lost. I did my best impression of a leprechaun and danced into the crowd. Ok, not literally.

Thankfully, Catherine was in the front, so I got to stand by a friendly face. Well, she didn't look so happy at the moment, but I was chalking that up to this trial bringing up all kinds of painful memories for her. Being ostracized for holding to the truth. What an awful way to live. How much easier would her life have been if she had just done what

Mercy had asked? She must have known that. Yet, she held fast to her ideals and instead let everything she loved disappear. Brutal.

While I was rolling the enormity of her sacrifice around in my mind, the High Council filed back in. Huh, that seemed quick. From the stirring and murmurs around me, it was clear I wasn't the only one who thought as much.

When all 7 members were seated, Raven again picked up the wooden hammer. "Sven Sivertsen, please come forward."

Sven moved forward, his head held high. My chest squeezed. This was it.

Raven looked at him for several seconds and said, "Of the charge Communing with the Fae, we The High Council, find you, Sven Sivertsen, not guilty." The crowd around me erupted into jeers and shouts. Someone snatched my leg. Smashing my elbow back, it connected with a rib, and a crunch as the hand fell away with a thud of something more substantial as my senses went on high alert. The catsuit policewoman dove into the mob. With a jerk, she cleanly lifted one vampyr straight off the ground. I slow blinked. Impressive. The pounding of the gavel came from the dais again. This time harder and more insistent. At first, nothing happened, but after a moment, the vampyrs around me quieted down.

When everyone's attention had turned back to Raven, he stopped smashing the mallet against its wooden plate. With silence echoing around him, he turned the ornate handle around in his hand as if mulling something. Finally, he said, "However, new information has been brought to light with the case." My stomach dropped. New information? My mind raced over the last few hours, desperately searching for what that could have been. "It has come to our attention that Sven killed his Master, not in a quest for power, but instead for one who is *not* a vampire. The law states you shall have no loyalty before vampire-kind." His words settled over the expectant crowd. Wait, it was acceptable to kill someone for power but not to save someone's life unless they were a vampire? What kind of twisted shit was that? "Therefore, we, the High Council, are bringing new charges against Sven Sivertsen. Breaking Loyalty. He will be tried in two days' time."

The gavel rang out a note of finality, growing resentment in my gut. Couldn't this just be over? Did we have to go through this again? Even worse, there was no escaping this time. Sven had given his Master's life for mine. Therefore, he'd given loyalty to me over vampires. And apparently, that was against the law too. Well, fuck. I hugged myself tightly. Just what would Sven have to pay for saving my life?

CHAPTER 10

The otherworldly sexy man in front of me slid his hands down his bare chest in an aching caress. When he reached his groin, my mouth went dry. He was a rippled, deliciously sinful morsel. Everything about him screamed, 'fuck me.' And oh, I want to.

It didn't have anything to do with me turning over a new empowered slut leaf, either. He was an incubus. His sole magic party trick consisted of making women's panties across the globe drop like autumn leaves in a thunderstorm. But I wasn't here to fuck him. I was here to send him back to Hell. I cracked the glow stick collar and shook it as he continued his seduction.

"What are you doing way over there? Why don't you come over here and get more...comfortable?" he asked, as he swiveled his hips and pressed his hands on the tops of his thighs. The black silk curtain of his hair spilled over his shoulders with the move, tickling his knees. Sweet Danu, what I wouldn't give to run my hands through that, as he sunk inside of me. I shook the necklace more vigorously. I blinked to clear the bedroom-thoughts racing through my head. Focus. Stay focused. Just because he was a lesser demon didn't mean I had nothing to fear.

All I had to do was open my eyes to see that. A dreamy quality tinged everywhere I looked. The mist swirling out of Sodom and Gomorrah pools wrapped around his ankles and snaked up his leg. Hazy and soft, it blended in with the now-lavender pond banks that framed his chiseled chest. And even though I knew the name of the geothermal pools behind him, they began to look unfamiliar, like everything else around me. Part of the incubus' spell was their ability to make you feel like everything was brand new, exciting. It made you more open to new experiences. Ergo, having sex with a stranger hot enough to fry eggs on. But I wasn't falling for it. I knew better. And right now, I knew I had to get this collar on that demon playboy.

"Just be a good little boy now, and come here so I can send you back where you belong," I said, right before I lunged for him. He dodged the move with ease, his hair fanning out in a spectacular display as it caught the sun.

He bit his lip and said, "Oh, I can be a good boy. Or... I can be really, really bad. What do you want inside of you, love? Do you want a good boy to treat you right? Or do you want a bad boy to make your wildest dreams come true? I can be whatever your heart desires. "

Couldn't I have a good, bad boy? I'd rather have someone who made my wildest dreams come true who would treat me right, not someone who treats me like shit and is just good in bed. Rather than debate all of the problems with women romanticizing men who treated them like shit, I dove at him. He jumped out of the way with the grace of a cat.

With a laugh that tightened things low in my belly, he said, "Come now, it doesn't have to be like that. You look stressed. Come over here and let me help you forget everything. You know you want me to. I can do it. All you have to do is let me wrap my arms around you. Then you can wrap your legs around me. And I can make-" I leaped at him. This time I was closer, but still, my hand met nothing but air as he slid out of my reach. He shook his head, a frown pulling at his pillow-soft lips. "That's not the way we do it. If you want me, you can have me, but we have to stop this cat and mouse game. Just let me give you what you want."

Since I'd been coming at him from the left, I switched to the right. The switch-up would've been successful with most people, but not with this guy. Yeah, this wasn't working. Time for a new game plan.

"You know, you're right." I bit the tip of my finger. Letting desire pool into my eyes, I imagined a different time, a different place, and a different man who gave me everything I'd ever wanted. I mustered the sexiest voice possible, but it sounded more like I was talking baby-talk to Gunny, my newly-acquired, gun-turned-cat. He had a bit of a temper. Trying not to sound like I had stolen the script for the world's worst porno, I said, "It's all part of the game for me. To see if you're good enough to be with me. And hot stuff, you sure are. You've got me so hot right now. "

The incubus bounced his wide finger against his lips. He was suspicious. Rightly, so.

"How do I know you aren't spouting lies. Wanting to get me close so you can attack?" he said, his lips flattening.

Damn it, there was nothing more frustrating than an intelligent demon. Clutching my breasts, I said in a breathy voice, "Come now. How could I do something like that? I can barely think past this need burning inside me. You're all man. Just what a woman needs. Just what I need. Please. Give it to me. I'll do anything to feel you inside me."

A slow smile, confident and sure, spread across his face. And why wouldn't it? For countless years, he'd been seducing woman after woman. Tor Mór, probably for a millennium.

And how many had turned him down? If I had to venture a guess, probably none. But what he didn't know was I wasn't just another victim on his tally board. Another human. I was a faerie. I had to give it to him, though. Even being aware and resistant, he still ate at the edges of my resolve. In fact, if it wasn't for the fate of humanity being on the line, would I have been able to? It was a thought I didn't want to think too hard about. My lips flattened before I remembered what I was doing and pursed them seductively again.

The doubt was in his eyes again. "I don't know. You feel off. No matter how badly I want to sink into your warm heat, I want to retain my form much more.

I pouted prettily. "Don't say that. I'll be good. No more tricks. I promise. just you, me, and heat." With the last word, I slid my fingers over the juncture of my thighs. He wet his lips as his gaze pinged down and then back up to my eyes. His smile wavered. He was close. "Here. Let me prove it to you. I'll lie down, and you can come to me. But you'd better hurry. I don't want to go off without you…if you know what I mean. "

The interest in his eyes flared. Thank Danu, energy from sex was how incubuses stayed alive. That meant him seducing me was a matter of life or death for him. To be fair, he could probably have any number of women falling all over themselves to be in his arms, but this particular incubus had more than a streak of pride in him. From everything I'd seen, it was more airstrip-sized.

I laid down and spread my hands out wide. "See? Harmless, I won't do anything. I'll just lie here and let you. Blow. My. Mind. "His feet shuffled slightly, caught in indecision. He wanted to come to me, but I hadn't sold it. I reached down slowly and unzipped my zipper, letting the top of my black lace panties peek out. "I just want you. Let me feel you. Don't deny me that. Give it to me. I want it so badly.

Come feel how hot you make me." Confident I was in line to win some award for bad porn, I rubbed my hands down my body to grip my calves. It wasn't until I came back up to tease the top of my panties that his expression broke. He moved forward on swift, sure feet.

Towering over me, his expression was dark and sensual. "Tell me. Tell me how badly you want it."

His words tightened things low. Part of me knew it wasn't natural. Knew it was his magic. But that didn't stop the sensations inside of me from being any less real. That's how I knew the words felt honest when I said, "I want you so badly it doesn't make sense. I want you to do things to me nobody has ever done before." And I meant it. I didn't want to, but I did. I knew what he was. Knew he couldn't give me anything even close to what Sven had, but that didn't stop the need from building inside of me anyway.

With a satisfied curl of his lips, his pants disappeared. As in vanished. Well, that was a handy party trick.

He looked deeply into my eyes as he lowered himself over me.

"You have far too many clothes on, love," he said, making my toes curl. With a snap of his fingers, my panties started to lower. I hissed in a breath as the cool air hit my belly.

"Yes, take me. Give me what I want. Make me yours." The words were not my own as I wrapped my arms around his neck to twine my fingers in his hair. Then I felt it. The hard plastic of the glow stick. Of why I was here. That's right. I wasn't here to make love to this delicious and imposter of a man. I was here to send him to Hell.

Concentrating on letting any rigidity out of my body, he kissed along my jawline and up to my earlobe. The world tilted dangerously as he licked and flicked heat there. A moan of pleasure snuck out as my hands wrapped the collar around his muscled neck. All of my muscles clenched and coiled as he dipped his hands below the line of my panties, reaching ever lower. If he had touched my center, I might have been lost, but I clipped the plastic glow stick connector in place at that very moment he covered me. A searing light pierced my eyes. I bucked and flipped him off me.

"You bitch!" he screamed and jerked at the blue light that seemed to emanate from within him.

Knowing what came next, I rolled out of the way. The whoosh I knew was coming threw my hair over my shoulder. I turned back around just in time to see him fully wrapped in fiery ropes. Wincing at the flare of light that I knew was coming, the intense blue still caught me off guard. Then he was gone.

Dropping my head onto the pebbled concrete, I fought to get my bearings, to clear the magic of seduction from my mind. Cheers and clapping came from all around me. What in the name of Dagda was that? Opening my eyes, which I hadn't realized I had closed, I remembered where I was. That's right, I was in Hell's Gate theme park to send back the goblin's numero uno bad guy, Cerberus.

I swung the one-shouldered bag to my front and zipped it closed as I turned to the goblins, who I had quite frankly forgotten had been here the whole time. Well, nothing like some foreplay to start the day. I had gotten here early because we had to wrap this up by 2 when the park opened. Looking away, I ignored the depraved congregation as I zipped my pants up and went to join them.

"They work!" shouted Mabye, the skull attached to his waist swaying precariously as he jumped up and down on his spindly legs.

"Yes, they do," I said as if it were the most natural thing in the world that I was wading through a throng of fun-sized monsters. "Which reminds me. I thought I told you to get me if any bigger demons came through." The goblins nodded, wide sharp-tooth grins matching on all of their faces. Clearly not catching my drift, I tried again. "May I remind you that an incubus is a demon. Being evil experts as you are," I allowed myself the teensy exaggeration and continued, "you at least know that he is from Hell, which also means you should have fetched me. "More smiles and nods bobble-headed all around me. Why did I have to be pseudo-god to one of the most patience-bending races in the history of the world? I rolled my eyes. Whatever, we had more important things to do, like keep all of the future creatures in Hell. "Nevermind, let's talk Cerberus. When does he come around?

Someone from the back piped up, "When he wants a snack, of course. When would you come around?" The goblins parted enough for me to see a group of goblins shaking their heads at each other as if that were obvious. Ignoring the part of the statement that made me want to throw him back into the caves where I first found the irritating race, I focused on the one part I could respond to. "Well, that's not exactly helpful because you all are the snack in this case. Last time I checked, we were trying to keep you guys on this side of the undead line." The more I thought about it, the more laughable it became. "I mean, really. What would we do, just dangle one of you out there for him to snap up?

The image of a goblin dancing with an apple in his mouth popped into my head. I laughed at the visual. Once I started, I couldn't stop. Tears squeezed from the corners of my eyes. After a moment, I caught my breath and regained my composure.

That's when I noticed nobody else was laughing. Instead, they were looking at each other and nodding their heads.

Finally, one asked what the other ones were obviously thinking, "Well, yeah."

Just when I was about to point out why that was a terrible idea, another goblin piped up, "Yeah, that's a great idea. "

A goblin in the front, with a dripping red cap, said, "Best idea ever!"

His portly friend next to him with a matching red hat jumped up with a gleam in his eye. "I'll do it! It'll be fun!"

Crossing my arms, I said, "It's going to be a lot less fun if you die." The volunteer rubbed the base of his neck, blood dripping down his arm as he pondered me. Looking around, I saw more of the same confusion. That's right. They thought I was their god. As a blood-thirsty race, I'm sure the suggestion made sense. However, we faeries prided ourselves on living for a century, so the idea of treating life so casually put a tack in my gut. I tapped my fingers on the back of my arms. I suppose if this was their culture, I had to respect it.

Still, for some reason I couldn't understand, I cared for the bugger, so I heard myself saying, "OK, fine. You can do it, but only if we follow some strict guidelines. First of all, we have to take precautions to make sure you…. what's your name?" I asked, feeling unreal as I pointed at the volunteer.

Excitement skittered through the group like a wave. I could almost see them vibrating with it.

And so went the push and pull between solid logic and unreasonable madness as we patchworked a plan together. An hour and a half later found us with a plan that lacked all reason and masqueraded as a compromise. The last hour alone had been outfitting the stubborn but endearing goblin I'd come to know as Tuelo. I stepped back and blinked the sting out of my eyes, assessing him.

Every inch of him dripped. Blood wept from that damn hat. After it had soaked our thirteenth attempt at putting together armor for him, I'd asked him to take the pain in the ass off, but he'd said no. When I asked him why all he'd said was, 'we never take them off. Not helpful. The rest of him was dripping because he was smothered in rotten food and trash that fell off him in plops as he walked down the boardwalk. My eyes were all but bleeding because of it. It was my fault. I'd opened my mouth and told him that Cerberus wasn't likely to want to eat a goblin that smelled of blood if the others he'd eaten hadn't worn the same hat.

"Well, not what I'd have put together, but it'll do in a pinch," I said to him, twanging the rope attached to the steel corset we'd trussed him up in.

"This protection band is the best idea ever," he said, his voice overly loud, fighting for space in my head with the clanging of metal as he thumped the chest piece.

Yes, I'd told him it was a protection band. It was the only way he'd agree to incorporate it into the design.

"This is a right good plan. You've really got this fightin' stuff down, don't you? Good on you. Real good. And the sun is shining. Blitz, what a great day for putting this beast in his place."

"Yes, it is. Just be safe out there," I said, talking through my teeth. The more he went on, the more fervently I found myself praying to Dagda this worked.

"Be the tempting morsel that I am. Can do," he said, his voice trailing away as I followed the rope around the rock outcropping to five goblins crowded together. They'd tethered the nylon cord around the waist of a goblin so big I questioned if he'd been adopted. The other four had ahold of the rope behind him, clinging to it as if their lives depended on it. Theirs didn't, but Tuelo's sure did.

"Ok, tell me the plan again," I said, sidestepping a rotten banana peel to check the knots were solid.

"If the rope jerks, we yank it back," said Dikeledi, who, to my utter shock, had volunteered to keep Tuelo anchored.

"Ok, yes, but only if what?" I held up a finger. Someone who wouldn't be named- Dikeledi- had gotten excited during the rehearsal and almost knocked Tuelo out on the rock outcropping by pulling when he wasn't ready.

"Only if the line is pulled twice first," said Tuelo's slender friend, Gofaone, bobbing his head in excitement.

Kut didn't bother to wipe off the blood that slung onto her shoulder with the move. While I appreciated the fighter's zen, my fingers itched to wipe off the impromptu Jackson Pollock impression. Nobody could accuse the goblins of being a sanitary bunch, that was for sure.

Doing my best to ignore the blood splatters, I asked, "Right. Are there any questions?"

Mogapi shrugged, the move shifting his chimera pelt he was inexplicably still wearing in this heat. "No. Seems pretty straightforward. Cerberus grabs Tuelo, you jump on Cerberus' back, slap that collar on him, and we pull Tuelo out while Cerberus is being sent back to Hell by your glow sticks."

I nodded, pretending there wasn't a hive worth of hornets in my gut. Yeah, that was it, just ride a hellhound, get everyone out alive, and send *the* hellhound back to Hell. No big deal.

"Right, looks like we're ready then. Remember to wait for Tuelo." Giving Dikeledi one final look that said, 'yes, I mean you,' I turned to the rock pile next to the eager group.

I lodged one foot after the other into the grooves up the steep incline. When I'd reached the top, I pushed the sweat-dampened hair out of my face. Sweet Danu, it was hot. They didn't call this a thermal park for nothing. Grabbing a glow stick out of my pack, I went to sit down but stopped and looked at the deceptive kid's toy again. It was awfully short for a beast's neck. Trying hard not to extrapolate that fun fact, I grabbed another necklace out of the pack. Snapping the two red and blue pieces together, I got ready to toss it if it gave any sign of activation. There was no way I was going to

Hell any time soon. I'd gained far too much notice from the Devil the last time I was there, and that was enough reason to stay away from the place. The last thing you wanted to be was a curiosity to the Devil and in his kingdom. That and it was Hell, let's be real.

Thankfully, no light show went off. Not trusting it, I stared at the deceptively innocent-looking plastic stick for a small eternity. Still, nothing happened. Ok, fine. Maybe, it wasn't going to whisk me off to Hell. Maybe.

I clutched the longer glow stick in my hand as I flattened myself onto the plateau. Peering over the edge, I spotted Tuelo right away. His juicy rolls bounced, spilling out of either side of the metal corset that we were all banking would save his life as he paced from one end of the boardwalk in front of the Hell's Gate pool to the other. Every now and again, he would stop to hold up his arm and waft it.

Much later, when the sun was high above, and I'd sweated a snow angel into the dirt under me, he was doing more of the same, just with much less vigor. The rotten trash long ago having dried to his gray body, nothing dripped off him, though. His feet slapped the boards, and he gave half-hearted rump shakes before he turned and went the other way only to repeat the lackluster move on the other side. I had to give it to him. We'd been out here for hours, and he was still at it. Hours that probably felt like a lifetime in that oven of a getup.

I'd just shifted to my other elbow when I heard it. A rattling of chains. On the heels of that was a lone howl. When it split off into a chorus of barks, I knew who was coming. Cerberus. The hairs on my arms stood up on end as my breathing stopped. In bounded a beast so large I understood in an instant why the goblins had referred to themselves as snacks. Our plan had worked. What had we done?

Tuelo, who with the skill of a veteran club-goer, had promptly dropped down to roll his fat bottom in front of the beast, was only half as big as one of its three heads. Its necks were collared by thick, scrolled bands held together by horned demon skulls with rings in their mouths. Door knockers. Spirit trails emanated from the collars and the chains dragging behind him on the too-ordinary floorboards. But it wasn't the spirit trails that bothered me. No, it was the tail. It was long and thick. And a fucking snake.

"Nobody told me it had a fucking snake for a tail," I grumbled as I watched the scene below
unfold.

I had to do something, and quick, or Tuelo was going to be the goblin equivalent of an apple fritter. Looking around, all I saw were rocks. Since I doubted bludgeoning a tail would be very effective, I discarded that idea. Instead, I tore my red tank top. I brought the strip round and round a few times until I had a solid length. Left with little better than a crop top, I tore it off. Testing the strength of it, I heard muffled arguing. When I looked back down, I saw the rope was pulled tight, and Tuelo was being dragged across the boards.

"Not yet! Stop! We're not ready!" Tuelo screamed, flailing as Cerberus followed him, stalking Tuelo like the predator he was.

It moved him out of range for my part of the plan. Of course.

"Dikeledi," I muttered as I tied the strip to my wrist in a slip knot.

Cracking the magic capsule in each glow stick, I moved back to the furthest part of the ledge. I grabbed where they joined together and shook them, making sure the potion flowed brightly through the tubes before shoving the necklace into my pocket. I had to keep my hands free. It didn't take a seer to know both hands would be needed to pull off this miracle.

Digging in for as much traction on the slippery pebbles as faerily possible, I took off. With one last push, I was airborne. My legs churned as I sailed through the air. Thanks to the extra zip of my vamp powers, I sailed just far enough. As I was angling my body to land on the back of the massive hellhound, Tuelo ran past. Unsurprisingly, the hellhound turned to go after him. Again. Instead of landing on the relatively cushioned back of a dog, my legs slammed into unforgiving boards, jarring my brain. I couldn't let him get away. This was our chance. In a desperate move, I reached out to grab the beast. To my relief, I connected, but it only took a flash of a second to realize I'd caught the one thing I'd been dreading. The snake.

Reacting on instinct alone, I slapped one hand over the other until I was left gripping the head of the snake. Its scaled body jumped and bumped under my fingertips as I squeezed the pulsing flesh. The maw opened wide, intent on sinking its fangs into me. Too bad for him, the frantic pressure I had on its neck made that only a prayer. Careful to maintain my grip with one hand, I brought my other over to loosen the slip knot with my teeth. After it was free, I slipped it off and made quick work of wedging it between the snake's mouth and using the tension around that and the snake's head to hold the knot into place. In no time, the binding was complete.

But there wasn't any time to celebrate. Confused at the jerking, Cerberus started to run. The slippery mud was the only thing that kept my brain from rattling out of my head as he slung me around violently. And just like that, the snake I'd been trying to avoid turned into my lifeline as I clung to it, finding myself on the unfortunate end of a land version of water skiing.

Just when I was deciding whether I should invest in a rose gold and diamond grillz or just let go, the choice was made for me. Cerberus flicked his tail. Only by the grace of my vamp powers did I manage to hold on. A twinge shot down my arms. To my utter shock, not only did they stay attached, but I found myself flying through the air. That's where my luck ran out.

On the downswing, the scaled tail was ripped from my hands. Momentum, also in the cosmic joke that seemed to be my life, pushed me forward. I tried to keep my eyes open, but it was a feat easier said than done when air is being blown into them. That's why I didn't know what I hit. All I knew was that it was solid, so I clung to it. And warm. And muscled. And...oh, shit.

The growl that vibrated my hands wasn't a surprise, but the hisses were. My eyes flew open. Red eyes, two feet from my face, greeted me. The spirit trails flowed faster as he let out a hair-raising growl.

I screamed. Sure, it didn't speak of courage, but it was better than shitting my pants. The fur-bordered, death-orbs didn't even have the decency to wince. Instead, the beast released the most terrifying bark I'd ever heard. Tendons under my (what I didn't realize were) shaking hands flexed as the beast tried to unseat me.

Too bad for him, I was seated firmly against his neck. And thank Danu too because it kept me just out of reach from the other head, snapping its viselike jaws at me. It did let me see the source of the hissing, though. Hundreds of tiny snakes grew from the hellhound's chin, forming the scariest goatee in existence.

More snakes. What kind of sadistic ass thought up this nightmare? Tor Mór, it didn't matter. I just wanted to put as much distance between this beast and me as possible. Yeah, the innermost circle of Hell sounded about right. Slinging my over-the-shoulder bag to my front, I grabbed a handful of extra glow sticks. I connected them all together before breaking the vial in each one and shaking them to distribute the liquid. Sounded simple, I know, but it was decidedly less so when a giant dog from Hell was doing his damnedest to make sure you knew he didn't want you riding him.

At last, it was ready. Using the curve of his existing collar made slipping the necklace around his neck as easy as chicken nuggets. Then Cerberus started to buck. With a desperate grip on the glowing plastic, I prayed the connectors would hold as I struggled to connect the last remaining piece. The world rotated and moved, its axis clearly now on a bouncy ball. Danu threw me a gift, though, because the connector snapped into place.

"Yes!" I screamed, pumping my fist. But my rush victory quickly changed to a panicked, "Oh, shit," as the familiar blinding light flared all around me.

Boosting up to a crouch, I started to scramble down the monster's spine. I had barely made it two steps when he sat. I jumped on one foot to catch my balance, but when he lifted a boulder-sized paw to scratch at his neck, I lost my footing. Air rushed past me. Angling towards the muddy embankment, I tucked my head in. Hitting the ground, I somersaulted, rolling once, twice, and a third time before finally coming to a stop. My breath came fast and hard. I worked to get it under control as the light show behind me danced all kinds of colors across the mud puddles around me. Finally, the colors flared, the same blinding light I'd come to appreciate so much. At least it was over. I dropped my head to the slippery mud as I struggled to get my breath.

It wasn't until my breathing returned to normal and I lifted my head that a faint waft of pungent air blew the hairs on the back of my neck. I went still. No way. It wasn't possible. I saw the necklace work. But as impossible as it might seem, I looked over my shoulder and saw Cerberus, nonetheless. Very much here. Very much still on our plane. And very pissed. Heat washed over me as he bared his teeth and growled. This was how I died. I expected my life to flash before my eyes. Instead, I thought about the cheeseburger from Upland's I wouldn't be eating again. The creamy avocado. The sweet kick of the peppadew peppers.

Just then, as if on a silent screen, the heart-stopping scene in front of me changed. To a goblin's butt. Tuelo's butt, to be exact.

"Hey, you cross-eyed kobold. What are you doing? Did you forget about this tasty dish?" Tuelo taunted, flapping his hands back and forth in front of the furious beast. Continuing his waving arms, he danced to the side.

Cerberus' eyes narrowed as he followed the meaty goblin.

"Tuelo, what are you doing? We have to abandon the plan. The necklaces aren't working." I hissed at him as I turned around and saw he was twerking inches from the hellhound's drooling maw. "Did you hear me? I said, get out of here!"

That's when Tuelo looked at me. The flash of excitement in his eyes had me doubting he'd heard me, but then he said in a low voice. "Get yourself gone. Tuelo's got this."

"No, Tuelo. Don't be stupid-" I said as he danced away, his intent clear as he trailed the giant dog after him. An acidic combination of fear and fury ate at me. I cracked my knuckles. "Oh, I don't think so."

I didn't think of the ramifications of taking out Cerberus, the guardian of Hell. All I thought about was the life of that frustrating-as-sin goblin who'd just saved my skin. I snatched in a heavy drag of ley energy. I'd need it for this beast.

I started to run after the pair but hadn't gone more than two steps when the world spun around me. I'd pulled too much Kundalini energy too fast. My steps faltered to a stop as I struggled against the sensation, and even though my feet weren't going anywhere, I couldn't stop moving. I mean, I was moving, wasn't I?

The beast lunged forward, and I knew we were out of time. Dizziness or not, this beast was going down. Holding my hand out in front of me, I blinked and tried to focus as I took aim and shot at his haunches. It was the only part of the monster I could hit from this angle. It let out two barks and a muffled whine but didn't move. Muffled? Oh, please, Danu, no. Dread ate at my stomach as I stagger-ran around the hellhound.

Sure enough, Tuelo was in one of its mouths. Thank Danu, the steel corset appeared to be working.

The fierce goblin had a cocky grin on his face as he punched Cerberus in the snout. "You dirty rotter. This one's for Goitsemedi. And another for Mmaabo. And two for Olebile."

While Tuelo continued to pummel the unfazed hellhound, the rope attached to his corset vibrated. It was too tight. Panic crawled up my throat.

"Hey! Be care-" was all I got out before the thick nylon snapped.

Cerberus' head jerked back with the force of it. It soon became apparent that had been the only thing keeping them tethered because the hellhound dashed off. With Tuelo in his mouth still hurling insults at the beast, the devil dog bound into Hell's Gate, leaving not even a ripple. And just like that, they were gone. With them vanished all our hopes for returning Cerberus to Hell for good. Because he'd be back. And there was nothing we could do about it.

CHAPTER 11

"*E*arth to Cy?" Kittie's voice drifted down from what had fast become her favorite spot to hang out on the ornate mirror of my home-away-from-home room at the Blood Spire.

A home I was looking to leave as soon as this trial business was all squared away. The second of which I was supposed to be getting dressed for but felt absolutely no motivation for. Even though I wasn't a scheduled witness in this hearing, I was still required to attend. Ugly words like "stand-by" and "in the event" had been thrown around.

"Yeah?" I asked, becoming aware Kittie had said something as I bent my back to spine popping relief. Despite my vamp powers, I wasn't a hundred percent back to normal after the cluster that was yesterday's events. My chest tightened. Damn it, Tuelo. Why did he have to do something stupid like save me? It made me want to bring him back from the dead to kill him again. Why would he do that? He should have let me handle it. Reality intruded, and I pressed my lips together to keep it together. Yeah, I'd been doing a bang-up job of "handling it." The little goblin had saved my life. I swallowed past the thickness in my throat.

Standing up, Kittie caught my attention fully this time. She planted her hands on her hips and said, "Do you understand what I am saying about the Queen? She's targeting your followers. Because you aren't there to protect them. As much as I hate Court shit, you need to go back and smooth things over. Time is running out for not only your relationship with your mother but your people."

"Look, I get things are bad. This trial is almost over. Go back to Knockaine. Talk to Anthony. He's the Royal Messenger." At her 'duh' look, I mentally shook my head. That's right; he's the one who had hired her in the first place. I waved a hand. "Anyway, see if there's anything he thinks I can do from here to make things better in the meantime until we finish up here and I can get back home. If he doesn't have any ideas, hang around the place and do what you do best. And no, I don't mean being a pain in the ass."

We both knew I meant spying. That's how I'd met the pint-sized irritation turned new-bestie in the first place. "While you're at it, I need you ask Iris for collars that do more."

"First of all, Anthony is MIA. No one knows where he is. Secondly, collars that do more what? Party tricks? Sing and dance?" Kittie asked, rapping her knuckles against the vanity to get my attention.

My gaze was pulled back to the mirror. Back to what I'd been staring at before. The diamond scar in the center of my chest. Well, it was more to the left than the actual center. Puckered around the edges, it smoothed out relatively quickly. It's where Oganess had given me Sven's heart. The scar bumped out as if Sven's heart had been bigger than mine. I wouldn't be surprised if it was. He had been one of the most thoughtful people I'd ever known. "Had" being the operative word. Before I'd taken his heart and rendered him the emotional equivalent of a mute. I was out of options where he was concerned. Nothing I'd done seemed to be making any difference. Maybe, getting his feelings back just wasn't something that could be done. My lips quivered. I pulled in my bottom lip to stop it.

I blinked, coming back to our conversation. "Remember Oganess' pet ifrit was a hellspawn?"

"Hard to forget a monster," she said, stretching high.

"Right, so we're talking about someone who flicked Redox across the room like he was a pushpin." I said, rubbing my forehead. "Well, we need something even higher up Hell's ladder than that. I did some research on Cerberus. Turns out he's the son of Typhon."

"Which would account for all of the snakey bits," said Kittie, refastening the straps on her knee-high combat boots.

Picking the last bit of mud out from under my nails, I sighed and looked up. "Right, and, more importantly, makes him the son of a demigod, which-"

"Makes him hard as shit to kill," She finished, pointing her finger at me and cocking it.

Frowning, I narrowed my eyes on her. "Exactly. So we need something-"

"That packs more punch," she said, driving a fist in the air to emphasize her point.

"Would you quit doing that?" I crossed my arms over my chest, the move shifting the most comfortable bra I could find, a sheer plunging number that at least didn't have an underwire.

She flew into the air and landed on my nose. Thrusting her hands on her hips, she said. "What would you like me to just keep ignoring your far-off stares and the half-assed conversations you've been having since you got back from Hell's Gate? Pull yourself together. You lost a goblin. So what? There's a dozen of the elf pukes to take his place."

Her words pricked my eyes. She was right, though.

Coming home had been hard yesterday. I know I hadn't been myself since. But she was missing the point.

"It's not just the goblin. Don't you get it? Whenever I get involved, things go to Hell in a head basket," I said, the words thick in my throat as I borrowed the goblin phrase. "Now, people are dying. Because of me. I'm not cut out to be anyone's god. Tor Mór, it's hard enough knowing what to do for myself. But what am I supposed to do? Just leave a whole race without protection? Protection they'd have, by the way, if it weren't for me?"

Kittie flew off my nose and hovered inches in front of my face. Her hands were balled into fists as she looked at me, shaking her head.

"Yeah, you fucked up. Ok? Is that what you want to hear? Because you did. Well, wake-up call. We all fuck up. Sure, you've left a good man an emotionless void. Sure, you've fucked over your entire race by exposing them to vampires. Sure, you killed off a god and left an entire species without a way to protect themselves," she said, waving her arm around heatedly. I leveled a flat look at her that said this clearly wasn't helping. She barely blinked before shifting her hand to a stop sign and continuing on, "Whatever, my point is. You're not walking away. You're still trying to do the right thing. And you will succeed at it because you achieve whatever you put your mind to. Because you're a good woman. And that says more than sparkles at a pixie parade."

My lips worked as I fought to not lose it. It always came around to that too. I felt like I wasn't good enough. Not strong enough. Not tough enough. Like I just wasn't *enough*. It was a fear that had lived inside of me ever since my mother had all but abandoned me after my Father and sister were killed. No matter how hard I tried to fight it, that black hole of a parasite came back again and again.

Reaching down to the table, I busied myself with closing

my makeup case and putting the brushes back as I tried to listen to the logic of Kittie's words. It was just hard to let the wise words sink in when a belief was buried so deeply. I stacked my palettes. Saying she had no tact would be an understatement, but the freight train of a pixie was right. I would find a way past this. I always did. All I had to do was keep my wits about me, even in the face of monumental screwups.

I let out a frustrated sigh as I moved the contour palette I never used. Underneath sat a fist-sized amulet I'd never seen before. Scrunching up my face, I picked it up. It was heavy. No doubt that had less to do with the thick, black chain and more to do with the mammoth blood-red gem in the center. It was framed in a black gothic setting that looked simultaneously refined and dangerous as fuck. No matter how elegant the metalwork, it was the gem that kept grabbing my attention. The stone was breathtaking. It sparkled in a way I'd only seen diamonds shine.

My mouth dropped open. It was the same necklace that had been stolen. It had to be. Red diamonds were rare. And for one to just show up here when another had gone missing was just too coincidental. A niggling feeling wormed into my gut. Shooting a glance at Kittie only confirmed my suspicions. She was beet red.

I waved the long amulet at her, "This is Ambrosia's, isn't it?"

"Who's Ambrosia?" This time it was Kittie's turn to cross her arms over her chest. I knew better than to fall for the innocent act, though. She was guilty as a one-legged rooster.

"Oh, you might remember her as the drunk vampire with the ten-inch silver stilettos." I shook it at her for emphasis. "This is her necklace."

She glared at me before finally sighing. "Ok, fine. Yes, I

took it. It got boring while you were all out for the count. I needed something to keep me entertained."

"So you turned to a little light kleptoing?" I swept the necklace around in disbelief.

"I wanted something to look at. Besides, it's no big deal. As pixies, we take things all of the time. Do you know how long it takes us to make something with these gnat hands?" she asked, fanning her nail-bitten fingers out.

That's when it hit me. "Where are the rest of them?" This time she glared at me. "Where?"

Apparently, taking a vow of silence, she thrust her hand down and pointed to the left side of the vanity. I opened and shut all the drawers, finding nothing until I gave the last one a tug. Even an inch in, I could see a dim glow. Time seemed to slow as I pulled it open the rest of the way.

Gems and jewels of all sizes lay inside. Necklaces, earrings, tie pins, cufflinks, garters, and Dagda knew what else crowded inside the tiny drawer. To the brim. Each one represented a vampire that was now pissed at us. Correction, at me, because they didn't know the little flying thief even existed.

Growling, I slammed the door shut. Taking the necklace, I shoved it in the inner pocket of my purse, making sure to bury it deep down as I said, "Not a big deal? I'll make sure to tell that to whatever wrathful vampire finds the stash. I would say you have to return them, but you can't be found flying around this place. Dagda only knows how you haven't been discovered yet. Just stop the stealing, or I will personally break each one of your wings. It seems fair considering you've set me up for getting my fingers broken, and that's if I'm lucky. Now, for Dagda's sake, just go talk to Iris. I have yet another trial to finish getting ready for."

The angry pixie dipped and bobbed in front of me, fury spitting from her eyes.

"Merlin's toe jam, good thing we didn't just get done talking about all the mistakes you've made." Kittie bit out sarcastically, her mouth pursed in anger. Then without another word, she took off in an explosion of purple glitter.

Caught up in the moment, my chest heaved as I ground my teeth against each other. Kittie had put me in danger for her own petty amusement, though. For something to look at, she'd said. That wasn't ok.

Seconds had passed before it dawned on me that she'd wanted something to look at while keeping me company. While watching over me to make sure I was ok. My jaw loosened. What was I doing? In her own messed-up way, she was just trying to take care of herself while being there for me. Tor Mór, you'd think after she was so kind to me, I could show a little understanding. She'd absolved me of way worse fuck ups not even five minutes ago. I rubbed my forehead. I'd have to apologize when she got back. The thought sat in my gut. I hated to admit I was wrong. But in this case, I was.

My mind put our conversation on repeat. Snapping my black-turtleneck bodysuit into place, slipping on matching black hotpants, and tugging on over-the-knee boots made for quick work as I came up with and discarded different things I could have said to Kittie. They all sounded terrible. I had to work on this being a friend thing. As of right now, I royally sucked at it. I was so absorbed in my thoughts I didn't even remember slipping on my floor-length gray and black brocade coat. All I recall was walking into the courtroom, feeling as conspicuous as a rabbit in a company of honey badgers as all eyes turned to me. I wished Sven were here. It would considerably lessen the chances of someone getting cute and trying to turn me into a light afternoon cocktail. As I scanned the crowd, I reminded myself he had more important things to do, like being part of yet another nerve-wracking trial. Besides, there was someone else I felt safe with. Catherine of Sienna.

That's when I spotted her in the back, apart from the crowd, nestled against a column. Outfitted in a dress made of layers of shimmering gold organza that only kept from being overwhelming by the simplicity of a Grecian style bodice, she looked right at home. She inclined her head when I caught her attention.

As if I needed any encouragement. I was already walking that way with such force my coat billowed back, only held by the catch at the waistline. I wasn't full of myself enough to think that's why everyone's eyes were on me as I made my way to her. No, their gazes followed me everywhere I went. Like they were just waiting for the moment I'd screw up and expose I was a faerie. Well, they'd have to just keep waiting. I wasn't about to do anything to put my life, or Sven's, in danger. My lips flattened into a thin line. At risk any more than they already were anyway.

When I reached Catherine of Sienna, she'd already turned back to watch the courtroom scene unfold. She didn't meet my eyes. Taking her cue, I leaned back against the column. Calm and collected was the look I was going for. I probably looked more like I'd swallowed a hive of murder hornets.

My stomach bubbled as the High Council filtered in. Sven was already on the platform. Had he been there the whole time? Or had he managed to sneak in behind me while I was on my way over here? I wish he would have stopped to say something. I was as nervous as a pre-teen at a Midsummer Night's Eve celebration.

My insides jumped as Raven cracked the gravel. And just like that, it started.

Raven didn't even have to raise his voice for it to reach the back of the massive courtroom. "Today, we will hear charges against Sven Siversten for Breaking Loyalty. Does the council wish to make any opening statements?"

"We do," said the same asshat attorney from before. So much for never seeing his irritating face again.

"Yes, your honors," Sven's lawyer said, bowing low.

I shoved my hands into the pockets of my coat dress.

"Please proceed," said Raven, with a nod.

As the prosecution gave his opening statement, I pinched my legs through my pockets. Everything would be fine. Just like last time. Still, I couldn't believe we had to do this. Again.

Unable to stand it any longer, I whispered to Catherine, "Why do we have to do this again?"

"You are asking why there is a second trial?" she asked, also not taking her eyes from the stage as she spoke.

"Exactly. How can they have another trial when he was exonerated of the charges already?" I asked through my clenched jaw.

"He has made a fool of her. Rest assured, she will stop at nothing to get her revenge," she said as if it were the most natural thing in the world.

Her words made me hot.

"Then why not just send goons into our rooms and be done with it?" My nails dug into my hands as the defense changed places with the prosecution.

She tsk'd. "Are you so eager for your own death? Your end doesn't come here, but I can't say the same for your...friend."

The comment froze my insides. My head whipped to her. "Are you saying that Sven is going to die?"

Her eyes tightened. But beyond that, there was no other acknowledging of my presence as she said, "Have a care. Eyes can turn to ears without the aid of magic."

Looking around, I saw that we had indeed caught the attention of a few vampyrs closest to us. Their heads were turned in contemplation. However, they weren't close enough to hear us. Yet. Catherine of Sienna was right. The less serious our conversation seemed the less notice we were likely to garner.

Closing my eyes, I turned my head to the other side. I made a show of stretching before turning back to the center of the stage.

"Yes, if deemed appropriate, death is a possible path for punishment," Catherine of Sienna said, looking for the world to be intent on the first witness as the prosecution drilled him. It was Joseph Blackwood. The member of Sven's coven. It was hard to make him out from this distance, but I could tell right away he was the same man as the last trial. My gut hardened.

"Yes, I was there the night of the fire," Joseph said, the lines of his body tense.

"And were you witness to Jerrick's, your previous master's, death?" asked the prosecution, looming over the sandy-haired vampire.

"Yes, I was there for his death," said Joseph, his voice grim.

My heart stuttered. Sven had committed murder as his act of Breaking Loyalty. Did that mean his life might be forfeit because of it? My hands went cold.

"How did your master die?" asked the attorney, walking away from the gargoyle witness box.

Joseph's hands balled into fists. "We all know how he died. This is-"

"Just answer the question, Mr. Blackwell." The arrogant lawyer said, turning back to him and pointing as if he were casting the wrath of God upon him.

"He was killed," said Joseph, crossing his arms over his chest.

"And is the person who killed him in this courtroom today?" asked the attorney.

"He is," said Joseph, the words stretching as if they were pulled from his core.

"And who killed your old master?" The lawyer's hands motioned wide as if we all didn't know the answer to this already.

"Sven did," Joseph said, not breaking his rigid posture.

"Mr. Siversten did!" Shouted the lawyer, leveling the justice finger at Sven with a triumphant crow. I wanted to go punch him in the teeth. I could almost feel the hard chiclets against my knuckles. He turned back to the witness box, he said, "And tell the court...*why* did Mr. Siversten kill his master?"

"Because he wanted to save his girl," said Joseph, defeat weighing his voice down.

"Because he wanted to save his girlfriend. And tell me, Mr. Blackwood. Is this girlfriend a vampire?" asked the asshat stalking towards the witness box.

"No," said Joseph so quietly I almost couldn't hear it.

"I'm sorry, Mr. Blackwood. You are going to have to speak up for the court. Was the woman in question, who Mr. Siversten killed his master for, a vampire?" asked the prosecuting attorney, resting his hand on the thumb of the gargoyle.

"No, ok. No, she wasn't. But she's a good person. Ok!" Mr. Blackwood all but screamed, dropping his hands.

"So what you're really saying is that Mr. Siversten broke loyalty by killing a vampire," pressed the lawyer, leaning towards him.

Mr. Blackwood's head dropped as he said, "Yes, yes, he did."

Gasps rang out in the courtroom. I wanted to line them up and slap them all. Of all of the pandering, self-indulgent bullshit. Joseph was being led around by his nose, no matter how he felt otherwise. It wasn't right, damn it.

"No more questions, your honors," said the asshat smugly, turning around and walking away.

"Would the defense like to cross-examine the witness?" asked Raven.

"No, your honor," said Sven's attorney, adjusting his shirt sleeves.

My insides knotted. Joseph's statements had been extremely damning. What did Sven's lawyer mean he didn't want to cross-examine the witness?

The events before me didn't wait for my fury to work itself out as it unfolded before us. The Prosecution called witness after witness. Even though none of their testimonies were eye-witness accounts, all giving similar stories. Apparently, Joseph had been the only surviving vampire from that night, except Sven. That fateful night where everything changed. Where this stopped being just a case and started being about something bigger.

"Yeah, he doted on that girl as if he would do anything for her. Quite sickening, if you ask me. I could for sure see him killing his own master for her, quicker than a vampyr spends a cool million on a house party." A man whose features resembled a weasel, and was single-handedly kicking dirt in the face of the idea that vampires were supernatural sex gods, spat on the ground.

"Thank you, Mr. Mezmarat. No further questions, your honors. The Prosecution rests," said the asshat lawyer, looking very much like a cat who had eaten the canary as he swaggered back to his post.

I wanted to reach down his throat and grab out that canary just so I could choke him with it.

"Would the Defense like to cross-examine the witness?" asked Raven.

My fists clenched even before I knew what he was going

to say, but that didn't stop my teeth from grinding against each other as Sven's lawyer said, "No, your honors."

While I was doing some heavy breathing to keep my shit together, Raven took this news far better and asked, "Does the Defense have any witnesses to call?"

I strained to see if I could get a read on Raven. He was a judge. What were his thoughts on the proceedings so far? Inexplicably, I trusted the mysterious vampire. Were things really going as badly as I thought they were? But it was no dice. I could barely make out his features from this distance, let alone get a read on him.

To my utter relief, the lawyer stepped forward and said, "Yes, we'd like to call Dextera Vanderheide to the stand."

The name sounded familiar, but I couldn't remember why. Out of the crowd stepped the first person I'd laid eyes on when I'd woken up here at the Blood Spire. The servant from the bathroom. Her black-slippered feet peeked out as she lifted her hoop skirt to climb the stairs. Why would they call her to the stand?

"Please raise your right hand. Do you promise to tell the truth, the whole truth, and nothing but the truth so help you lest you be struck down by Satan himself?" asked the badass bailiff I'd come to quite like.

Dextera, unflapped by the intensity of the woman's stare, said, "I do."

Sven's lawyer made his way over to the stoic woman. "You clean the rooms and tend to the occupants in the Eastern Wing, don't you, Miss Vanderheide?"

"That is correct," she said, barely nodding her head.

"As such, would you say that you spend a majority of your day there?" asked the lawyer.

"All day, to be precise. I am only not in attendance for a 30-minute lunch and overdays, when I am sleeping," she said. And even though I didn't like her on principle, I found myself having more respect for her. I'd hire her based solely on her attention to detail. Well, if I still lived in Knockaine, that is. I couldn't afford staff on my bounty hunting, private dick salary.

"Being that you are in the wing all day, would you say it is safe to say you see most of what goes on in the area?" The attorney paced back and forth as if deep in thought, but I knew he'd gone over the questions half a dozen times already.

"I see everything. Even what most don't think I see," Dextera added, and even though her inflection didn't change, I knew she delighted in that knowledge. It didn't take my years of observing people to know that. The palace servants had forever been giggling about that very thing. They heard everything. Saw everything. More power to them, I say. Take back your power wherever you can.

The lawyer nodded as if he, too, understood this. "So, have you seen Mr. Siversten and Miss Vanguard together?"

"I have," she confirmed, inclining her head.

"Where do you see them together?" the attorney pressed.

Stopping for a moment to think about it, Dextera said, "They are most often together when he goes to her room."

"And does he go inside Miss Vanguard's room?" he prodded, leveling a look at her.

"No, I have never seen him go into her room," she said.

"And what would you say their interactions are like?" Sven's lawyer started pacing again.

The pacing reminded me of my boss Sully, and I had a twinge of homesickness. I wonder what the crew at Bountyful Hunter and Private Investigator Services thought about me dropping off the map like I had. I wrapped my arms around myself. Honestly, probably not much, considering the last time they'd seen me, I'd been mourning the loss of Gaige, my best friend. I'd dragged myself in and took only one case before disappearing again. They had no idea I'd been kidnapped by a giant, fell into a coma, and whisked away by vampires. Not like I wanted them to. As far as they knew, I was acceptably human.

"He's very cold towards her while she, on the other hand, throws herself at him," she said, with a shrug of her shoulders as if the breaking of my heart was of no consequence.

I fanned myself as the room became ten degrees warmer.

He stopped pacing, "So you're saying Mr. Siversten doesn't go into Miss Vanguard's room, and he doesn't return her affections? That doesn't sound like a man that would do anything for someone. Those are the actions of a man acting out of obligation, not even desire, let alone an emotion as powerful as love. No further questions, your honors."

His words stabbed my heart like a knife in, digging around until he pierced my biggest fears. Sven didn't love me. He was just humoring me out of some sense of duty. It was the same reason anyone, up until the Kamikazes and Kittie, had ever been in my life. Feeling laid bare for all to see,

Raven gave him a nod and asked, "Would the Prosecution like to cross-examine the witness?"

"Yes, your honors," the lawyer said, striding up to the witness stand. "Miss Vanderheide, you have been employed at the Blood Spire for quite some time, have you not?"

"For 322 years," she said, holding her head high.

"That's a long time. One would assume you've seen plenty of liaisons between individuals, some of those being of a romantic nature," he said and paused, looking off contemplatively.

Even though it wasn't a question, she said, "I have."

"Would you say it is fair to say that some of those relationships have burnt hot and bright only to fizzle out shortly after?" he asked, holding his hands out delicately.

"Absolutely. Some even before the night is over," she said, her voice rising in pitch as if she was trying not to laugh.

"Before the night is even over. Isn't that interesting? Yet, the Defense would have us believe that Mr. Siversten couldn't have fallen out of love with Miss Vanguard in a matter of months. Well, that is just clearly not the case, is it?" He looked over the crowd. I could almost feel his eyes bore into mine before he said, "No further questions, your honors."

As the servant stepped down and a man with impeccable posture took her place, I couldn't help but feel a yawn in the pit of my stomach. It didn't go away as witness after witness came up giving accounts of how it was clear Sven felt nothing for me. I leaned my head back against the column, focusing on keeping my breathing steady. As if I needed a reminder. It felt like my heart was being pulled from my chest as it was. I didn't need to have that fact slapped in my face over and over again. A break in the stream of conversation brought my attention back to the platform.

Sven's attorney prowled around the stage. He must have been grilling another servant because the woman on the stand wore the same outfit as Dextera. The way she stood with her head dropped said she would rather clean a hundred rooms rather than waste one more second here.

Finally, he turned back to her. "It doesn't make sense that Mr. Siversten would go from committing a criminal act for Miss Vanguard to not even returning her affections. If all of the testimonies are to be believed, best case, you would be looking at a man consumed by lust. But you don't kill your master for lust, do you? Especially since Mr. Siversten is being painted as some criminal mastermind. He can either be a criminal mastermind or someone dim-witted enough to break the law for weak reasons. It can't be both ways, no matter how much the Prosecution would like it to be so.

Therefore, it does not follow that he would commit such an act. No further questions, your honors."

"Would the Prosecution like to cross-examine the witness?" asked Raven.

I dug my fingers into my palm. Please, Danu, let this be over. The asshat surprised the shit out of me when he said, "No, your honors. The Prosecution rests."

My stomach clenched even as my shoulders slumped, and relief washed through me that it was over. Finally. What didn't sit well with me is that this trial hadn't gone nearly as well as the last one. An eye-witness testimony versus speculation was hard to ignore. Crossing my arms over my chest, I held my biceps as I fought to calm the rioting of my stomach.

Part of me wanted to chat with Catherine of Sienna. I needed to occupy my mind with anything except the worst-case scenario that kept running through my head. Sven wasn't going to die. This wasn't the end for him, no matter how much it seemed like it. We had gotten through worse things than this. Bigger things than this.

That pep talk flew out of my mind when my stomach dropped as the High Council trailed back in. I had to fight to breathe evenly as they took their seats. Was it just me, or did Raven seem to look over the audience for far too long?

When he spoke, his voice seemed to boom throughout the room. "Sven Sivertsen, please come forward."

Sven walked to the center of the floor. I wanted to run up to the platform and fling him out of the way. Light the room on fire. Let in a pack of werewolves. There had to be a way to stop this.

Raven, his head arched, stared down at Sven. My stomach knotted.

He continued on. "Of the charge Breaking Loyalty, we, the High Council, find you, Sven Sivertsen, guilty."

My heart stopped. I didn't realize I'd also been holding my breath until Catherine of Sienna said, "Breath. Just breathe."

Sven, to his credit, didn't even flinch. He'd probably anticipated the verdict. Everything had been stacked up against him for it. Not surprising since he *was* guilty of it. But in the back of my mind, I thought we'd be able to get out of it like we had the other charge.

"Punishment to be determined. It will be communicated and meted out in three days' time," Raven smashed his gavel.

The crack reverberated in the courtroom, as did his words. Punishment. In only three days?

Past caring who was looking, I turned to Catherine of Sienna. "Punishment? What kind of punishment?"

"It varies," she said, looking to the side.

"Don't give me that bullshit. What kinds of punishment are we talking? And be straight with me. If I get one more vague answer from this place, I am going to lose my shit."

Her jaw ticked as she contemplated the ceiling. Finally, she turned to me. "Fine, you want specifics? It could be anything from being stuffed into a box in the bottom of the ocean to drowning over and over again to death by decapitation.

Panic tore apart my insides. I clutched my stomach. They would do that? To Sven? The man who was the best person who ever lived? I didn't even know what outcome to hope for. What was worse? What seemed like a dozen lifetimes of torture? Or death? Never in my life did I think I would pray for the death of someone I loved. Today, I did.

CHAPTER 12

"*A* demon on a diet, an imp with a limp, a lovebird familiar with an itch who's a-" said Mabye pointing to Hell's Gate.

"I get it," I said, wiping the sweat from my brow as the blinding light flared behind me. This stand in god stuff was for the birds. I shouldn't be worrying about this right now. I should be helping Sven through a difficult time. As a friend. Instead, I said, "Is that the rest of them?"

Mabye held up a clipboard that said, "I'm Bad. Be Jealous." close to his face as if the information on the paper might change before his very eyes.

After a moment, he dropped it with a satisfied nod and said, "Yep."

No sooner had the words left his mouth than a furry hellcat in a tiara flashed past. I raised my eyebrow.

"All the ones he wrote down," Kut corrected as she walked up.

Of course. I flapped my tank top to fan myself. If I had any luck at all, Kittie would be back at the Blood Spire by the time I got back and be able to tell us how to get Cerberus tied back to the gates of Hell. And maybe we could put them back for good. Sure, all of the Hell's residents we'd sent to the center of Hell hadn't come back yet, but it was only a matter of time.

"So, how many beasts are we looking at?" I asked her, not really wanting to know the answer. After the trial yesterday, I was emotionally and mentally spent. Physical exhaustion would make it the ultimate trifecta of misery. And just no.

"There's one at the Sulphur Spa, a handful by the Māori carving station, and two in the Mud Baths," Kut said, relating the information in true trooper style. All of the information and none of the drama. Thank Danu for people like her. A shrieking couple ran by in hiking gear. Humans. With a nod at their retreating forms, she said, "And at least one in the Geothermal Trails."

"You are no God. Our God would have rid us of these creatures and put Cerberus in Hell. Yet, demons are on the Earth and that demigod spawn walks free. You are an imposter," Dikeledi.

I jabbed a finger at his sunken chest. "First of all, Dik. Don't piss me off. You wouldn't like me when I am angry. Second of all, God helps those who help themselves. So make yourself useful and tell me how we're going to round up all of Hell's tourists."

"We can pretend like we're snacks and lure them out," said a squat goblin, his belly bobbing as he nodded excitedly.

I stuffed down my mounting frustration. "That's literally the worst idea. We tried that already. Where were you last time?"

"Relieving pressure from the tube, if you know what I mean," said the goblin with an exaggerated wink.

I scrubbed my hand in front of my eyes. "Never mind, I'm sorry I asked. Somebody else."

"We could dunk them in Baby Adam," said the goblin across from me, her severe ponytail brushing her shoulder as she nodded to the North. At my slow-blink she said, "It's the pool next to Hell's Gate."

"And what drown them? No, that's not going to work," I said, moving to the next hand.

"Well, it is a magic pool," she said, brushing her long ponytail over her shoulder.

That made me step back. "There's a magical pool here? What kind of magic?"

Dikeledi, "Some sort of divinity magic. Nasty stuff. Forget that. I say we get in groups. Beat them to submission. Then use your glowing plastic to make them disappear like frogs snatching firecrackers at the end of a fishing line."

Blinking past the visual overload, I first turned to the goblin with the ponytail. "What's your name?"

"Gorata," she said, her serious eyes never leaving mine.

"Gorata, I don't think the divinity pool is a bad idea, but we need time to test it. Time we don't have right now. Because what if it gives them the ability to see into the future or the power to enchant people? The last thing we need is to develop super demons that can manipulate people or the future. After we take these guys down, can you have someone test it and let me know what it's magic is?"

She nodded, "Yes, I will test it, myself."

"Perfect." I turned back to Dikeledi. "That's messed up. Also- I'm shocked to say, not a terrible idea. Simple and effective. Well, the glow stick thing. Not the catching frogs with firecrackers part."

Not trusting him to carry out such a plan, I turned to Kut. I waved my hand in front of her to get her attention. She was glowering at Mabye whose adoring gaze hadn't left her the entire time. There was no doubt he was head over heels for her. With her fierce quiet and thick braids hanging down one side of her face, there was no question as to why. She was a beauty by any standard. Even with her razor-sharp teeth.

"If I collar the ones in the Mud Baths, do you think you could organize the teams and tag the others?" I asked her.

Mabye blinked, coming back to the conversation. Hiking up his cow skull, he said, "No if and or butts, Pretty Pretty Princess."

Kut's expression didn't even change as she added, "We will do our best."

Her determination made me smile. You had to love the tenacity of goblins. Their sheer will in the face of adversity was on par with no other species I'd met.

"Good enough." Reaching into my bag to grab more glow sticks. I hesitated. There weren't that many left. How many did I leave them? Chewing my lip, I grabbed all of the glow sticks but three. When in doubt, go with three. As I handed them to her, I said, "Make sure to distribute these after the teams have been formed. These should get you through the night. It's all I have left, so keep a careful eye on them. To use them you'll crack the vial inside. It releases the potion, and then you snap it around whoever's neck you are sending back to Hell."

"As easy as crocodile tears," Mabye said, reaching for some glow sticks. Kut moved them out of his reach.

"After you clip the connector in place, run like a bat out of...well, Hell because you don't want to be caught by one of those bands and be taken back with them. Something tells me the demons we sent back isn't going to be so understanding," I added, as a note of caution.

Mabye's eyes widened with every word. By the time I was finished, he said to me, "You should do this."

"We will eliminate the threat," Kut promised with a half bow.

"I appreciate that. I will check back in after I am done and help out with anyone else that hasn't been disposed of. Bigger and scarier monsters are coming through, so be careful. Remember, you can always get more people to help but that's only if you are alive. So stay that way," I said, resisting the urge to shake my finger at them.

As I walked away, I heard Mabye say, "Give them to me. They can be a gift for the screaming monkey."

I shook my head. Goblins. A quick glance at one of the You Are Here plaques pointed me to the Mud Baths. Clipping down the boardwalk, I went over how things were going to play out. I'd send these two unwanted travelers back, check in with Kut to make sure all of the other escapees were sent back, and then I'd check back in with Kittie. Iris had to have come up with something by now. I mean, she had to have some family that she could talk with, didn't she? Suddenly, I felt like the world's worst friend, not knowing more about her. I'd have to change that. Then a white stick in my path caught my attention. When I went to step around it, it moved. I pulled back. Giving it another look, I saw it was enveloped in smoke.

Leaning closer, it turned bulging, eyes towards me. It had no pupils, but its eyes were so big it was almost cute. Its horns caught the glow of the mood lighting, courtesy of the thermal park's designer. I might not know what in the name of Dagda the being was, but I knew a lesser demon when I saw one. Slipping a glow stick from my pack, I snapped the vial and shook it, distributing the potion. The little monster stood up and flashed tiny, black tentacles at me, slapping them on the ground at my feet.

"Thanks, that's helpful." I reached down to grab the demon with smoke pooling around its chubby ankles.

He moved fast. If it weren't for my vamp speed, I probably would have missed him, but I managed to get my hands around him anyway and lifted him up. His mouth opened into a perfect circle as he hooted like an owl caught in a trap.

"Awww, you're just a baby. You're going to be so fierce when you grow up, little guy. I can tell," I said as I set the necklace in his clawed hand. It curled around the stiff plastic, holding it in place as if by rote. Its little tentacles flailed in protest, unwittingly helping me twine the glow stick around its tiny body. I'd just fitted the plastic connector in place when he placed one of his tentacles against my finger. "Awww, you keep that up, and I may just have to take you home," I said just as I was stuck with a dozen needles. "Ouch!" I dropped the little monster just as light shot from the necklace. I looked at my finger. Bloody dots appeared in a red circle. I looked back down just in time to see the tips of his tentacles glowing. "Ass," I said as the fiery ropes did their thing.

In seconds he was gone. Good riddance. Gritting my teeth past the fresh pain, I stepped over the charred space and walked even faster, as if speed alone would keep me from coming across even more escapees I'd have to send back.

Speed or not, I was thanking Danu's blessings as I arrived at the Mud Baths without coming across any more beasts wanting to stick me. Great. Didn't people go to bed? The pools were packed. But that didn't account for the eerie silence that greeted me. I knew the reason for that even before I saw everyone's eyes on the couple sitting in the farthest spa. With their arms twined around each other, two demons tipped champagne flutes back, laughing at the restricted movement. Sparkling liquid dribbled down their chins. It didn't matter to them, though. They were oblivious to the world as they rubbed identical rabbit ears, twice the size of their pointy-chinned heads, against each other lovingly.

Great. Personal demons, just what I didn't want to fight. My hands flexed around the glowsticks. Please, Danu, let these be enough to send them back. Personal demons were higher on the Hell food chain than hellhounds, and these damn suped-up kids' toys had been useless against Cerberus. Granted, he was the son of a demigod. The real question was in the divine bloodline, how did that measure up against Hell's hierarchy?

Taking a deep breath, I focused on one problem at a time. The first of which: how to get people out of here. Then I could kick some butt. When I spotted a martini glass on a table nearby, the perfect plan hit me. I snatched up the glass and stumbled over to the nearest bath. An elderly woman in a muddy floral swimsuit with a matching swim cap and a man with a beard so long he'd put a mountain goat to shame looked at me as if I'd quite possibly lost my mind. It was a fair assessment.

"Psshhht, hey, you Yes, you! They're giving out free alcohol, as much as you can carry for the next 10 minutes at the Devil's Cauldron." On the other side of the park, the boiling mud pit seemed like the best place. Maybe the fascinating steaming, burping pool might keep them there a little longer, even if there weren't any drinks. I lifted the glass high in encouragement.

"For only 10 minutes, you say? Come on, dear. As much money as we've spent on this vacation, I could use a gimmie," said the portly man, his beard blending seamlessly into his chest hair as he stood up.

His wife followed him, looking far less enthusiastic. I went to the next bath and then the next. After the first two stops, the baths emptied themselves, no doubt others curious to see what the commotion was all about.

Shortly, the entire section was empty, except for the oblivious demons. They were so wrapped up in each other, I doubt they would have noticed a Beyoncé concert blaring two feet from them. I thanked Danu for the distraction.

Maybe, I could send one of them back before they even knew what hit them. I'd have a prayer against one. Two would take a miracle.

"What would you have, my pet? Anything, you just say it." The pitch-black demon puffed, his voice husky with emotion.

"I couldn't help but notice the sulfur baths. The smell was absolutely divine. I'd die to go back there," said the pink demon closest to me, smiling like she had a hidden secret.

"So it shall be done," he said with a grand gesture.

"Oh, Percy. You're everything a girl could ask for. I can't believe you brought me here. This place is so magical." She lowered her head sweetly as I cracked two of the necklaces and waved them to distribute the potion.

"It's my soul mission to take your breath away for our entire lives, my pet," he said as I ducked off the boardwalk into the landscaping closest to the tub they were in.

I crouched low, moving from bush to bush as she laughed, a sweet-magical laugh, and leaned forward to tweak his pig nose. "Don't give me that sweet talk. We know that your goal in life is to make Jeff's life a living Hell. And you're doing a great job."

Looking away with a self-satisfied smile on his face, he ruffled the long fur on the back of his neck. Now was my opportunity. I put the orange glow stick in my mouth and crept out of the bushes, mere steps from my target. Slip it on her. Make it quick. I could do this. Holding the ends of the pink necklace in each fist, I willed my hands to stop sweating. I had one chance to have a prayer of sending these two back. And this was it.

"Pet, you're more important to me than he is. You know I'd do anything for you-" Percy stopped as he looked over her shoulder, at me, right as I'd dropped the necklace along the pink fluff of her neck.

He rose, his face a mask of pure rage. Mud matted into his fur as it ran down his heaving chest in clumps. He spread his hands wide, tufts of hair at his wrist only accentuating the silver blades that were his claws. Oh, shit. I yanked the ends of the sticks to snap the pieces together, but the woman grabbed it with her hands. Her boyfriend lunged at me. Acting on instinct, I moved back. Since the choker was around her throat, she came with me. Then suddenly, her grip slackened. Slamming the connectors in place, light radiated from around her as I shuffled back, ready to take on the still-free personal demon.

But he wasn't coming. He was staring down in horror at his girlfriend. That's when I noticed her pink fur had shed, and she was a sparkling black. That's when it hit me; she wasn't a personal demon. She was a doppelframer, a type of doppelganger. Unlike a regular doppelganger, who could just replicate someone, doppelframers had the ability to change parts of themselves outside of their original target. They were more devastating than hellspawn.

I thought that's why he was staring down at her, hopelessness written into his features. That she had deceived him. It wasn't until her now bald head dropped back that I realized the truth of it. He'd killed her.

"My pet, forgive me," He cradled her body to him, deep pulled-apart sobs wrenched from his body as pink lights from her glow stick necklace danced over him.

He clung to her as her limp body was wrapped in fiery ropes. When the light flashed bright, he didn't even flinch as he looked down with despair to catch the last glimpses of her mummy-wrapped body. Then she was gone.

He held up his arms, staring at the singed fur as if unable to piece together what had happened. Anguish twisted his face. Tilting his head back to the heavens, he let loose an unholy scream that raised all of the hairs on my body as he clutched his bloodied claws to his chest. He'd killed her. And it was because of me.

Panic fought to climb up my throat. Shit was about to get real. Fast. Well, in for a ruby in for a crown. Taking the other glow stick out of my mouth, I clutched it my fist. The movement drew Percy's attention to me. His eyes grew and then narrowed, spitting death.

"You shouldn't have done that, Demon Killer," Percy said, throwing his bladed claws out to the sides.

He stepped out of the pool, mud falling off his body in clumps as the world shifted. I blinked the feeling away and shook my head.

It took barely any time at all, but there was such little room on the walkway that he had reached me already. Razor-sharp claws swiped at me. I jumped back, right into the shrubbery. Lights swung wildly to the bushes and back as I kicked the floodlight. It let out a crack and fell, bathing the dirt in an ominous light. I grabbed at the palm tree. The sudden move jerked the glow stick out of my hand. I didn't have time to put eyeballs on it, though; he was already jumping at me with another cry. I used the momentum of my fall to swing myself around the tree and out of his path. When I was three-quarters of the way around the tree, I let go, tucking into a ball as I rolled as far away from the crashing monstrosity close behind as I could manage. The packed mud flew around me, coating me in wet goo. I threw my leg out to bring myself to a stop. Pain lanced up my groin as I got my desired result and stopped. However, the world around me was not so kind as it continued to spin.

Pushing up onto my knee, I knelt in the slick mud as I blinked to right the world. This time it didn't behave and continued to turn. Panic shuddered my chest as I tried to draw a breath. What was wrong with me?

The blurred nightmare walked towards me, orange and

green lights casting fear into my heart as they shone off his long claws and scrunched pig nose. Tapping the nearest ley line, magic rush into me, hot and ready. Gut-churning glimpses of faded and blurred images washed together as I tried to make out where the personal demon started and everything else in this tilt-a-whirl nightmare ended. I couldn't just light the place up without being able to see, though, could I? What if the mud bathers had come back?

Hesitation was all Percy needed. Suddenly, he was right in front of me. At least, I think he was. Staggering back, my foot snagged a rock, and I went down. I put my elbows out to catch myself, but hitting my head was the least of my worries. The demon was on me.

This wasn't the end of it. I was lighting this fucker up. Bringing my hands up to do just that. Percy snapped them up in his own punishing grip. Being so close to those deadly claws sent fear tearing down to my gut. Even as he brought them over my head, I shot energy into them.

He lodged both of my wrists in one of his furred paws as he snatched his other hand away. "Bitch, what kind of magic is that? A battery? Are you trying to juice me to death?"

What in the name of Dagda was going on? That was enough juice where it should have taken him down. Damn it, I didn't want to do the bomb thing when I was so messed up already, but what other choice did I have? Gritting my teeth to brace for the pain, I shot lightning out from my pores. Everything around me lit up like it was daylight before going dark again. I waited. There wasn't nearly as much pain as there should be. And to my absolute horror, Percy didn't do much more than grit those tear-stained teeth. The world around me was an entirely different story.

It swam in and out of focus as he lifted his pointed chin. "You just don't get it, do you?" His free claw sliced a rip in my shirt as he drug it from my collar bone to my shoulder.

"There is no getting free, and this is going to hurt," he said as he shoved the knifelike claw in. "A lot." Searing heat drove through me. He twisted his finger round and round. Bright red laced my dimmed vision as pain ripped through me. Then, he pulled it out. Cold air pulled, ragged into my body as I fought against the stinging as. "You took my pet from me. So your death will be slow," he said, as he inserted his claw ever so slightly into the wound and slid it diagonally down to rest against my abdomen. "And painful." It stung like I was being carved up with a needle. Letting go of my wrists, bringing his other hand down to meet his claw already half an inch deep in my torso. Wet fur left a cold trail of mud to mix with my blood as he moved to my belly. "You took my pet from me. You had no right." I reached down to pull the claw from me. It held like steel. My vision faded to a pinhole as I focused on the stars above. Everything spun faster. Something moved into and out of my sight. Was that a lion's fur I'd just seen? It happened again. No, wait. It was goat's fur. Wasn't it? "This is where you die," whispered Percy in my ear, and pain exploded as the world went black. My last thought was the one good thing that came from my death was he couldn't come back as my own personal demon. I'd had enough Hell in my life.

CHAPTER 13

*S*ven's blue eyes loomed over me. Not that they were floating. No, they were firmly embedded in his porcelain skin. A soft glow radiated around him. My insides warmed.

I blinked slowly, my eyes heavy with the effort. "Did I do it? Did I make it to Heaven?" His brow furrowed, and he sat back, moving out of my line of sight. That's when I saw the red brocade wallpaper. The Blood Spire. I groaned. "Nope, I'm in Hell. Funny, I always thought I'd end up here." Every inch hurt as I sat up. Wincing, I said, "That must be why I hurt so much."

"You're not dead." Sven had crossed his arms over his chest before bringing one back out again to wave it vaguely in my direction. "Though, I imagine with wounds like that you'd wish you were."

I ran my fingertips over my chest absently. Dragging over the rough comb of gauze almost immediately.

"What happened?" Still blinking the fog from my brain, I asked as snippets of my fight with the Personal Demon came back. My stomach dropped. "That's right, Percy. Well, here's hoping that he's enjoying his little jaunt on Earth and forgets all about little ol' me."

At that, Sven actually laughed, "Personal Demons don't forget. But no, Percy- was that his name? Has already been sent back to the Inner Circle of Hell."

I blinked, letting the information register.

"Well, that's a cute trick. How did that happen?" Thinking back, I remembered seeing a lion and a goat pelt. Then the pieces clicked. It had been a chimera pelt, and there was only one of those around. "Mogapi did it, didn't he?" It was a rhetorical question. I knew it had been him. The ranger must have picked up the glow stick I'd dropped. He'd gone up against a Personal Demon. A goblin. He could have died. He'd risked everything to save his god. I chewed my lip as guilt gnawed at me. The only problem was, I wasn't his god. Something told me he wouldn't have been so kind if he knew he'd put his life on the line for a stinking faerie.

Sven lifted his eyebrows and shrugged, "I'm not sure. All I know is Maybe- I believe that's his name-"

"Mabye," I corrected, not knowing why I did. I'd called Mabye the same thing. Was the irritating little goblin getting to me?

Sven inclined his head, acknowledging the correction. "Mabye told me you needed to be tended by faerie doctors because you'd been poisoned."

Doing a lot of blinking, I knew my voice rose as I asked, "Poisoned? What do you mean poisoned? Claws can't hold toxins."

"Unless they're attached to a gland of some sort, they can't. However, you weren't poisoned by the Personal Demon. You were stung by a Raum," Sven said as if I knew what that was.

"Ok, so what's a Raum?" I asked, knowing it was a long

shot but hoping anyway. They were only three and a half hours away from here.

"How it was explained to me was that it's a lesser demon who looks like an 'octopus mated with a walking reptile,'" he said, still acting as if that explained everything.

Which it did not. Far from it, in fact.

"I did pick up a scaled demon with tentacles and horns," I said, trying to remember the little creature I'd sent back to Hell. I held out my finger for his inspection. "It bit me."

He leaned forward enough to look at the tiny punctures that created a circle on the tip of my finger. Pressing his lips together, he said, "That looks just like they were saying it would. I suppose it's good they didn't give you an antidote. You can't trust goblin medicine."

"I don't suppose you took me to a faerie doctor?" I asked, feeling silly for hoping but doing so nonetheless.

His face was way kinder than mine would have been when he said, "I did not."

"I guess that makes sense. Even if you could find the local mound, they wouldn't let you in. You being a vampire and all," I said, pushing down the panic rising in my throat. It was fine. There had been plenty of times I'd been stung as a child and been just fine. Sure, it had never been by anything I didn't know. And I had never passed out because of it. I shook my head. What was I freaking out about? When did my life get so out of control that I had become afraid of a measly sting? Probably, the point when it became part of my everyday life to interact with evil beings. That especially included goblins.

Holding my breath to brace against the pain, I scooched up, bringing the red satin sheet with me. I settled back against the scrolled headboard, breathing evenly through my mouth to manage the throbbing pain. My hands shook as I pulled the sheet away from my chest. White gauze covered a solid line from my left shoulder down my breast bone and ended right above my belly button. Well, so much for wearing low-cut tops again. Well, maybe, it wouldn't be a scar. My eyes darted back to the pile of clothes, quickly dismissing that idea. Or maybe, I would just wear them anyway and say screw people's opinions.

Sven said, "Your clothes were stained in your blood. I've already burned them. I suggest you do the same when you change out your bandages."

Dropping the sheet back over my chest, I said, "Good call."

But my mind really wasn't on our conversation. Things were becoming too much. When would I get a break? Danu, when. All I wanted was one little, tiny break.

Just then, a butterfly flitted through the vent. Deep purple wings with thick black veins fluttered as its velvety body pitched from side to side. What was a butterfly doing coming through the vent? Its wings were rimmed in white dots. The same white shaded its hind legs. It made a bee-line for me, no pun intended. That's when I realized it was here for me. Also, its hind legs weren't white. The butterfly was actually holding something.

Finally, it hovered in front of me. Its black, beady eyes seemed to assess me. Then it dropped what it was holding. Barely lighter than a feather, it fell onto my leg and rolled into my lap. Its mission complete, the purple messenger beat its wings three times before flitting back to the vent. And it was gone.

I looked at Sven. He shrugged. Ok, it was a message. From who was anyone's guess. Sure, I had an idea or two, but just to make sure the message was safe to read, I fluffed the blanket. The roll hurled through the air. Bouncing twice, it rolled the rest of the way to my ankles. The message didn't explode or turn black. I shrugged. That was as good as I was going to get, I suppose. Reaching down, I picked up the tiny message. Unrolling the small parchment, it spanned an inch wide and an inch tall. The words were even smaller. I squinted, just able to read them. "Not able to come back. Iris clueless. -K."

My stomach twisted. Shit.

"Who can't come back?" asked Sven.

"Kittie," I said, pressing my lips together to keep them from trembling.

"Was she doing something for you?" he asked, a furrow appearing between his eyes.

I swallowed a bitter laugh. "You could say that. There's some kind of drama going on back at Knockaine. She was supposed to find out if there was something I could do while I was here."

"Well, the good news is since you haven't been identified as a faerie, you will be free to go back in a matter of days and can clear the matter up," he said.

"It's more than that. She was supposed to get me more information on how to tie Cerberus back to Hell." The words stuck in my throat. That was the hardest thing to admit. There was no cavalry coming. It was up to me to put Cerberus back in Hell and make sure he stayed there.

My hands trembled. How in the name of Dagda was I going to do that? Maybe, I could contact the King of the Patupaiarehe. Sure, the faerie mound wasn't known for being helpful, but they were known for getting violent when humans invaded their lands. I was betting they'd be just as pissed about demons overrunning their land, wouldn't they?

Sven leaned forward, his folded hands sinking into the plush comforter as he rested them on the bed. "And now, she isn't coming back," he said. I bit my lip and shook my head. Putting the pieces together, he gave a curt nod. "And that's what she meant by Iris being clueless? That she doesn't have a spell or potion to make Cerberus return to Hell?"

"It would appear so." Taking a shaky breath, I turned the paper over to make sure there wasn't any part of the message I was missing. Nope, it was blank.

"Can I assume that it now falls on you to make sure that happens?" he asked.

"That seems like a safe assumption. Unless I can convince the faeries in the mound 3 hours from here to help," I said, rubbing my arm.

He clasped his hands as if in prayer. "And are any of these faeries witches?"

"No, we're the only mound that has a witch. Certain types of witch magic mixed with ley magic make the Fourth of July look tame, so there is a huge disdain for witches in the faerie community." My cheeks heated at having to even admit something like that.

Thankfully, our sordid faerie witch history wasn't in question here. I knew what Sven was getting at. Even if we could convince the Patupaiarehe to help us wrangle Hell's denizens, how would we send them back? There would just be an unending flood of Hell's patrons overrunning our world. And that didn't even take into account hellspawn, greater demons, or even worse- the baddies everyone knew by name, like the Four Horsemen, Queen Lilith, or any of the other gods or goddesses. If they decided to pay Earth a visit- and let's face it, they were bound to if word got out about how they had free reign here, we might as well all just go live on Mars.

I worked to keep my breathing even. This was bad.

Running a hand through his hair, Sven lowered his eyes. I squeezed my fingers under the covers, trying to keep it together. A feat that was harder than it should have been. Then again, considering I'd just come back from the dead, maybe it wasn't that hard to believe. I just needed to stop. Take a step back. Could a girl just get a hug? Or some fries? Salty and mind-melting. Was that too much to ask for?

Sven seemed to process this information and said, "Well, let's say your friends aren't as...effective as you're hoping. Do you have any ideas?"

I threw the covers off as I threw up my hands. "Do you think if I had any ideas, I would have sent Kittie off to Iris in the first place?" Was that overreacting? Probably. Sweet Danu, what was wrong with me? I tucked my arms against my chest.

At my outburst, he sat back in the chair he must have brought in when he'd brought me back. We sat there in silence. Just what was I supposed to do? This was too much for one person to be expected to take on. My fingertips played over the gauze again as I rubbed my chest. It wasn't Sven's fault. He was just trying to help. He was the one thing that had been a constant in my life, and he was here, for me, despite the battles he had to face. That said something, didn't it?

Resting my hand against my throat, I couldn't quite meet his gaze, but I made myself talk anyway. He deserved more than to be a punching bag. "Look, I'm sorry. I shouldn't have said that. I'm just frustrated, and it feels like things just keep going from bad to worse. But I shouldn't have taken it out on you. You're going through enough shit. Tor Mór, in two measly days, you are going to die or be tortured for a small eternity. All because of me." The admission stuck in my throat, but I made myself push on. "You're the only one who's always been there for me. And I can't tell you how much that means to me."

A few moments passed. Quiet and long. My lungs ached, and I couldn't seem to catch my breath.

"Why are you crying?" he asked quietly.

"Because this is total, utter bullshit," I said, gritting my teeth as I swiped at the tears streaking down my face.

"What is?" he asked.

"I love you, damn it. I love you, and I've done nothing but hurt you. All I wanted was a future with the man I love. You. That's all I've wanted. From the start." My ribs squeezed. The only thing that had been in the way of that all along was me. It was a hard, gut-wrenching truth that just made the tears come faster.

When Sven didn't say anything, I cast my eyes at him. His hands were clasped, his head bowed.

"Say something," I whispered, wiping away the snot running from my nose noisily.

"What's there to say, Cy?" The usually calm vampire I knew threw his hands up in the air and looked at me. "The man you want is gone. He doesn't exist anymore."

"Yes, he does. He is right here. In front of me. You're amazing. Look at today. You brought me back and took care of me when I couldn't do it myself. Just like I'd do for you. You're still here, Sven," I took his hand in mine and held it to my heart.

He stood up, pulling his hand from mine. "You know very well what I mean. Don't play coy. It doesn't suit you. I don't love you. How many different ways can I tell you that? You keep looking for a way to make me love you. Well, I can't. Don't you understand? I can't love you. And I won't be able to. That part of our lives is dead. Gone. It isn't coming back. Ever. So stop trying to bring back things that aren't there. It's just going to ruin any friendship we could have."

The hand he'd flung to the side so casually burned. Cradling it to my chest, I let silent tears wet my face, not bothering to wipe them away. "You're wrong," I whispered to myself, unable to bring myself to look at him. I whispered it because I didn't even know if it was true or if I was just desperate for it to be so.

His voice was harsh as he said, "You don't think I want it to be different? That I wouldn't give anything for it to be so? I remember what it was like to love you. It felt like a piece of me that had been missing for my entire existence had come to me. I was half of a man. But after you...I felt whole. Complete." He thumped his chest. Where his heart used to be. Dropping his hand in disgust, he said, "Those memories don't just go away because I can't feel anymore. I still remember. Just now. It's hollow. Something I can see but can't touch. Every time I reach for it, it just floats farther away. Do you know what it's like to have no joy in your life? No happiness? Not even a scent of it? It's torture. I don't want to be numb all of the time. Remembering what it was like to be happy. Instead, now I walk around pretending to be a part of this life. Because that's all, I am doing. Pretending. Who wants that? To put on a mask every day? I don't want it. I want to *live*. Just tell me how to do that, and I will do it. But until then, don't come to me with talk of love. Because you're just reminding me of what I will never have again. And that is cruel, Cy."

As Sven strode away from the bed, I couldn't help think that he was right. Trying to make him feel something he didn't was wrong of me. However, I could still be a friend to him. It was the least he deserved after doing so much for me. And I appreciated him as a friend. Even if I couldn't have more.

The door handle turned. I sat up to tell him not to go, that we could be friends, as I heard the clanging of metal from the chute. No, not now. Not when my world was falling apart. I pressed the fluff of the comforter to my face. When I heard the familiar thud of goblin dropping to the floor, I dropped it back to my lap. This time there were two thuds, though. Had

Mabye brought Kut with him finally? There was the possibility that sanity reigned after all. In an attempt to collect myself, I drew in a ragged breath and released it before pushing myself out of bed. If I had to face more people, I wasn't going to do it in bed. I would do it on my own two feet.

Sven was still in the room. My gut pulled as I skimmed over him and put my attention where his was too. On the two goblins. Expectedly, Mabye was there. However, more surprising was the presence of Gorata, the goblin who'd helped in the battle last night. Or was that this evening? Tor Mór, I didn't even know anymore.

"Greetings, Pretty Pretty Princess." Gorata, her expression severe, bowed to me.

I wanted to roll my eyes. I didn't get anything other than somber vibes from her. No doubt she'd picked up Mabye's nickname for me and thought it was legitimate. Years of courtly breeding said I should be patient, but the bitterness that hit my throat was stronger.

"Could you all, I don't know, maybe at least give me a day or two to heal before you come barging in here demanding more shit?" I asked, throwing my arms wide.

Yeah, that was better. Anger was easier than sadness any day.

Gorata gave another unconcerned bow. I was just thinking how much I liked her when she said, "Your sincere pardons, Pretty Pretty Princess. You see-"

I dug my fingernails into my palms.

Maybe pushed her out of the way with his stick arms. "They're everywhere."

My stomach dropped at his revelation.

"Who?" Sven asked, confusion marring his forehead.

But I already knew. "Hell's residents."

"Hell's peeps, that's right," Maybe said, nodding furiously.

The violent motion sent his ears flapping.

Now, if only it would be enough to make him fly away.

"We wouldn't be here if it weren't an emergency," Gorata said, straightening the leather and bone necklace that kept her top in place.

In the back of my mind, I knew as much, but I crossed my arms over my chest, still wanting to be peevish. To not feel anything else. Not heartbreak, not hopelessness, not fear, nothing but just clean, simple anger.

That desperation made me ask tartly, "Let me guess? You all used all of the glow necklaces already."

"Yeppers," said Maybe, with a bright smile.

"Gone as a delicious baby on Christmas morning, Pretty Pretty Princess," confirmed Gorata.

My muscles were strung so tight, I could feel them quivering. I wanted to leave and never look back.

A bitter laugh bubbled from my throat. "I don't know what you expect me to do about it. I'm just one...person against all of Hell. Hardly a fair fight."

Everyone in the room stared at me with a head-pounding silence that screamed their expectations. I was their goblin god. I was supposed to protect them.

After a moment, Sven, who frankly I'd forgotten in my tirade, spoke up behind me. "I'd be willing to assist."

My heart skipped a beat, and my hands shook. I stuffed them under my arms. See? Amazing. He was worth so much more than anything I could give him. Maybe, it was just as well that he didn't love me. I didn't realize I was nodding along to the thought until Mabye asked quietly, "Does that mean you are coming too, Pretty Pretty Princess?"

Then I made a decision. Even if I couldn't have Sven, not only would I be worthy of him, I'd be worthy of myself. Snatching up my purse, I pasted a smile on my face. "Of course. I can't exactly leave all the fun to you all, now, can I?"

CHAPTER 14

"Get him!" a horde of goblins charging past screamed and whooped, following what I assumed was yet another of Hell's escapees.

I squashed my instinct to assist them. The most help I could be was right here. In a group of not-so-eager goblins, Sven, and one angel, who when I'd asked why a divine being was amid the evil gang, I'd been sourly told to 'mind your own business.' And so I did, no matter how much I itched to press the issue. I had more critical pickles on my plate. Like how to get rid of the pain in the asses that had come into my life. And I wasn't talking about the goblins.

"I know this looks impossible," I said, stopping to cough over the sound of a gurgling scream behind us. My feet itched to leave. To take me anywhere this nightmare wasn't. When it was over, I clapped my clammy hands and pasted on an overly bright smile. "But nothing is impossible. We got this. We just need ideas. So, hit me. What've you got?"

Nobody looked moved. Surprise. The pep talk had sounded fake even to my own ears. We were so screwed. I wiped my sweaty on my jeans. Phefo, the goblin who had suggested the bait ploy last time, raised his hand.

"And I swear, if someone mentions using goblins as bait, I am going to lose my shit," I said, looking at him, my eyebrows raising into my hairline.

He lowered his splayed gray hand and crossed his arms over his belly. That's what I'd thought. Unfortunately, he was the only one who'd raised his hand. Everyone else was as quiet as a pixie in a pea pod. That wasn't going to fly.

A goblin in the back raised his hand. "Forgive me, Your Badness, but why do they have to go back?"

My fingers curled around themselves. Why did goblins have to be evil? This would be so much easier if they were at least just decent beings. Very aware I was about to have the equivalent of the conversation about why people should be afforded equal rights, I said, "Because Hell's people belong in Hell. We can't exactly allow Hell on Earth, now can we?" At his squinty eyes, as if he were really trying to understand, I gave him the answer. "No, we can't. They are evil and would take out all of humanity." One by one, the goblins started to look at each other, coming alive with excitement, nodding and jabbing each other in the side. Ok, this wasn't going well. I tried again. "They don't belong here. Don't you think there's a reason Cerberus was chained to the Gates of Hell to keep them there in the first place?" The mention of the beast made some of them step back, but the majority still didn't look convinced. I threw up my hands. "Because your God knows what's best, and I said so."

After a chorus of shrugs and unenthusiastic nods of acceptance, I pointed to the guardian angel. I knew he was a guardian angel because he wore a helmet, breastplate, gauntlets, and greaves. They shone with a holy light. I knew it was divine because I couldn't look directly at him.

"You. What's your name?" I asked, squinting as I tried not to look directly at him. What if it was like the sun and could blind you if you looked at it too long?

"Ramiel," he said with a bow that just angled one of the beams directly into my eye.

I flinched. "Ramiel, nice to meet you. Do you mind toning the light show down a bit?"

Immediately, the brilliance dimmed down to silver so bright it could have been platinum. There was no mistaking the light that shone from within, though.

"Oh, my apologies. I'm not used to being visible to those…." Ramiel stopped to put his tongue against his teeth.

My jaw tensed. A gut reaction to living a life with pompous people. It may or may not have been an unfair assumption, but from the set of his chin, I was letting it ride.

"Unworthy?" I supplied, raising my eyebrow. Daring him to contradict me.

"Not of divine right," he corrected with a magnanimous bow.

Right. I had half a mind to call him out, but I'd learned long ago you didn't piss off people you were trying to get help from. And we needed all of the help we could get. I let it go.

I pointed at him again. Thunder rumbled my feet, and lightning crashed above, freezing the angel's mighty wings and harsh features in a fierce light. My jaw dropped. The big guy wasn't really taking his side, was he? I immediately dropped my hand. The lightning and thunder continued to crash. My heart in my throat, I looked up.

I don't know what I'd expected to see. God, with a big G, descending from the heaven above? Who knows. What I found instead made the tension visibly leave my body. Two ala demons, their bone-white eyes tipped in anger as they aggressively slammed into each other again and again, were snared in a battle of wills. A loud whirring snapped on, and my attention was momentarily diverted from the cloud-like demons to see two goblins wheeling over a massive shop vacuum. They held the gray nozzle up to the demons. It must have been a good vacuum because the creatures tried to swim away to no avail. Moments later, they were clinging to each other, screaming, their shouts sounding like the howling of the wind, as first their bodies and then their eyeballs popped into the small hose. Then they were gone.

I did a lot of blinking before turning back to the group. My eyes gaze went immediately to Sven. No, not him. I moved on. Right, Ramiel.

This time I nodded at him. Call me superstitious. "I don't suppose we could use you in this fight, could we?"

"Regrettably, no. I require orders to deviate from my assignment," Ramiel said without emotion.

Something told me he didn't want to help either.

I pursed my lips. Peevishly, I asked, "And just what is your assignment?"

"To keep him safe from harm," he says with a nod of deference at the angry-looking goblin who'd told me to mind my business.

That didn't tell me much of anything but whatever.

"Right, well. Using you in some way still isn't out of the question." I gave him a hard look. It wasn't up for debate. Even from this distance, I could see his eye twitch. He started to say something, but I turned to the rest of the group. "In the meantime, has anyone come up with anything else?"

Ramiel's lips thinned. Though pissing off someone with holy power wasn't on my bucket list, I wasn't about to let go of any string that might have some pull in this impossible situation. All I was met with was more blank stares. The dead had to be more active than this group. I suppose that's why I was the leader here.

Squaring my shoulders, I said, "I get it. It's not an easy problem to tackle. Let's break it down to what we know. We know we can't outman them. There are just too many. We know there are more coming, so we need to take care of the ones who are here as soon as possible because the fact is that the farther down circles of Hell of the real mean bastards." This got a gleam of appreciation and some excited nods from the goblins. That better be anticipation to fight. I didn't want to entertain any other possibilities. "So our best solution is magic." When we'd been standing here last time popped into my head. I snapped my fingers and turned to Gorata. "What about that magic pool. Do we know what it does yet?"

"Yes, we are...mostly sure whoever is dipped gets what they need," she said mater-of-factly.

My chest lightened. Nodding, I knew it was premature, but I couldn't help the smile that crept onto my face. "Ok, that seems useful. Has it been tested?"

"Kind of." The serious goblin's wide mouth turned down. She crossed her arms over her chest, sending a gold medal swinging back and forth. Had she been wearing that earlier? With its bright yellow ribbon, it seemed like an odd fashion choice for a goblin.

Sven frowned. Which was fine. I wasn't paying him no mind anyway.

The slapping of feet passing by sounded too large for a goblin. Damn demons. Goblin war cries sounded close behind. I put my foot out. Something solid the size of a small tree connected with my leg. I caught myself on Mogapi. With his help, I was able to stay standing, and the mass went down with a thump and a groan. Seconds later, one by one, a trio of goblins hurled through my peripheral vision.

When a series of hollow thuds and crunches followed in short order, I turned back to Gorata. "What do you mean, kind of?"

"The first tests were unpredictable. Bontle fell immediately asleep when she entered the waters. She had to be pulled out of the pool. Until this, she had been sleepless because she had hit her head as a young goblette. And there's…." Gorata screwed up her lip and pointed to the guardian angel. He was standing next to the angry goblin. Odd, the other goblins were giving a wide berth around him. Looking around the group, I noticed they were giving the same space to Gorata. That was strange.

Blinking to stay focused, which was becoming increasingly difficult by the second, I asked the question I'd wanted to ask since I'd gotten here. "But why a guardian angel?"

Gorata's ponytail fell over her shoulder as she leaned forward. I did the same, noticing a sweet smell almost like freshly baked cinnamon rolls wafting from her. She whispered, "Itumeleng is often mistreated by his family unit. It is my belief the angel appeared to keep him safe."

Itumeleng must have realized we were talking about him because he started kicking the dirt with such force it sent pebbles skittering past our legs. His body was still rigid with fury but bowed in shame at the same time. My heart went out to the little guy. Abuse was never ok, no matter the situation.

Gorata passed a hand through the air as if to wipe away this new goblin Rip VanWinkle and surprise angel. "The key to the spell is asking for exactly what you want. But you have to mean it with all of your being. If you don't, the waters will give you something else."

My eyebrows shot into my hairline. "That seems like quite an assumption. How do you know that's how it works that way?'

Her gaze dropped as she held the medal around her neck out for me to see. Pulling it in close, I read it aloud. "It says, 'In Recognition of being a Valued Member of the Finsch Clan.' Ok, while that is a great medal. How does that prove anything?"

"I asked to be Queen of the clan, but in reality…" she held up the medal again with a shrug and dropped it again.

"You just really wanted to be acknowledged for her efforts," I said, seeing how she'd come to the determination she had about the spell. She was very bright.

Her chin dipped, and she cleared her throat before saying, "Pretty much."

"Well, that is great!" I said, my voice coming out more chipper than I had intended. I just wanted to help the embarrassed goblin past her embarrassment. And it really was the best news I had gotten since I'd arrived. I let out a deep sigh of relief just as a one-eyed monster ran past. Quick on his toes, Phefo jumped out of our little group, barely snagging the prick. Somehow, he managed to wrestle the beast to the ground.

To the background of grunts, whacks, and moans, I continued on. "Granted, it could use some more tests, but it sounds like our best plan of attack so far. Let's go down and make some big dippers out of you all!"

Sven stared passively at me, which wasn't a surprise because he'd been in some sort of one-man statue contest since we'd gotten here. All of the other goblins exchanged uncomfortable looks. Why did this have to be so painful? Why couldn't it be easy? Like chicken nuggets? Soft and greasy and warm.

I sighed and tried to look a lot more reasonable than I was feeling. "Ok, what's the problem?"

Clearing her throat, Gorata said, "They refuse to go into the pool because it stinks. They are afraid the smell will never wear off."

I wanted to cry. We were being invaded by Hell. Actual Hell and the gating item for saving the world was the smell? Counting to ten, I looked to the heavens and reminded myself everyone had their own problems. Just because I didn't understand it didn't mean they weren't valid. I mean, that applied to the end of the world, too, right?

After a minute of furiously searching my mind for alternatives and deserted islands where I could go be alone if I got out of this alive, the solution hit me. "Fine, we'll dip weapons into the pool instead of ourselves. Does that work for everyone?"

Gofaone's head was tilted to the side, contemplating this as blood dripped from his red cap and pooled at his feet. After a moment, he nodded. "As long as I don't have to touch the wet weapon, this will work for me."

To my shock and relief, his concession was met with more and more until most of them agreed. The others were elbowed until their heads started nodding.

I tossed my hands to the side in relief. Thank, Danu. "Done. Now, let's go before this nightmare gets out of hand, and there's no chance for a sequel."

"Remember that everyone is required to kill at least one. I'll be keeping track!" I shouted to Dikeledi as Sven handed him the sock full of what had to be rocks.

I didn't trust the wanna-be king. You could never really count on people who didn't want to get their hands dirty.

Another goblin took his place, handing Sven a broken beer bottle. Unphased, Sven took it and handed it off to me in what had become second nature. We'd been doing this for at least 20 minutes. It was the arrangement we'd come to after the goblins still refused to take the weapon after I dunked it. Apparently, two people between them and the divinity pool was better than one.

Bent over the embankment with trash bags tied around my kneecaps and elbow-length gloves, I was making damn sure none of the bubbling liquid splashed on me. I didn't know if it was necessary, but I wasn't taking any chances. After the train wreck I'd gone through over the past few months with spellwork, I was playing it safe. Because who's to say I wouldn't be spellbound for eternity or until I could get to Iris again? Then again, maybe she wouldn't even be able to help me. Hell didn't appear to be her forte. Not that I held it against her. Hell shouldn't be anyone's forte. Except for maybe the Devil. Besides, that was assuming Knockaine hadn't turned into Lucifer's playground by then.

Cradling the improvised weapon, I lowered it into the deceptively innocent-looking water. With any luck, the bottle wouldn't slip out of the grip in these impossible-to-maneuver gloves because I wasn't reaching in there to grab the improvised weapon. They could just find another one.

I focused on the one thing that truly mattered right now as I submerged it fully into the hot water. The prayer.

"Please protect the bearer of this weapon and use it to kill any of Hell's creatures that may roam Earth," I murmured under my breath.

I'd said it so many times it was hard to mean the rehearsed words anymore like Gorata said I had to for the spell to work, but I kept putting all of my heart into the script. I'd initially prayed to send them back to Hell, but when the Test Demon, as I liked to call him, had fallen dead, that fell into the good-enough category. If we made it to the end of this, we'd throw the bodies into the Devil's Cauldron. The bubbling, spitting pit was the perfect place to hide bodies. Kind of like quicksand, except you needed a couple pokes to get them fully submerged since it was thicker. Test Demon had proved that. I just had to have faith. And I did. As I pulled the bottle back out, I reminded myself they were beings from Hell. I wouldn't lose sleep over it. Well, much.

I shook off the excess water before passing it to Sven. It didn't even have the decency to glow to let you know it had a divinity spell attached to it. How many animals were walking around this place enchanted out of their minds?

Sven passed me a toy wand, complete with a star attached to the top with the same seriousness as he'd handed me the broken bottle and the sock full of rocks before it.

I gave it a double-take. I shot a look at the chubby, little goblin, standing there with pride in her shoulders and her full hips.

"Hey, what's your name?" I called to her.

"Kefilwe," she said, with a beaming smile.

"Kefilwe, no offense, but I think you should find another weapon. We're looking for something that can actually function as a weapon if the spell doesn't work." Because her expression got tighter and tighter. I tried to be the picture of reason, even going as far as to turn up my palms.

She crossed her arms over her chest. "It can be used as a weapon."

I opened my mouth to argue the point, but from the savage expression on her face I finally just shrugged and held out my hand to Sven. Maybe, she could kill someone with it. Still, when the cheap plastic hit my hand a giggle bubbled up. Sven looked at me and raised an eyebrow as if to imply nothing was ridiculous about the 'weapon.' However, I could see his lips twitch. Ducking my head to hide the warmth I knew was in my eyes, I went back to the pool. After our conversation in the Blood Spire, he'd made his feelings very clear. I dunked the glowing, multi-colored wand into the water. I just wished I could make him love me. If only it were that simple.

"Please protect the bearer of this weapon and use it to kill any of Hell's creatures that may roam Earth," I mumbled, the words quiet across the water.

Sighing, I pulled the magic wand out. It still lit up. The wonder of LEDs. Handing the toy back to Sven with more care than I ever thought I'd give a kid's toy, I avoided his gaze. He wasn't going to love me. I had to get over it. As the days passed, I would. Time healed all. Right?

"That would appear to be all of them," Sven said, reaching his hands out and stretching.

I blinked in astonishment as I looked to the shore. He was right. There was nobody else in line. I thought back to the goblins who had come through. After some corralling by Kut, that had been all of them. Well, except for Mabye anyway. Against my better judgment, I'd sent him to the Patupaiarehe. Hoping against all logic, the bearded king would at the very least hear him out and send over scouts to assess the questionable goblins' claims. But I wasn't holding my breath.

Untying the bags from around my legs, I put them in a pile along with the gloves. We needed to be able to dip more weapons at a moment's notice, in case we missed anyone or, Dagda forbid, they lost their weapon. Which with all-over-the-place goblins was probably the more likely scenario.

Well, this was it. This was when we went against Hell on Earth. With a sigh I felt to my bones, I picked up the whip Oganess had made me from the dirt. I'd grabbed it on impulse when we'd left Blood Spire, never dreaming I'd be dipping it into a divinity pool. Sven had the runed knife one of the goblins had given me- I mean their god- as a thank you. Even though he was a vampire and as such had links to Hell, he'd agreed to help us. There were so many crazy rules in vampire society. I couldn't help but wonder if helping us broke yet another law and could be used against him in tomorrow's sentencing. Assuming we got to tomorrow, that is. If we were lucky, Hell on Earth would send the entire world into chaos, and we'd all be dead before that happened. I let out a dry laugh.

Sven looked at me at the sound. His lip cocked up, and he said, "It's not going to exactly be a walk in New York City, is it?"

"No, it really isn't going to be. There are so many. It's overwhelming, you know?" I shook my head.

"Yeah, I understand that feeling," he said, tucking the knife in as he crossed his arms over his chest.

We sat there in silence for a moment, each formulating our plan of attack. Then it hit me. There was one thing I could do to help him. One thing he didn't have. One thing that, if it came down to it, just might be able to save his life.

Confident he wouldn't appreciate me insinuating he couldn't take care of himself, I tried a different tactic. "I think the quickest way to take them out is to paralyze them with lightning and then slap them with the whip. The cracker on the whip can be changed out, so I only dipped that."

He nodded his approval and then said teasingly, "Is it possible you've had your fill of magic that isn't your own?"

I laughed, smoothing the hair below my ponytail. "More than my fill, that's for sure." When he turned quiet in reflection, I knew that was my chance. All traces of humor fell away. I had to pick my way through this to make sure it didn't come out wrong. There was so much taboo about the conversation. Not the least being our current Hands-Off status. I kept my voice quiet as I said, "I think you should do the same thing."

As if I'd flipped a switch, he shut down. I let the silence sit between us, thick and uncomfortable. Finally, he said, "Cy, that isn't going to happen."

"Listen, I know it is uncomfortable because…." I faltered. How could I put this any other way than what it was?

"Because you like it," he finished for me. And there it was. Heat crept up my neck. His lips thinned, his dark brown hair falling over his brow. Then he said, "I'm not going to bite you."

"Now, you're just being stupid. That I..." the admission got stuck, and I cleared my throat past it before continuing on, "Might get something out of it has nothing to do with it. You know as well as I do, we're outmatched here. We need all of the help we can get. Tor Mór, we don't even know if this divinity spell will work against the bigger and badder denizens of Hell. And if it doesn't, I'm sure they aren't going to wait around while we do all of this song and dance then." His lips were still pressed together, but there was uncertainty in his eyes. I pressed on. "The best-case scenario is we can hold them off until Mabye and the rest of the faeries get here. But that's three and a half *more* hours from now. You and I both know a lot can happen in that time. Your having lightning just makes sense. Hey, I'm open to anything besides biting if you know of another way to get the damn stuff to you."

I know I sounded bitter as I said the last, but I didn't care. That Sven was rejecting me on every level pricked a bit.

He ran a hand through his hair, his brow working as he stared at me. That he was having such a hard time accepting even a part of me just twisted the knife deeper in my heart. Finally, he shook his head and said, "You're right, of course. It just makes sense. And besides opening a vein into a glass, which has...complications, biting you really is the most efficient way. It is my hope that we can keep this on a transactional level."

Dagda forbid I have feelings for the stubborn ass vampire.

"Might I remind you that you're the one who mentioned biting in the first place? I'm just trying to help," I said with a forced smile, feeling strung as tight as a tuned harp when it hit me; he was really going to do it. He was going to bite me.

"You are right, again. I apologize. It is I who assumed," Sven said with a slight bow.

And he meant it. My chin wobbled. I was quick to hide it by ducking my head. Why did he have to be so damn kind? It only made everything more painful. Taking a deep breath, I looked away. Really, I was lucky to have him in my life. Even if it was as a friend. I was just being petty. After a moment, I regained my composure. See? I could do this.

Feeling better than he was at least going to be taken care of and maybe, just maybe, we might be able to salvage our relationship as friends, I crooked a smile at him. "Just come bite me, so we can light up some bad guys."

I expected him to smile, but he was somber as he walked over to me. All in all, I don't suppose I blamed him. This was probably uncomfortable for him. And that was partly my fault. Well, that was about to change. I was going to be good from here on out. A model friend. But first...I turned around so I didn't have to see him and pulled my ponytail to the side. The crunch of pebbles under his boot let me know when he was right behind me.

My breath quickened in anticipation. Cool air breathed over my exposed neck as I waited. Without a sound, he bent my neck farther to the side. My heart was in my chest as I felt his lips on me. Lips I never thought I'd feel again. The world went dark as my eyelids fluttered closed as the moment swept me away. A wave of sensation flooded through me as his teeth pierced my tender flesh. First, there was the pain. Always the pain. Following it was an arousal so intense the world tilted. At first, his lips had been soft, hesitant, but then they pulled rougher, sucked deeper. Tighter. I moaned, the sound vibrating his lips against me. He grabbed me and yanked me close, hard against him. My breath caught. I reached up to run a hand through the softness of his hair. It felt like down. Then he stopped. His body was tight under my fingertips as he growled. It was like a splash of cold water. I dropped my hand. I'd crossed the line. Again. Stupid Move 75,003.

I went to step away, but his hold was firm. My heart took off, pounding in my chest like a bird trying to escape. I held my breath as I turned in his arms. His eyes were heavy from the drug of my blood. But that was it. Not love. Not even affection. Just good old-fashioned, blood lust with a faerie kick. Of course, it was. What did I think? Merely from tasting my blood, that all of his feelings would come rushing back? That was like thinking if you screwed a guy, he would fall in love with you. It didn't work that way. He needed to actually have feelings for you. And not just your vagina. The only way Sven would get feelings again was if he had a heart. I froze. How dumb could I be? The solution to our problems was five feet away.

"Sven, you should use the divinity pool to get your heart back," I said, trying to keep the hope out of my voice, but instead, it just came out soft, scared. Dagda be damned, I was scared. Scared of being pushed away. Again. Just how much rejection could a girl take? But I had to try. At least one more time.

At first, I didn't think he even heard me until he cleared his voice and disengaged himself from my arms, which I hadn't realized had come up around him. Immediately, they felt empty. I wrapped my arms around myself, my whip tickling my stomach.

Blinking the lust from his eyes, he said, "No matter how tempting that may sound. We don't really know what the pool does. A few questionable goblin experiments, two of three which went terribly, isn't enough to make me want to spell myself. Besides, I have no idea what is going to happen tomorrow with my sentencing. I don't want to risk doing something to myself that will make it unbearable. You don't realize I could have this punishment for a lifetime. Pardon the phrase considering what we are about to go up against, but there's no sense adding Hell to eternity."

I'd completely forgotten the black shadow that loomed over him. How insensitive could I be? Despite everything he was going through, he was here. He had to be so overwhelmed. And I was just making it worse.

I put a hand to my throat, never good at apologizing for being an ass. "Hey, sorry, I can't believe how insensitive that was-"

He stopped me with a hand. "Hey, it's ok. We have more important things in front of us right now than what tomorrow may bring."

He was right. We needed to deal with what was in front of us. I smiled at him, wanting to thank him for being understanding for being kind.

Instead, I held up my whip in a mock salute and said, "Hell, yes we do. In fact, I bet I take down more demons than you."

Catching on, he returned my smile, even if it was a little empty. "In your dreams."

"Look who's talking," I said and pushed him out of the way as I loped off to the North.

His footfalls were right behind me. I hadn't gone farther than the adjoining Spraying Pools when a praying mantis appeared on the walkway. It wasn't the milky eyes, razored legs, or the bony protrusions jutting from its arms that ticked me off that it was a demon. It was the fact that it was the size of me. I cracked my neck. Might as well get to it. This was why we were here, after all.

True to what I'd told Sven, I summoned my kundalini energy as I ran down the path towards the evidence of nature going overboard. Heat filled my body like I'd opened a gate. I let the current flow from my spine to my hands when I was close enough to the monster that I wouldn't miss. Lightning shot from my palm. It moved its arms into the path, the bone spurs absorbing the bolt harmlessly. I gritted my teeth.

"What in the name of Danu?" I huffed as I tried again, this time shooting at its feet as I ran down the trail.

He dropped his other arm into the dirt, and it soaked in the energy again. I shook my head, my ponytail bobbing behind my head. Unbelievable. Well, at least I could be relatively sure it was the bones sponging up my magic.

Snatching the whip from my waist, I unfurled it with a crack. The last time I'd used this thing had been mildly successful. Let's see if I could repeat that. All I had to do was snap it with the end. Theoretically.

I got as close as I dared before planting my feet. The green beast reared up on his hind legs, green-black slime stretching down from his forearms to glop onto the path with a sizzle. That wasn't comforting. It swiped at me.

I bobbed and weaved around them, dancing off the path as I asked, "You don't have any tentacles or needles or anything, do you?"

Paranoid? Me?

Unraveling my whip, it trailed after me as the monstrosity followed. I cracked the whip at him. Or that's what I thought would happen. The tail flew to the side with all of the force of a spaghetti noodle. Ok, maybe not. With a flick of my wrist, I sent the leather jerking like a snake having a seizure. Steam scorched my ankles, telling me I'd gone too far. The good news was I stayed on dry land. I didn't trust that there weren't any other magical pools around here. The bad news was I couldn't back up any further. And he was coming closer. Why hadn't I dunked something else? The answer came even before the thought did. It reminded me of Oganess. During a time fraught with uncertainty, there was nothing like the memory of my kick-ass, adopted family to give me a shot of much-needed energy. Suddenly, the giant insect stopped moving. I jumped back as it slumped forward. Its sickly green form crashed the ankle-high wood fence bordering the path. Behind him stood Sven.

"One," he said with a crooked grin.

"Your ego might want to move out of the way of that sizzling black stuff. Something tells me it's more than for looks," I said with a laugh, pointing to the spreading black ooze.

As if to prove my point, the fence it dropped on shuddered and fell to the ground. Yikes. Definitely, corrosive. At least it was off the path. Well, mostly.

"You're right, as usual," he said with an easy bow. His body language changed in an instant when he looked over my shoulder. As if on cue, my ear started ringing. Grabbing my ear, I gave it a couple shakes to stop it, but it kept on.

I didn't want to turn around. I really didn't want to. It was a demon; I was sure of it. And if it was freaking Sven out, I was confident I didn't want any part of it. I squared my shoulders. Insanity seemed to come hand in hand with saving the world. That didn't stop time from slowing as I turned around.

In front of me was a giant skeleton. It had to be fifteen times taller than us. But it wasn't just a set of bones. It was made up of thousands of other skeletons, all clinging to each other.

My mouth had dropped open. I closed it with a click. How was that even possible?

"It's a Gashadokuro. I've only heard of them in myth and legend. They're said to be made of people who have died of starvation or in battle without being buried," Sven said, his hushed voice barely carrying over the wind.

"That's awful," I said, and I meant it. And though it was awful, he had to be taken down, and like now, because the longer he was alive, the more likely the public was to see him. A behemoth that towered above the trees was hard to do damage control around. The buzzing in my ear grew louder as the monster approached, and I couldn't help the awe in my voice as I added, "He's massive."

"He may look scary, but he's a lesser demon," he said, with a determined smile.

"I like what we did last time. Why don't we do what we did last time with the giant praying mantis," I said.

"You mean the mantid?" he asked.

I waved my hand through the air. "You know what I mean."

"Indeed, I do. And I think it is a fantastic idea," he said.

"Why don't you be the damsel in distress this time? You're faster," I said, pushing him forward.

The giant skeleton honed in on the movement.

"I think I get where you are going with this," he said. And he was off, his coat flying behind him as he darted to the side.

Why he wore a coat, I had no idea. It was way too hot for one. Wait a minute. Did vampires feel hot and cold? Probably not.

I stayed still. The Gashadokuro followed him. Sven kept moving until the creature turned around completely. All I had to do was catch him with the popper. Since he was a lesser demon, that should kill him for sure. If he indeed was a lesser demon like Sven had said. I looked way up at the giant. I sincerely doubted he was.

When I was sure he couldn't see me, I pulled my arm back and sent my whip flying through the air. Or flapping, to be more exact. It looked like I'd thrown out a dead serpent. Snatching it back in, I clenched my jaw. I could do this. It was too late to go back now. Letting out a deep breath, I snapped out the tail again. This time, it worked, cracking through the air. But it landed a few feet shy of the skeleton that made up the nightmare's big toe. Its head moved, and then its shoulders were turning. Great. I'd gotten its attention. Not exactly my intention. Then the bones started to rattle and shake. Praying I'd get to it in time, I sent another snap of the whip screaming through the air. And I did get to it but not because I'd been quick enough. The beast hadn't moved. Just as the tip connected, I realized lightning webbed between its skeleton joints as its body danced. My lips quirked up. Good old Sven.

That's the last thought I had before skeletons started falling from the sky as the Gashadokuro broke apart. With two giant leaps, I catapulted onto the path and ducked into a ball. I somersaulted twice before stopping. Swinging my hands up, I covered my head. Splinters flew through the air as the remains smashed against the ground. Even though I knew I was in the thick of it, shock still roiled through me as one of the skeletons slammed into my already sore shoulder. I hissed in pain.

Finally, the crashing stopped. When I was relatively sure it was safe, I raised my head. Skeletons blanketed the entire area. Tor Mór, what a mess. Throwing a femur off, I uncurled myself and looked for Sven. Bones rumbled and clattered as they slid down the bone pile as he popped out. A giggle bubbled in my chest. Covered in bone dust and dirt, he looked like a damn mess. Unable to contain it, I burst out laughing. When he saw me, he started laughing too. I'm sure I didn't look like a runway model either.

"Might I suggest you work on your whip skills? Indiana Jones, you are not," he said, shaking his head as he walked up.

"That's not a bad idea," I admitted, rubbing my eyes.

"And so it goes," Sven said.

"So what goes?" I asked, taking my fingers out of my eye sockets. His focus was on the bridge. Squinting, I looked too. It took me a second to see it, but after a moment, I did. A post seemed to bump out just a little too far. At second glance, a pair of giant eyes swiveled around, taking in the surroundings. I looked at Sven. With a raised eyebrow, he returned the look. I nodded.

"So the hunt continues," he said, with the blood-red runes shining in the setting sun as he saluted with his knife and stalked over.

The demon must have known the gig was up because he detached himself from the pole, changing to immediately blend in with the pavement. It looked like floating eyeballs for a fraction of a second before he skittered off in the opposite direction. Sven picked up the pace.

Shaking my head with a ghost of a smile on my face, I stretched my shoulder out, contemplating what Sven had said. He was right. I wasn't good enough with the whip as it stood. The grim reality is anything that even resembled a weapon had been used already. Which meant, even if I could find something else to use, the improvised weapon would probably be terrible. Yes, it would be spelled, which should take care of any of Hell's denizens, but there was still the reality that the divine magic wouldn't work on the more evil tourists. I just needed to practice my whip skills. I'd been able to use it in the Never.

Ducking into the trees, so I didn't have to worry about being snuck up on, I did just that.

The motions came back to me like riding a bike. Before I knew it, I was snatching leaves off branches and sending rocks flying. Ok, not every time. Indiana Jones, I was not. But it would do. Coming out of the trees, the happiest demon I'd ever seen walked past. Her ruby-red eyes, crinkled in anticipation, shone almost as bright as the pile of garbage she was carrying. Well, trash to me, but her long serpentine arms were wrapped around sheets of charred tinfoil, gum wrappers, and pop cans as if they were a chest of treasure. A steel tumbler fell out of the pile and rolled to me, only stopping when it hit my foot. Welcome to Hell, it cheerfully proclaimed.

Yep, that about summed it up. There seemed to be no end to the demons. How were we ever going to take them all down? Shaking my head, I unfurled my whip and made good use of my practice. After thanking Danu for her favor, I went on to make even more use of my gift.

I knew Sven was joking about me being no Indiana Jones, but I have to admit, I was starting to feel a little like it after four calling Baigujing demons, three french hydras, two teuthidas, and a partridge in a pear tree. I wiped the sweat from my stinging eyes as Mogapi, and I squared off against an Achaieral. Ok, kidding about the partridge, but not about the Achaieral. This particular one was doing his damnedest to bring back the nightmare of Sven's case by taking on the form of a gargoyle. I'd been cracking my whip at the monster while he'd been having a grand old time teasing me by dipping and rising just out of my range. I'd been more than happy to accept Mogapi's help when he'd offered. We'd been engaged in this frustrating cat and mouse game for longer than I could afford. Demons were coming in faster than we were taking down, and just like I'd anticipated, they were getting higher and higher up the food chain. I hated being right. And even though we'd been able to handle everything that came through, so far, we'd reached an official code red status due to the sheer number. And no, that wasn't about the goblin who'd apparently become bored with killing demons and had appointed himself the official ticker of monsters. That consisted of him calling out Hell's patrons by number and running up and down the boardwalk crowing out siren sounds. No, code red as in that damn faerie king with the red beard could show up at any minute.

Noticing Mogapi had crawled up the awning and was in place, I readied my whip. He nodded, signaling he was ready. I shook my head. The demon's black, leathery wings blotted out the night sky still. He was too high. A wide grin split the gargoyle's face. How those razor-sharp teeth didn't bust open his lip was beyond me. Even though he looked like it, he wasn't made of stone. Then he dipped, and I got to smile my own cocky smile. I gave the go to the ranger. With sure feet, he ran down the awning and jumped. His cloak floated behind him for a brief moment only to come back with a slap as he jarred to a stop when he seized the demon's foot. The monster's roar shook the metal roof with a wong. He jerked his foot to get the unexpected weight off. The ranger bounced up and down, his legs dangling like twigs under his pelt. The unexpected nakedness I wasn't concerned about. I was more worried about those blade-like talons inches from his hand. Even a nick was enough to sever any body part, no matter how much you wanted to keep it attached.

"Be careful," I whispered. My heart in my throat, I watched the beast sink lower. I readied my whip. The gargoyle's face twisted in anger as he screamed and kicked and thrashed. Please, Danu, just a few more feet. The demon sank lower. I gritted my teeth. Was he low enough? I couldn't risk hitting Mogapi. Just a foot or two more, then I would do it. Slick with sweat, my fingers slipped along the metal handle as I swung the whip behind me. With another bellow, the beast drew his wings down in a desperate pull. Impossibly, he inched up, but then the determined goblin started to swing back and forth. The movement jerked on the tiring monster. It wasn't long before it became too much for the achaieral, and he dropped. Now. Elation soared through my veins as I snapped the leather out, aiming for the farthest spot I could reach. I prayed it would land above the heroic goblin. It hit the monster's calf with a crack. Then it fell. The two creatures plummeted to the earth below. The fiend shrank in a twisting, turning blur.

"Mogapi, jump!" I screamed, even knowing I'd be too late to warn the ranger.

I recoiled back as if I'd been slapped when they hit. Thankfully, the wily ranger was way ahead of me and had already let go. He was already rolling away, safe as a destructive puppy. The would-be gargoyle hit the earth with a crash. When the dust cleared, his body was all that remained. He'd dissolved into the form of a man. Lifelessly, it stared up at the indigo night sky through giant winged eyebrows that stuck out well past his temples. I smoothed a shaking hand over my scalp, brushing back strands that had crept loose. These creatures were a trip. Just what else was in the depths of Hell? What else would we have to face this night? The ranger came over, dusting off his knobby kneecaps.

I uncrossed my arms and gave the goblin a salute with the butt of my whip. "Mogapi, you are quite the fighter."

"The honor is mine," he said with a bow. Then he nodded at the whip still cemented to my hand. "That's quite a weapon you have there. What's that drum there for?"

I held up the whip. It was a truly unique invention. All black, it effortlessly blended the stiff leather of the fall with the smooth metal handle. The scrollwork around the small chamber tucked against the handle made it look like a work of art more than a killing machine. Even though she'd created it in a hotel room on the fly, the seams between the metal parts were effortless. The glass clinked as I tapped the futuristic chamber. "It holds ley energy."

"Now, that's a handy weapon to have," he nodded in approval, crossing his hands over his tunic.

"I still have to test how to work it on our plane of existence. The incredible woman who made it for me was an aetheral, so I only know how to use it in The Never. Which, no offense, is a place I am hoping to avoid for the rest of eternity," I said with a rueful grin. I don't think anyone would begrudge me that. I'd died there, after all. Nothing like having the very air you breathe eat you alive to make you want to strike it from your travel plans.

A monster that looked like a black yeti with spider legs skittered past, cutting our conversation short. This time Mogapi was the one who sighed as he pulled out a short sword from its holster. Did I really just see that? I'd never thought I'd see the resilient ranger tired. He seemed to have a never-ending supply of energy. If he was like this, how were the others fairing? More to the point, how were we all expected to keep this up? We weren't machines. Would everyone abandon the mission like the ticker goblin already had? Or would they make stupid mistakes because they were exhausted and killed off one by one until no one was left? No one but demons and monsters. My stomach knotted. I'd rather have them all abandon the operation first. Live what life they could before the inevitable end.

He started off after the demon with a salute, but I stopped him with a hand, my morose thoughts eating at me. "Do you want some help?'

Laying his hand on mine, he said, "Not with this one, but many thanks. Take you care, Protector of Goblins and All that Is Bad."

Guilt sat heavy in my gut as I gave him a nod, and he strode off. I watched him. I wasn't his god, but at that moment, it hardly seemed important. There was way too much to worry about to add silly things like labels to the mix.

"Fifty-two and a half!" screamed the goblin counter, his

wide feet sending pebbles clattering down the boardwalk as he ran by and started his siren wail.

Flinching at the piercing sound, I shouted to the goblin. "How do you get half a demon?"

He didn't answer; he simply disappeared around the corner. On second thought, did I even want to know? I grabbed my hair in my hands and held it for a second

Rubbing my forehead, I headed to Hell's Gate. I didn't bother hurrying. If there were fifty-two more Hell's tourists, my running wasn't going to make that big of a difference. Conserving energy was the name of the game now. We just had to wait for the other faeries to get here. I wasn't even going to say 'if' anymore. They had to come. We were out of other options.

Rounding the corner, the uplit sign for Hell's Gate loomed ominously. I rubbed my arms. But as I turned into the exhibit, I stopped cold. A fiend crouched over a half-eaten corpse, her white hair blending seamlessly with her white robes as they flapped behind her in a breeze I could neither see nor feel. Behind her Kefilwe, branding her plastic wand. And behind her was a horde of beasts, closing in. That got me running.

Sprinting towards them, I yelled, "Behind you!"

The pale woman swung demonic, black eyes at me. Blood painted her dainty chin and dripped down her kimono. She only stopped on me for a moment. Swinging fully on the determined goblin, her pale white and ceremonial red makeup danced in the LED lights of the plastic wand. Then Kefilwe touched her with it.

Well, that was one down at least. I picked up speed, praying I reached the gang behind her in time. But then I saw something far scarier than anything I'd seen so far tonight. The woman didn't fall. She didn't even falter. How was that possible? I'd spelled that wand myself. Despite that fact, the monster's fragile hands reached out and grabbed the goblin by her thick throat. Lifting her high, the petite woman pulled the squirming gray goblin close. Little feet kicked in vain at the blood-soaked robes. When that didn't work, the goblin hit the unfazed creature over and over again with the flashing toy. That's when it hit me. This was one of the big baddies. Because of the glow stick necklace resistance, I'd been worried the spell might not work on this very type. And it hadn't. Fuck, fuck, fuck. I was so caught up in my thoughts that I almost missed the next surprise.

One of the terrors that had been closing in on the pair swam around them and yanked the goblin out of the greater demon's hands. With quick movements, he pushed the spitting-angry goblin to the side, out of harm's reach. The filmy creature probably wouldn't have been able to even do it if it weren't for taking the still-blinking woman off guard. But she wasn't for long.

Just as the angsty goblin was dusting herself back off, the little creature slammed a well-manicured hand into the chest of the would-be rescuer and pulled out his blue heart. That's when the rest of the horde reached her. They crashed into her, pushing her over the corpse of her victim. She threw her arms out to balance herself but to no avail. Lost in the billowing robes and hair, she fell. Her body slamming into the boardwalk was the last thing I saw before the troupe descended, blanketing her one on top of the other. They fought to get at her. Bits and pieces of white flew from the mass hysteria. It wasn't long before her screams finally stopped.

That's when I realized shock had stopped me in my own tracks. I wasn't the only one who was struck by the events. The goblin was staring at it all with huge eyes. If I hurried, I could still save her. Hastening to close the distance, I pumped my arms. She wasn't going to be torn apart like that greater demon had been. Not if I had anything to say about it.

As it turned out, I didn't. I was almost there by the time the pack was up and stalking towards her. My heart dropped.

"Behind you!" I shouted as I took off in a run, unfurling my whip as I went.

That's when the mob noticed me. Breaking off from her trail, they turned to me. Fine by me. I could take them. Knife-like claws high, one broke off with a gleam in her catlike eyes. I swung the whip around and cracked it at her. Hit. She crumpled and fell like her strings had been cut. That spurred the others. This time they came at me all at once. Four demons. Well, I guess we were about to figure out how good I really was. Swallowing hard, I braced my feet.

"Stop! Not her!" screamed Kefilwe, who dashed across the space to almost bowl me over as she threw herself in front of me.

As if switched off, the demons stopped. I blinked. What was going on here?

"But she was going to attack you, my darling. I vow to keep you safe," said a demon with tentacles for arms with a grand bow.

I stepped back.

Kefilwe managed to wrap her thick arms behind her and clung to my legs like a child. "This is a good one. She means me no harm."

Various eyes looked me up and down, measuring.

A humanoid with red curls and a snake tongue dropped to his knees at her feet and said, "Dearest heart, this wretched woman is a demon killer. She will kill you. Let me slay her for you to prove my love for you."

His declaration sent the others falling all over themselves.

Kefilwe stomped her feet and screamed, "Stop!"

And they did. As well as what I realized had been

scuffling next to us. I looked over to see a goblin and a demon froze mid-grapple, wide-eyed, staring at us. Never breaking eye contact, the goblin stabbed the monster with a fork, and he folded in on himself. Shaking my head, I turned back to the Kefilwe who held the creature's rapt attention as she berated them.

"Nobody needs to prove their devotion," she said, shaking the wand at them, the plastic tip wobbling as if to emphasize her point.

Then it dawned on me. "Wait, all of these," I point to the four demons with a sweep of my grime-covered finger, "are in love with you?"

"Watch where you point that, Demon Slayer," growled one covered in so much hair I couldn't make out where its legs began.

I brought my gaze back with a shake of my head. You kill one demon, and now you have a label forever.

"So it would seem," responded Kefilwe, brushing her stringy hair out of her face with the hand that still clutched the wand.

I shook my head, unable to comprehend it. "But...how?"

She shrugged her meaty shoulders. "Got me. All I do is touch them with this here star, and they're immediately in love with me. Not sure why it didn't work on the one, though?"

"I'll love you forever, my heart," said one with tears streaming down its face. Come to think of it, the thing had been crying this entire time. If he was crying because of love, I got that. My face screwed up in a grimace. Was I really commiserating with a demon? The very kind who would prefer that my head be rolling around on the ground rather than attached to my body? Love. Tor Mór, why didn't it hit me sooner?

The confused look on the goblin's face would have been

comical if I wasn't in the middle of berating myself. Obviously, I'd messed up while dunking the makeshift weapon. I had been thinking of Sven, no doubt. Again. I really needed to let that shit go.

Blowing out a sigh, I looked over at the bigger fish the goblin hadn't been able to take out with her weapon. It was torn to pieces. Courtesy of the monsters currently giving her calf eyes. In a way, it was funny. A very small, is-this-really-happening way.

"If I were still up for the idea of goblin bait, I'd say we come get you if any bigger demons come down," I said with a dry laugh.

With a toss of her hair, Kefilwe puffed out her chest. "Oh, yeah. I'll take them out-"

I held up a hand to cut her off. "We're not doing that. Some beings are far more powerful than even twenty of your new admirers could take out." The thought was a sobering one because it really wasn't an exaggeration. "Now, unless you want a different weapon, get yourself gone and round up more of Hell's tourists. We have 49 of Hell's denizens here now, and that was only after they started keeping track."

She only hesitated for a second before grinning broadly. "Nah, think I'll keep it."

With a sly wink, she sauntered off, her harem trotting after her. I laughed to myself. Well, that was one way to own it.

My thoughts stayed with the impetuous goblin even after she left. What if I did the same thing to one of the other makeshift weapons and they weren't having...good results? What if one of my courageous recruits died because of me? I scoured my mind to try to remember if I'd been thinking of anything else when I was dipping the equipment. Nothing came to mind. Then again before Kefilwe, I would probably have said the same thing. I massaged my tiring wrists as I stared out over the still waters of Hell's Gate. I couldn't chance it. The blood of innocents wouldn't be on my hands tonight. First, I'd spell a couple more weapons, so I could have them on hand. From there, I'd go around the thermal park and switch out the bad ones as I went. There couldn't be more than a couple, could there? I'd like to think I was more in control than that. Then again there was a goblin walking around with a toy making people fall in love with her. Shaking my head, I turned to go when something orange caught my eye. And it was rising out of Hell's Gate.

Great. Another one. Was I really going to take it down instead of help the goblins fighting so valiantly for their lives? No. They needed me more than I needed to take down yet another demon. Just as I was thinking about walking away, the ticker goblin ran up.

"Fifty-three and a ha-" When he laid eyes on what was behind me, he stopped. His face froze into an expression that would have been comical if it wasn't followed by an ear-piercing shriek. He didn't stop yowling as he ran out of the exhibit.

Instinct took over and even though I hadn't seen what was behind me, I called after him. "Get help!"

There was no response. The screams just kept fading until they were gone entirely. My jaw worked. Well, I guess it was just me and whatever was behind me. If a creature garnered that kind of reaction from someone who'd seen at least 52 demons, I couldn't just leave. That was a plan change. No matter how much I wanted to right the wrongs I'd done. No matter what I wanted. Heat grew behind my eyes.

"Fuck!" I shouted, kicking a plastic bottle.

It jumped across the boardwalk. Then a familiar roar shook the ground, jarring me out of any would-be pity party. Turning around my worst fears were realized as I came face to face with an ifrit. It wasn't the lovable-but-fierce ifrit I'd come to know as family, though. This monster was bigger, the gold cuffs on his wrists wider, and the expression on his face meaner. If that was even possible. The embers glowing beneath his black fur flared in the dark of the night. It looked like he had been born of the night. My nightmare come to life.

The tendons on my neck stretched as I flexed my sore shoulder. I could do this. It would be fine. Totally, fine. Maybe, the divinity magic would work anyway. The ifrit's legs sizzled, blowing a gush of steam as he shifted back on his heels, looking me up and down. Nothing said it couldn't work on hellspawn, right? The other wretch Kefilwe had come across had been a greater demon, so she'd been an exception since those were higher on the food chain. Right?

Gnawing my lip, I unfurled my whip. The movement caught the beast's attention. After a moment of lazy assessment, he looked away. He was dismissing me? My lip curled as my blood boiled. Nobody marginalized me. I allowed myself a steely smile. Lucky for me, anger helped me focus.

Quieting the part of my mind that pointed out those tree trunk-like legs could cross this distance the space of a heartbeat, I cracked my whip. It snaked out like lightning, a direct hit to the center of his chest. He didn't so much as flinch.

Pushing down rising panic, I hit him again. And again and again. Sweat poured from my brow as red-hot embers floated down through puff after puff of smoke. The black cloud would have blended into the night if it weren't obscuring fire that flared from him with each blow. Even though, he didn't so much as flinch, I didn't stop. I was out of options. This had to work; there was nothing else. Waiting for the other faeries was no longer an option. Then he started to move towards me, each step releasing a hiss until he finally stepped onto the boardwalk. It groaned with the weight but held.

"I need help over here!" I shouted, hoping anyone could hear me as I drew in a deep drag of ley energy.

No sooner had warmth flooded me that I shot it at the fast-approaching monster. This time he felt the sting. His roar split my ears. I winced, but didn't let up the steady stream of energy pouring out of me and into him. Putting his giant horns down, he pawed the ground, his claws digging gouges into the wood. He was pissed. That was the last thought I had before he charged me.

Screams sounded behind me. High pitched ones. Human ones. When had they gotten here? Dagda be damned, I knew the park was operational, but couldn't they find somewhere else to be? Launching myself out of the ifrit's path of destruction, I ducked and rolled into the entrance coming to a stop just as three pairs of goblin feet entered. I looked up. Kut, Mogapi, and Kefilwe all stood there together, wearing expressions of eagerness, determination, and terror respectively.

I sprung to my feet, slinging out orders as I rose. "Kefilwe, get the humans out of here. Kut and Mogapi help me take down this giant hemorrhoid."

Loose dirt fell from me as I turned around, not bothering to see my orders carried out. I didn't have time to. The nightmare had already extracted himself from the covered seating. Kut, Mogapi, and Kefilwe came up alongside me as he was turned back our way.

"What are you doing? Go take those people to safety," I bit out to Kefilwe my voice getting reedy as I started to pull ley magic in.

"No can do. You need me and my studs," she retorted,

cracking her wand against her hand, sending every color of the rainbow dancing across her fierce expression.

As if on command, demons flanked her, pressing Mogapi back. There had to be 6 of them by now. Unfazed, Mogapi went to stand on the other side of me. I shook off the irritation that pricked at me. If the humans couldn't save themselves, so be it. Kefilwe was right. We needed her and her little entourage here.

"Guys and girls, this hellspawn will try to kill me. Who's willing to lay down their life to save me? Who's willing to prove they love me the most?" she screamed holding her plastic staff high.

At her war cry, undistinguishable appendages of all shapes and sizes lifted. Whooping rang from either side of her. The over-zealous demon with the tentacles shot forward. I may not be a huge fan of tentacles anymore, but I could appreciate the urgency. With a shrug to the others, I fired my lightning at the ifrit who'd taken two steps forward to meet the demon who was alive with righteous fury. He slapped the muscled torso, leaving fiery streaks where the embers blazed brightest.

Pumping lightning into him, I tried to stay high, so I didn't juice up any of the other demons who were hot on the first's trail. Mogapi and Kut chose a different tactic, coming up behind the fiery ifrit they hacked away at him. His roars grew louder and louder. We were winning. We were going to do it. Hope soared in my chest. Striding forward, my whip trailed behind me until I was close enough. This was it. He was weak enough. I flicked out my whip. With a prayer, I swung it around my head and let it fly. It hit with a crack that inexplicably could be heard above the war cries, screams of pain, and thuds of every weapon imaginable hitting hard flesh. The ifrit's body went silent and caved in on itself. Everything went silent, the attackers stepping back their breaths coming hard in the sudden silence that stretched the air like taffy. My breath held in my chest.

Then the beast threw his arms wide and let out a bellow that was only rivaled by the percussive burst of fire exploding from his body. Shockwaves knocked everyone off their feet, but since I was farther away, it only knocked me to my knees.

Raising my head up, everything was silent as a piercing ringing echoed around in my head. I pressed my hands to my ears and screamed in pain. Watching helplessly as the ifrit stepped over bodies that lay, unmoving at his feet. I did my best to blink away the pain and stand on my feet. Backpedaling to get myself more room, I needed time. More time to think as the ifrit looked at the carnage around it. A smile widened his furred maw. The maliciousness of it took me aback. Iffy had never been like that. He'd been fierce, but protective. Good.

My heart squeezed. Iffy. If only that part of my adopted family was here today, he could give us the advantage we desperately needed. If only Oganess's spell saying I'd never be alone was literal. I could use more literal than feel-good magic right about now. I know it sounded ungrateful, but I would give almost anything to be able to call Iffy to help right about now.

The thought made me stop. Wait. Had Oganess done just that? She'd never struck me as someone who was overly sentimental. What if she had meant for me to call on the Kamikazes whenever I needed them? I wished to Danu I'd asked her when I was in the Never, but I'd been so out of it. Not that I think anyone would blame me. After all I'd just died and been brought back to life.

The ifrit brought me back to the present by dragging a claw against the wood, peeling it up as he cocked his head at me, a gleam in his eye. I swallowed hard. He was done playing. I needed to get out of here. Looking around, I spied the awning. When in doubt, copy success. I pulled a Mogapi and climbed the shelter.

Thinking furiously, I fitted my fingers into the metal grooves. If Oganess had meant for me to summon the Kamikazes, she would have already told me how. She wouldn't have left that to chance. Could I use the same spell I'd used to parts of myself? It was worth a chance to save our asses. Whoever was left, I thought grimly, praying my little diet coke of evil subjects were still alive.

Reaching the roof, I looked back down on the enclosure. People were huddled in the corner as fire roiled off the monster staring up at me. He was so big he could still me. Thank Danu, it was only his eyes that peeked over the roof. I was cornered. Everything in me wanted to run, but I held my ground. This was the best I was going to get.

Well, no time like the present. Let's see if this worked. Tugging my clothes into place, I relaxed my muscles as much as possible with a monster staring at me mere feet away.

Even though it had been months ago that I'd spoken the spell, my mind retrieved the words with ease. Funny how your mind holds on to trauma.

Keeping my voice even, I spoke the words that haunted my dreams, changing them just enough for what I wanted. "By air and earth and fire and water, binded are we, The Kamikaze. By three and nine, our powers are bound. Come to me, Iffy." The air crackled. But nothing happened. Then a hand as big as my head swiped at me. I stumbled out of the way, its razor-sharp claws just missing me as metal bit into my knees as I fell. I braced my boot against the nearest post, so I didn't slide off. My chest heaved as I furiously searched my brain. Ok, what was I missing? There had to be something. It made too much sense. What had Oganess said? She'd said something about our powers being sealed and revealed. Our powers. Not their powers. Ours. Well, the only power I had was the ley line magic. What if I was supposed to use that along with the words? What if that was the key? Something to focus the spell, like the meditation and visualization had in the Never? The furred hand came up again. This time, it pulled on the roofing. My foot slipped as the metal started to buckle.

Gripping the post as the roof bowed, I pulled Kundalini energy and said, "By air and earth and fire and water, binded are we, The Kamikaze. By three and nine, our powers are bound. Come to me, Iffy."

In a burst, a circle of rolling fire appeared in the air- mere feet away. It flared and blew my hair back as it flashed then sent a giant column of fire shooting into the sky. Then a thick blanket of smoke snuffed out the fire. The curtain of black dissipated into the twinkling night sky revealing the one, the only, Iffy. He dropped to the ground with a rumble that shook the earth.

I whooped in victory. "Iffy!"

My victory was short-lived though. A loud yawn screeched and the roof crumpled, with it my lifeline.

No, no, no. My gaze darted around. There was nothing for me to grab onto. The world shifted as I plummeted through the air. I screamed. Iffy closed the gap between us with quick strides, plucking me out of the air. I screamed as his massive hands seared my torso, catching my shirt on fire. Thinking quickly, Iffy rolled me towards the crowd in the corner. I hit the ground hard enough to pull a grunt from my chest. Sky and wooden planks rotated in and out of my view before I came to a hard stop. Searing pain blossomed as flames engulfed my shirt. I whipped it off and slapped it to the ground. Gasps from the onlookers made me look up. They were looking at my chest. I rolled my eyes. Right, a creature from Hell was fine. But Dagda forbid they see a woman in a bra.

Standing up, I absently ground the flames out of my shirt with my foot as I looked back. Iffy looked the larger ifrit up and down, sizing him up, as if he wasn't impressed. The subject of his perusal flattened his mouth. Then Iffy ducked in, grabbing the big ifrit's shoulders. What was he doing? You always wanted to be on the inside. Maybe Iffy could sling him down first. But it was as if the bigger hellspawn read my mind. He braced his hands against Iffy's chest. I winced. The move seemed to stalemate them, though. Their muscles flexed and bunched as they braced against each other. The long black fur matted under Iffy's hands as he fought for purchase. Finally, seeing he couldn't win, Iffy butted his massive horns into the head of the other beast. Not accepting defeat, the black ifrit angled his head down. A hollow thunk was the only sound in the breathless clearing as they locked horns. Their angled racks clacked and scraped as they entered into a struggle of wills. They spit fire with the effort, their teeth grinding together with such ferocity as if that will alone could win them the fight.

Finally, the bigger ifrit used the better leverage of his hold to throw Iffy. He went sailing into the woods. Trees and shrubs folded like a house of cards under his weight. Shit, get up, Iffy. That's when I noticed movement off to the side. Very much alive, Kut and Mogapi crouched low in the tree line, looking the worse for wear. I nodded to them. Kut saluted me with her bloodied staff. Apparently, she felt more comfortable killing the demons the old fashioned way. That made two of us.

My attention was brought back to the fight as Iffy roared, eliciting shocked gasps from the onlookers behind me as he pulled a full-grown tree out of the ground. I had half a mind to tell the humans to leave, but really, where were they going to go? The entire park had to be overrun with demons by now. This had to be the safest place for them now. Which was a sad commentary in and of itself.

Chest heaving, Iffy stalked back into the fight. Cocking the tree back, dirt from the roots flew into the pool with little splooshes. When he was just in range of the bigger ifrit, he swung the tree like a Louisville Slugger. His target reached out a hand to stop the makeshift bat. Still, the swing must have been faster than he'd anticipated because it caught his arm and on the follow-through and then his midsection. He bowled over, and Iffy took the advantage, slamming him across his bowed spine. The behemoth roared, shaking the leaves in the trees as the tree broke across his back with a crack.

Launching the broken tree back into the forest, he turned back to the fight to find the dark haired ifrit gone. A crunching of stone to the South placed him at the rock outcropping. When I saw what he was doing there, my legs tingled in fear. He'd lifted the entire top half of the formation in one solid piece, exposing what was left of the landscape Iffy had squashed.

"Everybody, duck!" I screamed, throwing back a hand, as the ifrit hefted the slab in the air.

But he didn't throw it. Instead, his muscles balked under the weight as he walked it over to Iffy.

The Kamikazee bobbed to the left and right, but unless he came over here and put everyone in danger, he was trapped in the court. And the big ifrit knew it. An evil smile strained his face as he hefted the rocks up. Iffy braced his hands against the inevitable, but it was too heavy to be stopped. The slab smashed over Iffy's head, crumbling into a thousand pieces. Iffy hit the ground. Hard. Struck down, he blinked, dazed, unfocused. Then he closed his eyes and threw his hands out to the side.

Suddenly, a giant circle appeared around his massive opponent.

The bigger ifrit's maw stretched in a grin. When he released a low chittering as his eyes closed, I realized he was laughing as he stepped away from ifrit. What was going on? A circle that looked like fire shining through cracks in dried lava glowed from all around the black ifrit, highlighting the satisfied look on his face. I looked back at Iffy. Whatever he was doing his opponent clearly liked. But why? I looked back to Iffy. He was staring straight at me. Then he curled his fists and a massive blaze erupted, engulfing the circle in a curtain of fire. But the fires of hell wouldn't hurt the ifrit, would they? Wasn't he, himself made from the same fires? Glancing back at Iffy, I noticed he was trying to tell me something. When he held up the cuff on his left wrist and nodded to the ifrit currently behind the flames, I knew what I was supposed to do.

Picking up my shirt, I tore it in half and wrapped it around my hands, tying it off as I ran over to Mogapi and Kut. After some hasty whispers, they followed me to the trees closest to the hell fire. The already burnt flesh on my chest stung as we took up our positions. Mogapi tore his cloak into fours, and they mimicked my wrapping. Iffy had turned to watch us, and as soon as I gave him the nod, he dropped his fists. On cue, the flames around our adversary dropped. They weren't down for a fraction of a second when Iffy was on the smug-looking ifrit.

We ran too, but we didn't even register on the brute's radar because Iffy sunk his teeth into his arm. Above the golden cuff. His meaty arm went to tear Iffy off him, but we were already there. Mogapi grabbed his hand before he could reach it around. It gave just enough resistance and Kut and I were quick to latch on. Immediately, we tore at the bracelet. It didn't budge. An inscription engraved in them in a language I couldn't read. Was it some sort of protection? The beast roared and shook his hand. He sent my teeth clacking even as we held tight. We wouldn't be able to keep this up for long. Iffy, seeing our dilemma, grabbed the bigger ifrit around the neck with his free hand. Whipping his head, the monster tried to unseat the clawed hand from around his throat.

Turning our attention back to the impossible cuff, I turned it over. On the underside was a small niche. The beast's thick forearms flexed, threatening to rip it out of our grip again.

"Why doesn't he just rip out his throat?" asked Kut, through gritted teeth.

Holding the beast's arm close, sweat dripped down my forehead as I nodded to the indentation. "Mogapi, use your sword!"

He was on it in a flash. Fire reflected on steel as he brought the weapon up and worked the tip into the hollow. With a jerk of the ifrit's arm, the blade slipped out. Squinting he tried again. My arms began to shake.

"I don't know how much longer I can hold him!" I shouted through gritted teeth.

He continued to move it around and dug it in harder, his muscles straining under the effort. Suddenly, it popped free. I grabbed the cuff as the ifrit let out an unholy howl that echoed into the night. Seconds later, with far more skilled movements, Iffy released the other cuff.

"Good enough. Now, let's go!" I didn't even bother to push the sweat out of my eyes as we let go and ran for safety. Or what little the exhibit could provide anyway.

When we looked back, I saw just how ridiculous the escape had been. The embers under the ifrit's fur had died. In its place smoke rose like a snuffed fire. Iffy grabbed him by the neck with one hand again. This time the smoking ifrit was no match for him and even though he pulled at the claws clutching his throat, he was no match for Iffy's strength. Not anymore. I turned over the gold cuff. It was bigger than my entire hand. So the bracelets were the source of their power, huh? A scuffling brought me back to the action. Iffy drug his hellspawn brother to Hell's Gate. Without ceremony, Iffy shoved him into the muck. Dropping a knee into his back, he pinned him down as he held his head under the water. The ifrit writhed and bucked, but Iffy mercilessly held the invader. I don't know how long passed before his body gave one final shudder and went still. Iffy continued to hold him for a minute longer before he finally let him go. The creature's head floated, face down, in the pond as Iffy ambled to his feet.

Everyone was silent. Even the humans, who were staring at it all wide-eyed, blinking furiously to take it all in. From their horror-frozen faces, I could tell they'd failed. Miserably. I got it. You couldn't see someone be drowned and be the same after.

Iffy ambled over. Now, that the action was over, I didn't know what to say. I'd never spoken directly to the ifrit before, only his charge, Oganess.

"Well, that was...effective," I said, with an overly bright smile.

He pointed at my burnt chest, his brow furrowing.

I laughed it away. "It's ok. It looks right at home with my demon scar."

Just as I finished laughing, I heard the one sound that I wasn't ready for. The rattling of chains. Even though, I knew it was coming, the haunting howl that followed to split off into a chorus of barks sent goosebumps down my spine. Cerberus bound in, crashing through the toppled tree line. His three heads sniffed, two on the ground one in the air. Crouching low, he prowled over to the first scene of the massive fight that had went down. Blood soaked the ground. I looked around. Gore slicked the boardwalk too. My eyes fingers went cold and my eyes flew open as it hit me.

"He was drawn by the blood." Dropping my voice, my heart pumped in my chest. I lowered my voice, working through my thoughts out loud. "No offense, but can a hellspawn kill a demi-god?"

"Does it even matter?" asked Kut, darting glances at the giant dog prowling the area. "We need all the help we can get to kill that thing."

"We can't end its life. It has to be tied back to the gate," Mogapi reminded her, moving to keep the monster in his line of sight. He wasn't about to be a snack.

I ran my hand through my hair. "Mogapi's right. And frankly, I don't want to lose you guys, Iffy, or anyone else. Dagda be damned, why can't he just go home?"

"No kidding. Why wouldn't he want to go home? There's nothing better than sitting on a nice couch with your pet, giving them all the lovings," said a familiar voice behind us.

"Kefilwe!" Kut exclaimed, a flush staining her skin.

And though I was excited to see the over-the-top goblin too, what she'd said had released a freight train in my head.

"You're absolutely right." I said, as Cerberus came into view to sniff the dead ifrit.

Lifting his head, he let out a soulful howl.

"We need a couch?" Kefilwe asked, coming around to where I could see her.

"No, that pets have owners. And every dog with a collar is a pet." My pulse slamming in my throat, I turned to the ifrit at my side. "Iffy, do you know who Cerberus' owner is?" His horns scraped the palm trees behind him as he nodded. Adrenaline shot through my veins. "Yes! Ok, I need you to go to Hell and let him know Cerberus has gotten loose. Can you do that?" Fire flared from his nose as he gave a snort of approval. "Ok, and hurry! Cerberus has been here before. He's bad news with a capital B."

Without another word, embers flew from Iffy. Swirling around him, growing in numbers until they covered him in a tornado. Suddenly, they stopped and turned to ash, falling to the ground.

"So...that means he's going to find the Cerby's owner, right?" Kefilwe asked, her brow crinkled.

"Yes," I said with more conviction than I felt. Sweet Danu, I hoped so. "Listen up, we have to keep Cerberus here until Iffy gets back." I pointed to Kefilwe. "You don't have any more of those handy demons, do you?"

She screwed up her face and held up her palms to indicate she had nothing in them. "Afraid not." she said pointing to where we'd come from. Sure enough, demon bodies littered the ground, crumpled and unmoving. "How long are we supposed to keep the pup here for? Should I go wrangle some more up?"

"No, we need to keep him here, but I have no idea how," I said, crossing my arms over my chest.

After all the action, I was drained. Out of tricks.

"Should we keep him here with bait?" said Kut with a shrug.

Using goblins as bait she meant because he wasn't interested in anything else but blood. Frankly, it was the last thing I wanted to do, but how else were we going to keep Cerberus around for his owner? My stomach knotted. She really was right. As much as I didn't want her to be.

Growling, I said, "Fine, but we go in pairs and pull the baitee out as soon as Cerberus comes near. Absolutely, no letting him bite anyone. Got it?"

To make sure everyone knew I meant what I said, I levelled a look at each of them. They nodded in unison. Mogapi and

Kut sprinted away together. I squashed the feeling that said this was a very bad idea and walked with Kefilwe, nodding to the tall fence. Mogapi and Kut had already gotten the dog's attention by the time we'd hoisted Kefilwe up.

"Ok, let's go over this again. Make sure you fall before he snatches you. I will catch you," I called up to her as she climbed the rest of the way up.

"But I'm too big!" she hissed back.

I rolled my eyes. Why were beings always worried about their weight?

"Don't be ridiculous. You're a goblin. It will be fine," I whispered back, as Mogapi cartwheeled out of Cerberus' snapping jaws. I whispered back up to her. "Ok, you're on!"

"Hey, Cerby!" Kefilwe called, sticking out her tongue at the massive dog when he turned around.

Spirit trails from his collars flowed faster as he spotted the fleshy goblin turning the first, second, and then the third head our way.

"Dinner's up. Come get it!" she said, slapping her meaty bicep.

The thick feet of the beast made sucking sounds as they pulled out of the muddy battlefield as he turned towards us. Mogapi and Kut went to work behind him to get into the next position, climbing one of the tallest trees. Come on, guys, hurry. Then I really looked where they were. My stomach turned. What were they doing? They were going too far up. As if to put weight to my fears, the tree bent even as they climbed higher. I gasped. If they didn't fall to their deaths, they'd never get down in time before Cerberus reached them. The very dog who was padding over to us even now. He could be here in a second if he moved any faster. But he was playing with us. Maybe this wasn't such a good idea. Apparently, the two thought they were in position because Kut gave the nod. Quieting my racing heart, I decided then and there to have faith in them.

I hissed to Kefilwe, "Ok, jump!"

But she didn't. Instead, she grabbed her belly in her hands and jiggled it. "What's the matter? Too much of a meal for you? Going to get a stomach ache? You can't handle this."

Cerberus' chains rattled as he stepped up on the boardwalk. A bright look was in his eyes as he assessed the brass goblin.

"What are you doing? They're in place. Get. Down!" I ground out, shaking the pole.

"Where they are isn't safe," Kefilwe whispered back, never taking her eyes off the monster eyeing her with such intensity.

A thick trail of drool fell from the mouth closest to us as Cerberus' teeth flashed in the moonlight while he crept ever closer. He was toying with us.

"They're skilled warriors!" I argued even though I'd thought the same thing. When she didn't move, I wanted to scream. This was a nightmare.

I smacked the pole, and my hand stung. Shaking it, I barked up to her, "Kefilwe, if you don't get down from there, I am going to break every bone in your body!"

This entire situation was well past out of control. Where was Iffy? What was he doing? My eyesight blurred. Not right now. I couldn't do this now. Swiping at my eyes, my hand came away wet.

Cerberus was ten feet away. Screw this. I wasn't going to stand around while Kefilwe got herself killed. I'd be damned before I lost another goblin under my care. Decision made, I wrapped my hands and forearms around the pole. Bracing the ball of my foot against the post, I started to climb. My jaw ached as I gritted my teeth. This had to be ten thousand times harder without help. I hadn't quite gotten to the top when the massive dog was within lunging distance. Blindly, I reached up. I was able to swipe at and eventually grab the stubborn goblin's ankle.

"Hey, let me go!" she screamed as I pivoted my foot against the pole and swung her off the column.

Ignoring the nagging guilt, I aimed for the group of rapt humans. They could catch her. Nobody would get hurt. Too badly.

Kefilwe hurled through the air. But it turned out I was right; Cerberus was too close. Massive jaws snapping out, he snatched her out of the air. The little goblin let out a piercing scream as fear knifed through my chest.

Full of spit-fire, she flailed around. The knife in my chest faded to a dull ache when I realized he'd just managed to snag her furred skirt. Hope lifted my chest. I could still save her.

Sweat beaded on my skin as I pushed off from the post. Tucking and rolling, a chill chased over me as he turned back to Hell's Gate. Not again. I ran towards his front, towards Kefilwe. I hadn't gone two feet when the dog stopped up short, his entire body going rigid. Whatever had his attention didn't matter. The only thing that was on my mind was the spunky little goblin who'd tried to save us all. My nerves on end, I sprinted through his legs, narrowly avoiding the snapping jaws of his serpent tail. When I broke through his forelegs, I saw only an animal skin skirt but no goblin. Thank Danu.

With trembling hands, I pushed my hair back as I scanned the area for Kefilwe. That's when I saw her bare butt disappear into the bushes. Pride blossomed in my chest. She'd gotten out, all by herself. But if she hadn't been why Cerberus stopped, why had he? All I had to do was look to Hell's Gate to find my answer.

A demon, not much taller than any other average man,

stood on the embankment of Hell's Gate, but he had to at least weigh as much as ten overweight men put together. He held his arms behind his back in a pose that spoke of a commanding authority that abided no questions. But there was nothing human about the power radiating off him. It flew off in hot, thick waves. As he stared the hellhound down, his thick, pudgy lips pursed, sending his double chins quivering in fear of the disapproval.

"Do my eyes deceive me? The idea was laughable when I'd first heard, but now…." His eyes flashed, and the dog's heads dropped. The general never moved. The silence thundered louder than if he'd rallied and railed. "Dear Cerberus, are you really on Earth instead of guarding your post, as I have instructed?" The dog shook in fear, mud falling off him to slap around me in giant mounds. The stiff fabric of the man's suit, black as night, relaxed and then protested, stretching taut over his protruding belly before falling back in line as he lifted his hand. "I have put you in charge of keeping our people in Hell. We are at war, my pet. It is I, and I alone, who calls the shots. I will be obeyed, above all. If you have jeopardized my battle plans, you will know what true pain is. Now, be tied back to your post, never to leave again. I will deal with you later."

Putting his lips together, he gave an eerie whistle that stretched through the trees. The chains trailing on the ground around me grew an intense red, and with a pop, the dog disappeared. To reveal me. I swallowed. Hard.

His horns, sticking out of a tall general's hat, black as night with red piping, tipped as he regarded me. He pushed the shiny silver symbol, an infinity sign on top of a two-barred cross flanked by giant bat wings, in the center of his hat as he continued to assess me. I held my breath, resisting the urge to squirm.

"Cy Vanguard, Demon Killer and vampire lover," he said, pausing to regard me.

He knew who I was? This general? My stomach dropped.

Continuing on, he said, "And now, not only are you the self-appointed protector of our little friends, it would seem you have befriended one of our hellspawn. You are making quite the name for yourself." He seemed to roll a thought around in his head. What could be going on in his mind that I would warrant this much consideration? Finally, he said, "Consider yourself on my radar. I will be watching you. Until we meet again, for we will."

While I was trying to figure out if that was supposed to be out of respect or warning, he raised his fingers.

Before I could stop myself, I shouted out, "Wait!"

His eyes grew wide. Dancing in its black depths, I could see two urges warring. One was the urge to laugh out of sheer disbelief, and the other was to snap me in two for merely speaking.

While everything in me screamed that he was obviously high up on the Hell's food chain and I should stay as far away as my faerie butt would let me, I knew I needed something from him. Earth needed something from him. "Pardon the forwardness, but I think you should know that there are already Hell's...people on Earth. I thought you might want to know since you'd mentioned that it could interfere with some of your...plans."

He laughed. Outright. The sound surprising even him as it sent his double-chins scattering.

"Your words do not fool me. I know your true intent is to rid my people from your plane." His jowls fought his starched collar as he stretched his neck forward, daring me to deny it.

Since he was right, I kept my mouth shut. For a long while, he stared at me. Just when I was contemplating whether it was wise to pull ley energy when a magical being could most likely detect it, he closed his eyes. The air around me grew thick, and I felt the crowd behind me shift. My attention went to them. They were safe. The goblins hanging from the trees and bushes were also safe, if- disturbingly, a little star-struck. But then I noticed something else. No corpses of dead demons remained. Not one.

"However, since you are correct that their presence here disrupts my plans. I have abided by you. This time. Take heed for it will not happen again," he said, then he snapped his fingers and was gone.

I scanned the area. People were looking around, and Kut, Mogapi, and Kefilwe were wandering around. The bodies of Kefilwe's would-be lovers were gone. I waited. No other monsters came in. Was it really over? Well, I supposed we should go tell the others. And just maybe look for some stray demons. Looking back to the entrance, no one came in. Letting out a shaking laugh of disbelief, I rubbed my forehead. Was it really over? I turned to see all of the humans, still huddled in a terrified group staring at me as if I'd grown two more heads myself. Oh, right. Them too. Well, I didn't have any amnesia spells here, so I suppose there was only one thing I *could* do.

I threw my arms wide. "And that folks, concludes tonight's performance of Hell on Earth. Be sure to come back for more one-of-the-kind, unique, unbeatable, can't be believed ummm...theatrical pieces that will have you questioning...well, everything really," I said, with a bow. When I righted, nobody moved. Everyone just stared at me, their eyes never losing their wide-eyed shock. Frustration ground my teeth against each other. I really just wanted them gone, so I could work through this last little bit of my pseudo-god duties. So I added with a grand sweep of my hand, "Now, if you would kindly move to the Pool, Spas, and

Concession area, so that we may clean the area for the remainder of your visit, it would be much appreciated."

I paused. This time a few claps came from the back, unsure. Then slowly, more and more claps joined. After some relieved laughter, it wasn't long before everyone was whooping and hollering.

"So realistic!" said one man, his voice lifting in excitement.

Another woman gushed. "Can you believe it, Tom?"

"*The* best vacation. Ever!" screamed a little boy, pumping his fists.

Relieved that I finally had them buying it, I stood up there, bowing as long as I could stand it before waving and heading out of the exhibit. If they weren't leaving, I would. As grateful as I was that the threat to goblins and all humanity was passed, I had to find the others and let them know. Because I'd nodded to them on the way out, my little crew was hot on my heels as I left.

When we were far enough away, I motioned for Mogapi's tunic. He removed it without a word and handed it to me.

Since she was still naked on the bottom half, I wrapped it around Kefilwe's waist as I couldn't help the first thing that came to my mind. "Ok, someone tell me who that scary demon was."

Kut moved a thick braid that had fallen over her left eye as she said, "That was Beelzebub. It is a very short list of those above him in Hell."

"You kidding? You don't give him enough credit. He's one of *the* Princes of Hell. Not to mention the chief lieutenant of the Devil himself. And don't forget he's Gluttony of the Seven Deadly Sins fame." Raved Kefilwe with dreamy eyes. "He's literally *the best.*"

I shoved a hand through my hair, trying to pretend like this fan-girling of Hell wasn't making me all kinds of uncomfortable. "Ok, all fancy names aside. Can we trust that he brought all the demons back to Hell and is keeping Cerberus there?"

Kefilwe snorted and blinked her eyes rapidly as if personally offended that I was questioning his word.

"Yes, Beelzebub only operates to please himself. He is not a player of games. He would not say anything he didn't do, and he wouldn't do anything if it isn't in his best interest." Mogapi confirmed, crossing his arms over his hollow chest.

I pushed away the thought that reminded me that a Prince of Hell promised we would meet again as I dealt with the immediate issue that needed to be dealt with. "We need to find Sven and the rest of the goblins. They need to know the threat has been neutralized." Mogapi and Kut nodded, but Kefilwe looked up from pulling at the edges of the tunic, just barely covering her bottom. For her benefit, I added, "That the demons and Cerberus are gone. Also, I need Sven to meet me back at my car. I need some rest before the trial tomorrow."

Even mentioning the judgment made my stomach twist.

"On it," said Kefilwe, swinging her toy wand around.

I eyed it. "Why don't you give me that while I'm thinking of it?"

"I'll be sure to let everyone know!" she said, talking over me as she scooted away, moving just a bit faster.

I narrowed my gaze at her fast-retreating form. Kut covered a cough with a laugh and nodded before also leaving.

"I will not rest until the entire clan has been told and Sven has been returned to you, Protector of Goblins and All That is Bad," Mogapi said with a bow.

My chest tightened at his words and the endearing light in his eyes. I reached a hand out to him. Our connection stayed him. He looked back at me with questions in his eyes.

"Mogapi, listen. You have to stop calling me that. I'm not

your god. He got…" I stuffed my hands in my pockets, unable to put words to what happened. "Lost along the way. I…I thought you should know. I'm not him. I'm sorry."

My throat closed off as my guilt choked me. Well, there it was. Now, he knew that I'd deceived him and his entire race. I respected the ranger, and losing his respect would hurt, but he deserved to know the truth. Mogapi just looked at me. I scratched my shoulder. Why did I lie to them? I should have been honest from the beginning.

Pulling my hand back, I said, "Say something."

"What would you like me to say? I already know. But let's not spread it around. My kind needs a hero. And you'll do just fine," he said with a rare smile.

My mouth dropped open. I was stunned. He knew? He knew and never said anything? As he jogged off, my heart swelled. For evil beings, they really weren't so bad.

Changing my mind, I made my way back to Hell's Gate. I wanted to grab my purse, so I could jet as soon as we were done. If I could still find it in the wreck that was the exhibit anyway. Hopefully, the park had insurance. That way, I could leave as soon as everyone was told. No sense in staying in this place any longer than necessary. I could really use a nap before the trial tomorrow. And a shower. And a shirt.

On my way back, one of the humans bobbed a selfie stick around with barely restrained gushing. "Guys, this place is off the charts incredible. They have the most amazing events. There was just a Hell on Earth event with demons and everything chasing us. You all, it was SO realistic. Definitely. 10 out of 10 crowns. You've GOT to come here!"

As I walked into Hell's Gate, I prayed she hadn't recorded anything else. The last thing I needed was people recognizing me on the street. Talk about making my day job hard as a diamond. To my surprise, there were plenty of goblins here already. It crossed my mind to tell them to minimize exposure, but that seemed too-little-too-late considering the crazy night we'd just had. Besides, I'm sure that was being addressed by their own leadership. I wasn't trying to get involved more in the goblin culture than I already was.

Some people stood to the side, giggling and pointing at the goblins. One lanky boy with pimples walked back and forth with his legs spread wide like a monkey, no doubt mocking how the little goblins walked. Dick. The group let loose peals of laughter. I looked back again to where they pointed. That's when I noticed Kefilwe was at the center of it. Her and her wand. She walked over to one of the male goblins with wavy locks. As he stared thoughtfully into the trees, she hit him over the head with the toy, sending colors of all kinds dancing over his head. Without hesitation, he turned around. After laying eyes on her, he fell to his knees. Throwing his arms up, he looked at her with abandon. I thinned my lips. Demons were one thing, but any other being was another matter entirely.

With quick steps, I walked over and snatched the toy wand out of her hand.

"Hey!" she shouted, trying to grab it back.

I deadpanned a look at her. Immediately, her hands stopped, and she crossed her arms over her ample chest. Then she looked around at her new harem.

"I mean. Whatever, I have all I need here. Come on, boys," she said with a wink.

They followed her with ready grins. I shook my head, unable to help the chortle that bubbled up. Talk about incorrigible. Then I remembered the love shining in their eyes, and it wiped the smile from my face. My next thought came unbidden on its heels. What I wouldn't give to be in her position. But I'd just want one person to fall in love with me.

Tapping the wand against my hand, I went behind the rock outcropping and found my purse right away. Jackpot.

Falling to my knees, I unzipped the bag and dropped the wand in. I stared at the lights flashing in the dim interior. Unable to bring my eyes away from it, I couldn't help but be half-tempted to try it on, Sven. If only that was the real problem. No, the real problem wasn't that he didn't love me. Sure, that part affected me, but his inability to feel any emotion was more important than that. That was the big issue. But if he loved me, wasn't that better than feeling nothing? My mind argued. No, it really wasn't. It was a forced, fake thing. Not real emotion.

Determined to push the thought aside, I buried the hard plastic farther in my purse. I didn't want to make Sven love me again. What he'd said in my room had really hit a chord. All I really wanted was for him to feel again. I wanted to give him as much as he'd given me. I'd no sooner finished the thought than the amulet caught on my thumb as I pulled my hand out. It came with me and dropped into my lap. Picking up the cool chain in my hand, the diamond caught the glow from the exhibit's floodlights. It really was a beautiful piece. I almost didn't blame Kittie for taking it. It was so big it looked like it could be someone's heart.

I was about to drop it back in my purse when my hand froze. A thought came to me, and I knew I was going to do it. My heart beat fast in my chest as I slipped the amulet around my neck. Slinging my handbag over my shoulder, I had to work to keep my pace even, so I didn't start running.

No sooner had I exited Hell's Gate when I ran into Dain, King of the Patupaiarehe. He had a troop of warrior fae behind him, dressed in loose loincloths. In addition to a loincloth, he wore a wide sash of tiny bones and feathers. It covered his left shoulder, sticking out like a shoulder guard before dropping down to expose his ripped abs. Upon seeing me, his eyes crinkled into a welcoming grin. But he wasn't the one in front. Mabye was. And if it was possible, his smile was even bigger than the fae in behind him.

"Good work, Mabye," I said, nodding my approval.

He bowed, almost losing his balance but catching himself, the smile never leaving his face. "Was nothing."

The pale king's red eyebrow rose. I winced. If he could have said a worse thing, I didn't know what it was. The Patupaiarehe had immense pride, and a statement like that could be taken as a great offense. I think that was the Diet Coke of Evil's cue to get out of here.

"Mabye, we need to collect all of the...weapons used in the fight. They need to all be burnt," I said, patting his shoulder, praying that Dain missed the pause. The last thing I needed was for them to realize a divinity pond was on their lands. Who could foretell how they would use such a powerful magic? Not I. I didn't know the Patupaiarehe well enough. Not to take that chance.

Ducking, Mabye slid out from under my touch. "On it, Pretty Pretty Princess."

As he walked away, his chest puffed, Dain looked at me with a smirk on his face.

"Don't ask," I said, twisting my lips to fight the grin that wanted to break free. I wasn't used to such free banter with the king, but the giddiness of the night made me feel more free than usual. "Thank you for coming. But we have it all under control. Your kindness will not be forgotten, though."

"As it shouldn't be," he said, his man bun moving as he gave a slight bow of his head.

His words weren't intended to be a slight. Expectations set in the Court pretty much said as much anyway. The words were teasing if anything.

Looking into his blue eyes, I said, "Listen, I just want to say thank you for listening to a goblin. I know it's quite unusual, so just know how much I appreciate it."

"It is that. Truth be told, it was the only reason I came at all. It intrigued me." The king's eyes flickered down, taking in my semi-nude state.

It wasn't an offensive or leering look, just a glance that showed he'd noticed I was all female. With his strong jawline and thick wavy locks tacked away with feathers into a bun that begged to be let loose, it could be easy to imagine being in his bed. What would it be like to be his wife? As a strong, brave mound, I can imagine his home would be much less formal than my own home in Knockaine. Since Sven didn't want me anymore, I had to ask myself, could I marry for political gain?

Shaking the thought from my head, I blinked. What was wrong with me? If I was thinking along those lines, I must be more tired than I thought. Even if Sven didn't want me, I wouldn't marry for anything other than love. Saying out loud didn't make it any easier, and I knew a shadow had fallen over my face by the way the glint in his own eyes dulled.

"You have done an exceptional job here, Princess Cy. If you ever need me, you know where to find me," he said with a half-bow. Then after a searching look, he nodded to his warriors and turned away.

I watched the wonder of a king go. He was intriguing, to say the least. But I had more pressing matters on hand than mild fascination. Clutching the diamond necklace against my chest, I finished the small trek to Baby Adam.

The rising sun's rays glanced off the pool, which was only partially obscured by the steam rising from it. Making quick work of the gloves and tying off the trash bags around my knees, I removed the necklace from around my neck. It glowed in the soft morning light. I took my time on the rocky embankment as I contemplated the enormity of what I was about to do. Like all magic, it could either go miraculously or tragically.

After all of the life-or-death moments I'd had over the last few months, was I really going to play with magic again? My brow furrowed as I stared at the red diamond. My mouth worked, thinking of the lives that had been lost. The sacrifices that had been made on my behalf. My heart slamming in my chest like a bird trying to get free, I made my decision.

For Sven and what he'd given up for me, it was worth it.

Rocks poked my knees as I knelt on the embankment. Pulling off the necklace, I dipped it into the crystal waters.

"Please God, give Sven his feelings back. Give his emotions back. Give him his life back. For there is no man or creature on this planet who deserves it more," I said, whispering harshly as I looked to the heavens.

Fighting tears, I looked down as I pulled the amulet back out of the water. The diamond glowed a bright gold and then turned back to red. Did that mean it worked? What did it mean that light had shone from it when nothing else had? My hands shook as I stood up. Whatever it meant, it was done. Would it be enough?

CHAPTER 15

The moon shone big and bright through the skylights. It was all you could see out of the darkened cathedral ceiling. The rest of it matched my mood. Black. Sweat slicked my palms as I stood in the Blood Spire courtroom.

"We are here to carry out judgment against one Sven Siversten for the crime of Breaking Loyalty," rang out the somber voice of Raven from his place in the panel. High Council.

I was a fool.

"It has been many years since we had to try one for Breaking Loyalty," he continued, his voice echoing throughout the vast hall.

I was a coward.

"So it took time to decide on a fair…" he paused, his gaze flickering Mercy's way for only a split second before shifting back, "and reasonable punishment."

My whole body ached as I looked at Sven on the platform, small and alone. Sure, his chest was puffed like they couldn't take away his pride, but emptiness radiated from him. It was a shell of a man from the vampire I knew. He wore a simple black button-down, black trousers, and nothing else.

The necklace burned in my pocket. I should have given it to him. But without knowing what his sentence would be, how could I? What if having feelings just made his punishment that more unbearable? After everything he'd gone through because of me, I couldn't bear the thought of being the cause of even more of his suffering.

"The sentence is 100 years as the Midnight Ghoul with direct report to the High Priestess. Sentencing to be carried out immediately," Raven said, smashing down his gavel.

Two men with leather hoods and black robes strode in, carrying an iron pole. Cuffs on each end flopped back and forth. Shocked murmurs swept through the crowd.

"What is the Midnight Ghoul?" I asked Catherine of Sienna, unable to take my eyes off the scene in front of me as they walked towards Sven.

Raven cracked the hammer repeatedly. The noise level quieted.

As Raven spoke, thick chains lowered, birthed from the blackness above. "While it is true some considered the punishment of Midnight Ghoul too extreme and thus it had been banished for thousands of years, due to the severity of the offense, we believe it to be a just punishment in this case."

Everyone started talking once again. This time louder. More fervently.

"What in the name of...." Taking a deep breath, I stopped myself before calling out a faerie god. That was the best way to get Sven and me both killed. I struggled with the pain ripping me apart. What could get this many people scared? Because they were frightened. It radiated off them in waves. My voice was barely even a whisper anymore as I said, "In the name of all that is holy, what is the Midnight Ghoul?"

One of the men took the chain suspended from above.

The heavy shackles clanked against each other as the first man handed him to his partner. Somber, he proceeded to weave the chains around Sven.

Catherine of Sienna's ordinarily stoic face worked as she watched the proceedings. Finally, she managed to say, "The Midnight Ghoul is the Executioner, at the command of the High Council."

Over, under the thick chains wrapped. "Executioner? So he has to kill people for them? That doesn't sound...too bad, I suppose. Isn't there a lot of violence and killing in the vampire community anyway?"

When the chain wielder stepped away, Sven was wrapped in chains binding his chest, over his biceps and swirling up each of his arms to join together at the center. His arms high, he looked out, impassioned out over the crowd. I blinked in surprise. Wasn't that a bit overkill?

"You don't understand," her voice broke. "He'll be turned into a mindless killing machine. He will no longer be Sven. He will be a mindless puppet. At the complete beck and call of the High Priestess."

Yanking Sven's legs into place, the men none too gently wedged the pole between Sven's feet. My nails dug into my palms. Their unnecessary roughness made me want to knock their lights out. Sven wasn't even resisting. With tugs to ensure the restraints and the chains held, they stepped back. Then a man in white walked onto the platform. He carried the cross of Satan high, his robes ballooning with each step as he strode up to Sven.

"But surely, he will be himself, on some level." My heart spasming, I reached in my pocket to clutch at the amulet. Its metal ornamentation bit into my palm.

The massive clock behind me vibrated the wall, chiming. Once, twice, three times. The white-robed priest stepped in front of Sven. Making movements over Sven's body, his chants reached us clearly. This couldn't be happening. Four times, five times, six times. Straining to hear what he was saying over the strikes, I realized it was an ancient language. One I wasn't fluent in, but I knew some of it. Obey. Blood. Curse. Death. The need to stop the cleric wrapped around me like a boa constrictor. No. This couldn't happen. Not like this. Not to Sven. He was such a good person. He'd saved me. Why couldn't I do the same for him?

But I stayed. Because there really was nothing I could do. If I went up there, death would be the fate of both of us. The gong continued until the twelfth peal faded away. Midnight. The incantation died at the same time. Sven had fallen, held up only by the chains suspended from above. I knew this because his kneecaps were visible on either side of the man's robes. Robes that suddenly seemed far wider than they had before.

The hushed silence of the room provoked Catherine of Sienna to continue. "He will only be himself during the break of day. At midnight is a different story entirely. He will transform into the Midnight Ghoul. My dear, you have no clue what is in store for your love. Ghouls are unfeeling, unseeing. As the Midnight Ghoul, he will be given strength and power to rival no other in this Veil. But it will be the Mercy's to wield. Not his."

With her words, the priest stepped away. I stumbled back, gasping. My voice was swallowed by the reaction of the crowd. Whispers rose to a dull roar as everyone stared at the stage. The delicate vampire beside me reached out a steadying hand, but I was made of sterner stuff. Wasn't I?

I stared in horror at what could only be Sven. His skin had decayed before our very eyes. Black, it sagged from his flesh. Flesh that had sunken in to hang off his bones and had pulled away from his mouth. It looked like his face was frozen in a wicked smile. However, his hair had shot out like a navy-blue weed. When he raised his head, his hair was down to his shoulders. Covered in sweat, it hung in chunks past his red eyes as his shoulders heaved with pain. I stared at him for a long time, shock rolling over me in waves.

"He will need to feast. Ghouls have no thoughts beyond what is forefront in their minds. They take what they want. And the Midnight Ghoul is no different. The only difference is the High Priestess tells him what he wants," she said, her voice dropping in sadness.

Mercy. That heartless bitch. I could only imagine the atrocities she'd have him commit on her behalf. Things the real Sven would never do.

The men with the leather masks unchained him. He fell to the ground.

"Will he...remember what he does at night?" I asked, not wanting to know the answer but not able to help myself.

"Every horrific detail, yes," she said, her lips and her eyes thinning like the mere thought brought back memories too painful to bear.

So the acts he committed at night, against his will, would haunt him throughout his days. How could he live like that? Wasn't this worse than a death sentence?

"That can't be true." I shook my head in denial as I stared at the man I loved panting on the ground. Broken.

If she responded to my denial, I didn't hear. I barely registered the gavel crack or noticed the High Council adjourn or the departing crowd, who shot hasty glances over their shoulders to the stage where Sven knelt. Motionless. The touch of Catherine of Sienna almost didn't even register. My mind worked. What could I do? There had to be something. She'd said ghouls (I swallowed past the thought) did nothing beyond what they wanted. Since Sven didn't have emotions, that meant he didn't want anything outside of the needs of an animal. But what if he could feel again?

What if the amulet worked? Would he want other things? Could he fight the curse?

I didn't realize I'd been walking towards the stage until I hit the bottom step. Then I sprinted up the stairs, my steps echoing in the now-empty cathedral. Empty except Sven and I. The gargoyles loomed over us as I slid to my knees. Sven didn't meet my eyes. He simply stared past me, unseeing. Vacant.

"Sven," I pleaded a broken word.

I swallowed as I looked him over. Up close, he was even more grotesque. One of his eye sockets was slightly recessed, making his glowing red eye look even more hideous. His black flesh, though shockingly smooth, showed every bone and rib. Though, inexplicably. He looked stronger. Like he could break me in half with all the effort of one breaking freshly baked bread.

"What did they do to you?" I whispered, despair deepening my voice.

He didn't even flinch.

My hands flitted about the clothes hanging off him. Ghosting around the bony parts of his arm, where his sinewy muscles had once been. The stringy hair that had been so vibrant, so touchable. "I'm sorry. So incredibly sorry. I had no idea. I'd never let them..."

Unable to complete the thought, I trailed off. I spread my hands out in front of me to focus. When I could continue again, I took a deep breath to collect myself. We could try now. This was the time.

With shaking hands, I withdrew the amulet from my pocket. "Sven, I have an idea. I dipped this amulet in the divinity pool. I had hoped that...that...." My voice cracked, and I waved the idea away. "Anyway, I think we can use it to...help with the curse."

Still, he didn't move.

"Sven," I said, hoping the mere sound of his name would trigger him. "Sven, I think we should try it. It can't be worse than this," I said, gesturing desperately to his unmoving form. "But I need you to tell me it's ok. I don't want to do anything without your permission."

His vacant expression remained. The shell of the man I loved remained. My lips quivered. He hadn't wanted to try the divinity pool, but he couldn't have known they would turn him into...this. Could he? Surely, he would change his mind. But he couldn't tell me. He couldn't do anything. Apparently, until sometime in the future where he had a physical need or was summoned. And then he would turn into a raging beast. That nightmare would repeat. For a hundred years.

"Fuck this," I said, my voice thick with unshed tears as I lifted the necklace with trembling hands.

Because of the sweat slicking my hands, it took a few tries to get it settled around his neck, but I finally did. My heart in my throat. I waited. Nothing happened. I observed him. Nothing happened. Gritting my teeth to still my quivering lips, I adjusted the large amulet in the center of his chest. It shone, beautiful in the soft cathedral light, like the wonderful man he was. And he was that man. Even if he couldn't physically be that man anymore, it was a memory that deserved to be cherished. Because he was extraordinary and everyone should know it. I moved his hair off his face and behind his shoulders, busying myself to make sure it nestled behind his ears.

"It's ok. I will take care of you. You need someone. And I will be there for you. I won't leave you to go through this alone. I promise. I love you, Sven." I brought my hand down to cup my heart as wetness trailed down my cheeks.

I would not cry, damn it. Not now. The man I loved needed me. Even if my heart was breaking.

Cold hands came up to enfold mine. My head shot up as my heart raced. Sven was staring down at me. Yes, it was still the Midnight Ghoul with black skin, blue hair, and red eyes. But it was Sven. I could see it in the love that shone there. My heart swelled. Love. No sweeter word existed in this world.

His hand came up to thread into my hair, and I rose on my knees as he pulled me close. My heart sang as his mouth came over mine. I opened my lips, and his tongue darted in, sweeping out all of the sadness and doubt. He was mine. He was himself. He was home. After too short of a time, he pulled away.

Looking deep into my eyes, he said the one thing I wanted to hear for the rest of my life. The one thing I'd never thought to hear again. "I love you too, Cy."

CHAPTER 16

*P*ulling Sven into my room, I slammed the door behind us.

He laughed as I moved my hands over him. My heart soared. Well, the heart I'd been gifted. I couldn't believe he was here. All of him. In the flesh, so to speak. And all of his emotions were his. They were real. He was whole again. Ok, minus some meat and plus some extra pieces but here nonetheless. Who knew what the future would bring. At least we were together. Finally.

I pushed him onto the bed. After a slight resistance, he let me. From the immovable wall he'd been before yielding, it became apparent Catherine of Sienna hadn't exaggerated when she said that as the Midnight Ghoul, he was stronger than any being I'd ever met.

"Don't you want to wait until dawn to have your way with me? Or are you into half-dead men?" he teased.

I jumped onto the bed after him. The mattress bounced him under my weight.

I looked up, pretending to contemplate it.

"Maybe, in 50 years or so. But for now, I vote you hold

me until dawn. *Then* you can rock my world," I said, snuggling up to him.

Wrapping an arm around me, he nuzzled the top of my head. "That sounds like a splendid plan."

My blood sang through my veins. We'd done it all. We'd braved it all. And we still came out of it on top. Together.

Just as the happy thought warmed my bones, a flash of blue and an explosion of glitter rained down on us.

Squeezing my eyes shut, I groaned. Why now? Ex issues aside, all I really wanted was to be alone with the man I loved. Well, the intruder could just be on his way. I sat up to tell him just that, but what I saw made my heart stop. Anthony, Messenger of the Crown, former lover, and refriended best friend collapsed on the ground, covered in blood.

"Anthony!" I screamed, pushing off the bed.

Rushing to his side, I turned him towards me. Sven was there in a heartbeat, and he helped ease the giant blue wings around until Anthony faced us. The pain there sent my heart careening.

His eyes slits, he reached out to me.

"The death cart has come. Your mother….you've got to…" Then he trailed off and went still.

When a forgotten god brings Cy back home, she must decide who is

more important. A mother who never loved her or a people who have no one else to turn to.

To read BANSHEE BONES, the epic finale in Cy's whirlwind adventure, Click Here now!

MESSAGE FROM THE QUEEN

Queens & Kings, thank you so much for reading *BLOOD VEIL*!

I hope you loved reading it as much as I did writing it.

Reviews help readers JUST LIKE YOU choose great adventures to fall in love with!

Pop on Over to Leave a Review Today!

ABOUT THE QUEEN

Erica Reeder is a *USA Today* and International bestselling author of Urban Fantasy who uses glitter as a territorial marker. Kids, boyfriend, you name it. If it's got glitter on it, it's hers. Besides an infatuation with glitter and all things fantasy, she is a Queen with an unreasonable passion for writing. Whether throwing her characters a demon or hiding pixies in pants, there's always fun to be had. Come be a part of it in so many places either at www.ericareeder.com, where there's merchandise that will spellbind you, and of course, books that will steal your breath and enchant your heart. Or you could join our Facebook Group: Erica Reeders Fae Court to have daily fun. OR for less interaction but no fewer goodies, you could JOIN THE NEWSLETTER, WHERE YOU'LL GET YOUR VERY OWN FREE BOOK *TODAY*! Click here to join!